W9-COU-814

Ryan Foley

Perseus

Destiny's Call

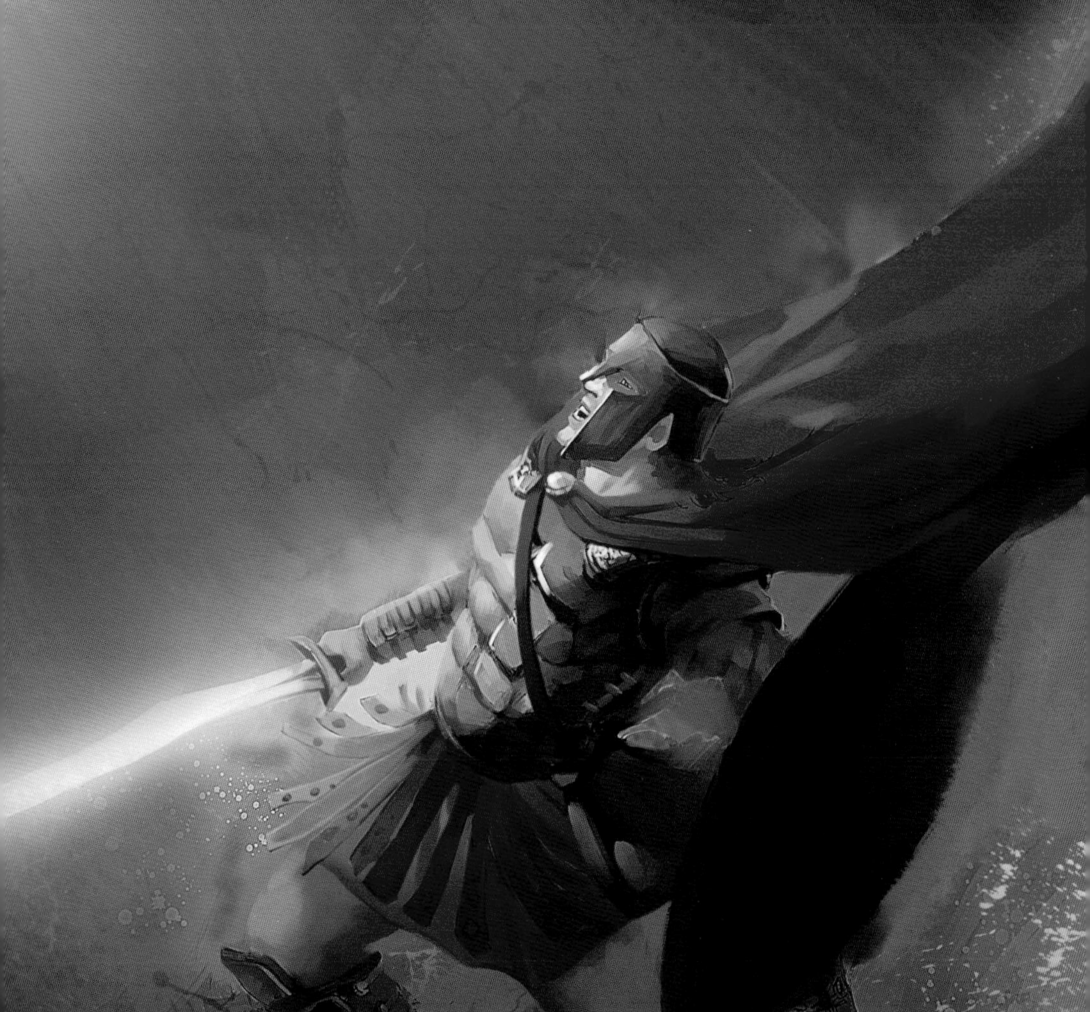

CAMPFIRE™

KALYANI NAVYUG MEDIA PVT LTD

New Delhi

RYAN FOLEY

PERSEUS
DESTINY'S CALL

Sitting around the Campfire, telling the story, were:

WORDSMITH **RYAN FOLEY**

ILLUSTRATOR **NARESH KUMAR**

INKER **JAGDISH KUMAR**

COLORIST **MANOJ YADAV**

LETTERER **BHAVNATH CHAUDHARY**

EDITOR **SUKANYA MEHTA**

PRODUCTION CONTROLLER **VISHAL SHARMA**

COVER ART **JAYAKRISHNAN K. P.**

DESIGNER **VIJAY SHARMA**

ART DIRECTOR **RAJESH NAGULAKONDA**

www.campfire.co.in

Published by Kalyani Navyug Media Pvt. Ltd.
101 C, Shiv House, Hari Nagar Ashram, New Delhi 110014, India

ISBN: 978-93-80741-08-6

Printed in India

RYAN FOLEY

Born in 1974 in Toms River, New Jersey, Ryan Foley's obsession with comic books began during his childhood when his mother introduced him to characters like Spider-Man and Batman. He cites R. A. Salvatore's science fiction, *The Crystal Shard* (and its character Drizzt Do'Urden) as having influenced him the most, for it drew him into a world of fantasy and inspired him to become a writer. He has worked with Image Comics and Arcana Studios on comic book series such as *Masters of the Universe, Dragon's Lair, Space Ace, and Tales of Penance: Trial of the Century.*

Having adapted several stories from myths and legends for Campfire, such as *Legend: The Labors of Heracles, Stolen Hearts: The Love of Eros and Psyche, The Treasured Thief. Perseus: Destiny's Call* is his next book for Campfire.

NARESH KUMAR

A resident of Delhi, India, Naresh describes himself as a seeker who is continuously trying to learn as much as he can, and his art is an expression of his curiosity towards the world. A firm believer in humanity, Naresh brings an experienced hand to the drawing board. His work features in a number of other titles from Campfire, which include *Robinson Crusoe, A Christmas Carol, The Adventures of Huckleberry Finn, Frankenstein, and Kidnapped.*

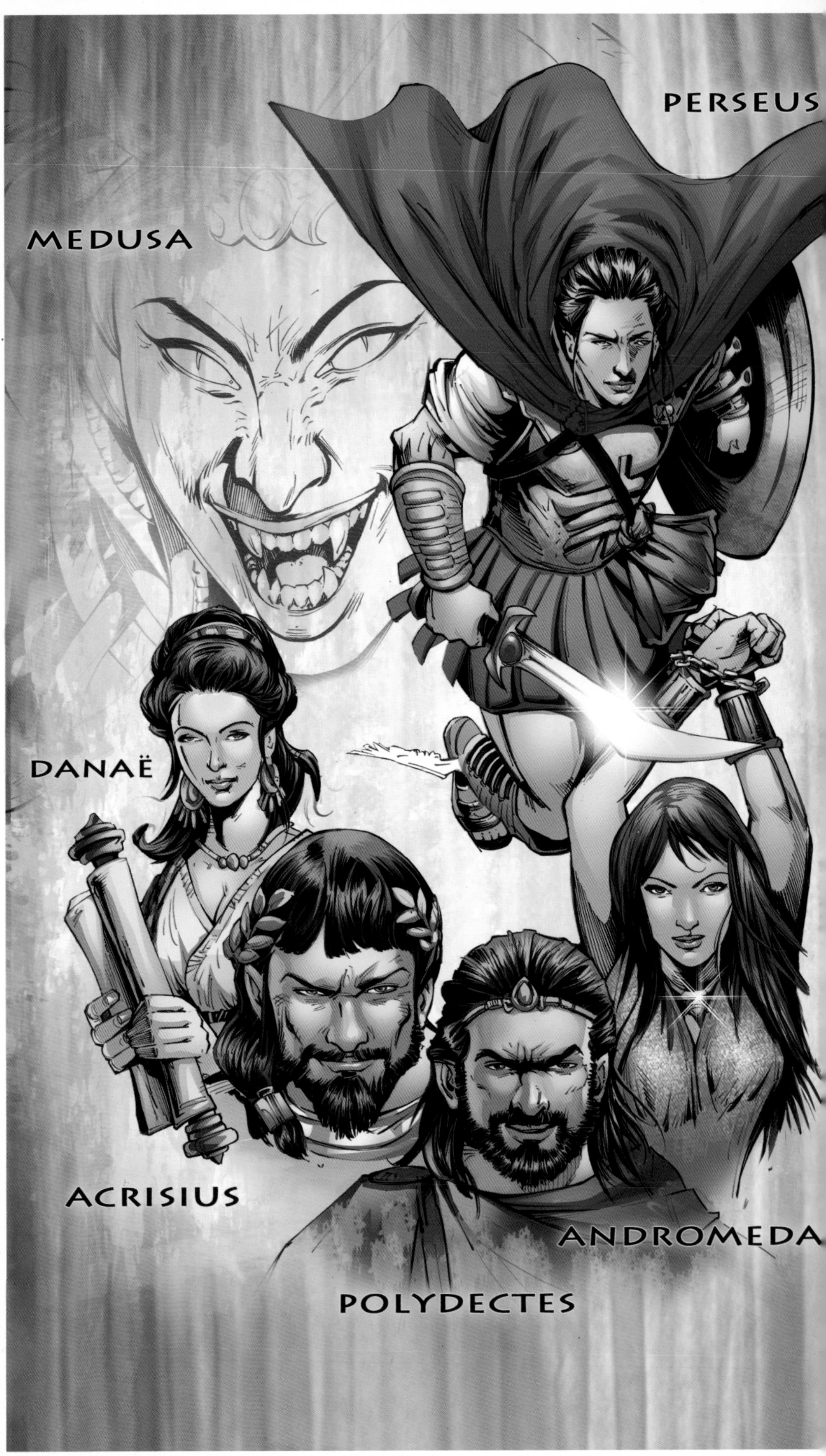
PERSEUS
MEDUSA
DANAË
ACRISIUS
ANDROMEDA
POLYDECTES

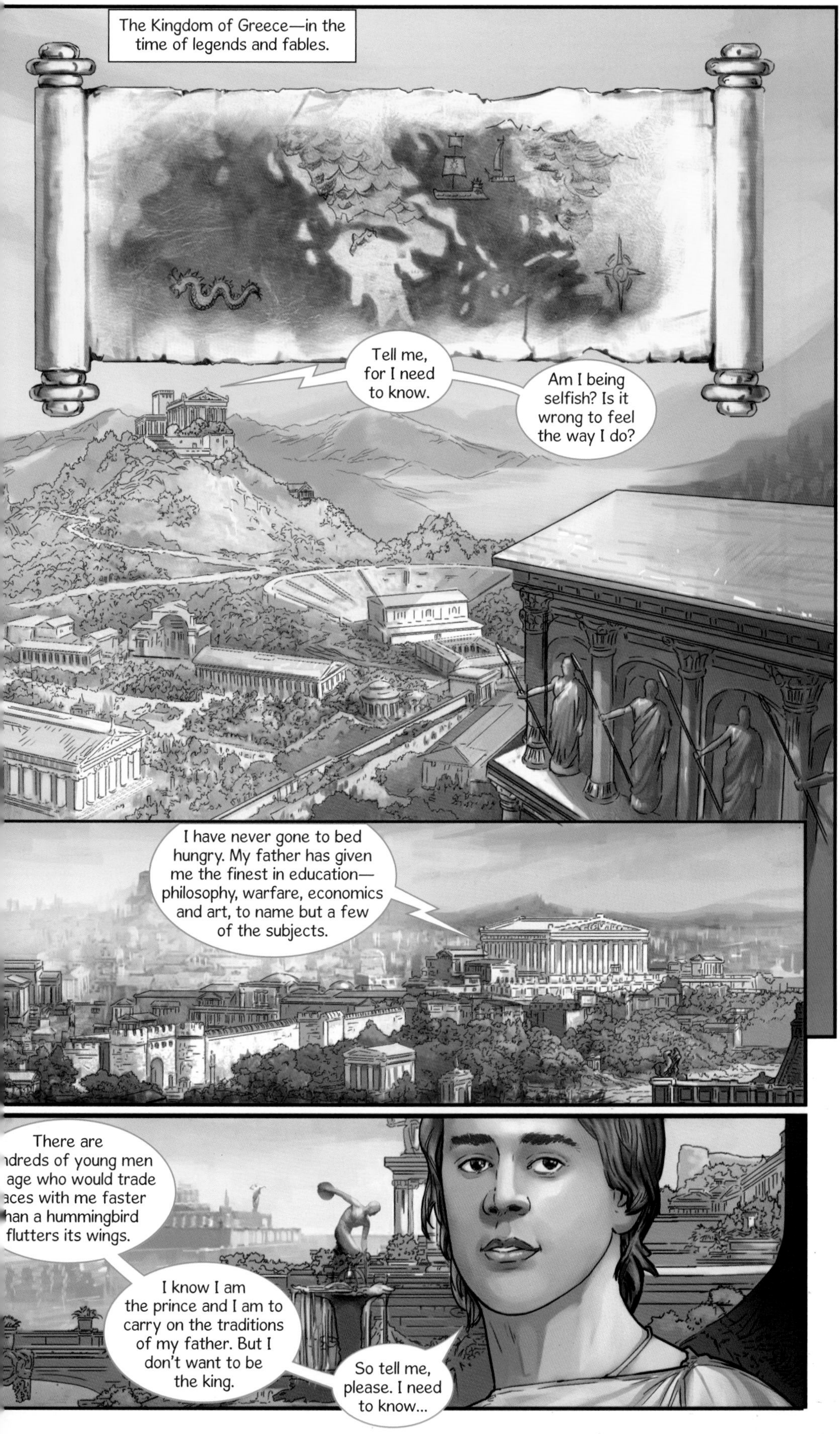
The Kingdom of Greece—in the time of legends and fables.
Tell me, for I need to know.
Am I being selfish? Is it wrong to feel the way I do?
I have never gone to bed hungry. My father has given me the finest in education—philosophy, warfare, economics and art, to name but a few of the subjects.
There are ndreds of young men age who would trade aces with me faster han a hummingbird flutters its wings.
I know I am the prince and I am to carry on the traditions of my father. But I don't want to be the king.
So tell me, please. I need to know...

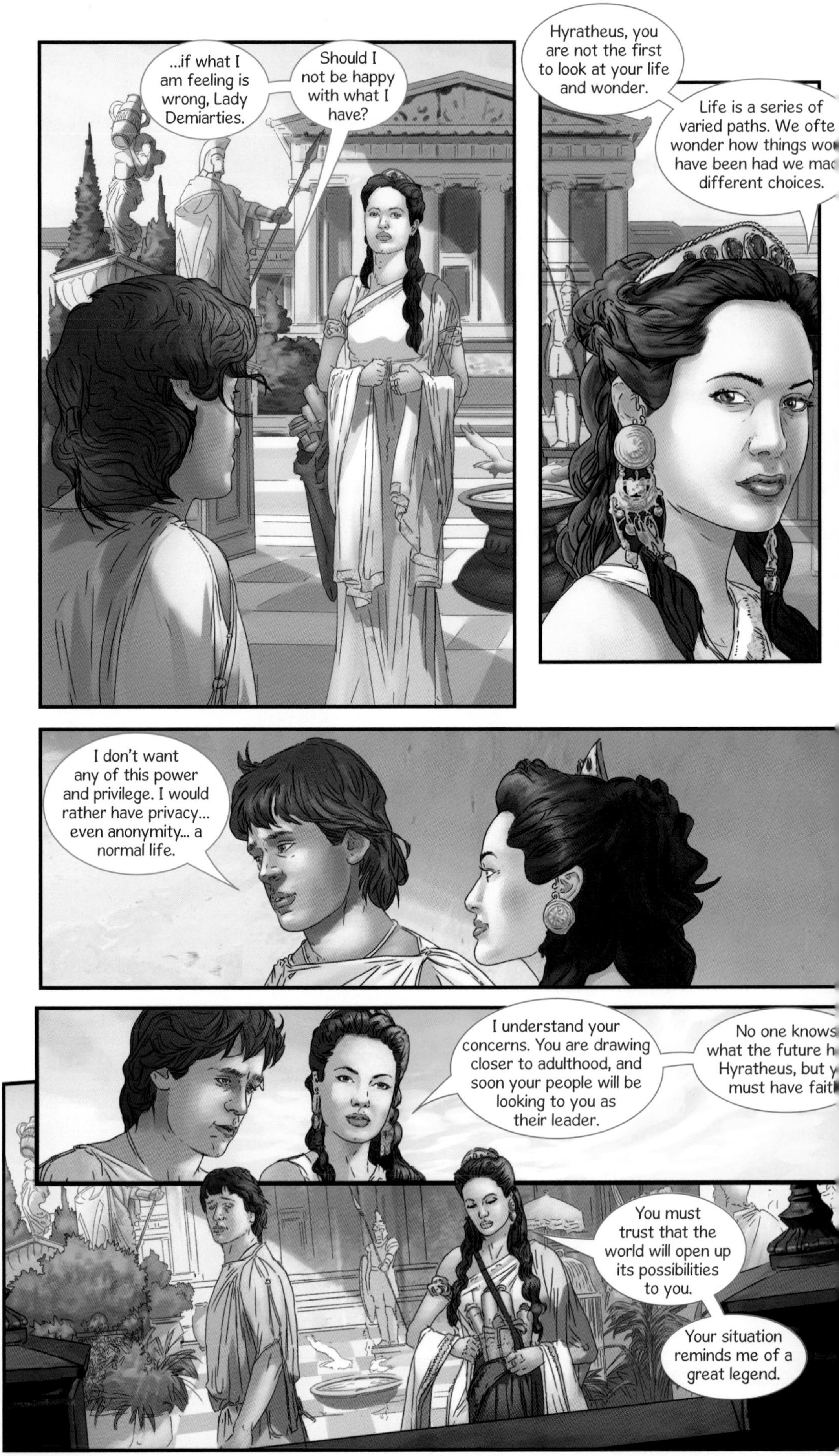

...if what I am feeling is wrong, Lady Demiarties.
Should I not be happy with what I have?
Hyratheus, you are not the first to look at your life and wonder.
Life is a series of varied paths. We ofte wonder how things wo have been had we ma different choices.
I don't want any of this power and privilege. I would rather have privacy... even anonymity... a normal life.
I understand your concerns. You are drawing closer to adulthood, and soon your people will be looking to you as their leader.
No one knows what the future h Hyratheus, but y must have fait
You must trust that the world will open up its possibilities to you.
Your situation reminds me of a great legend.

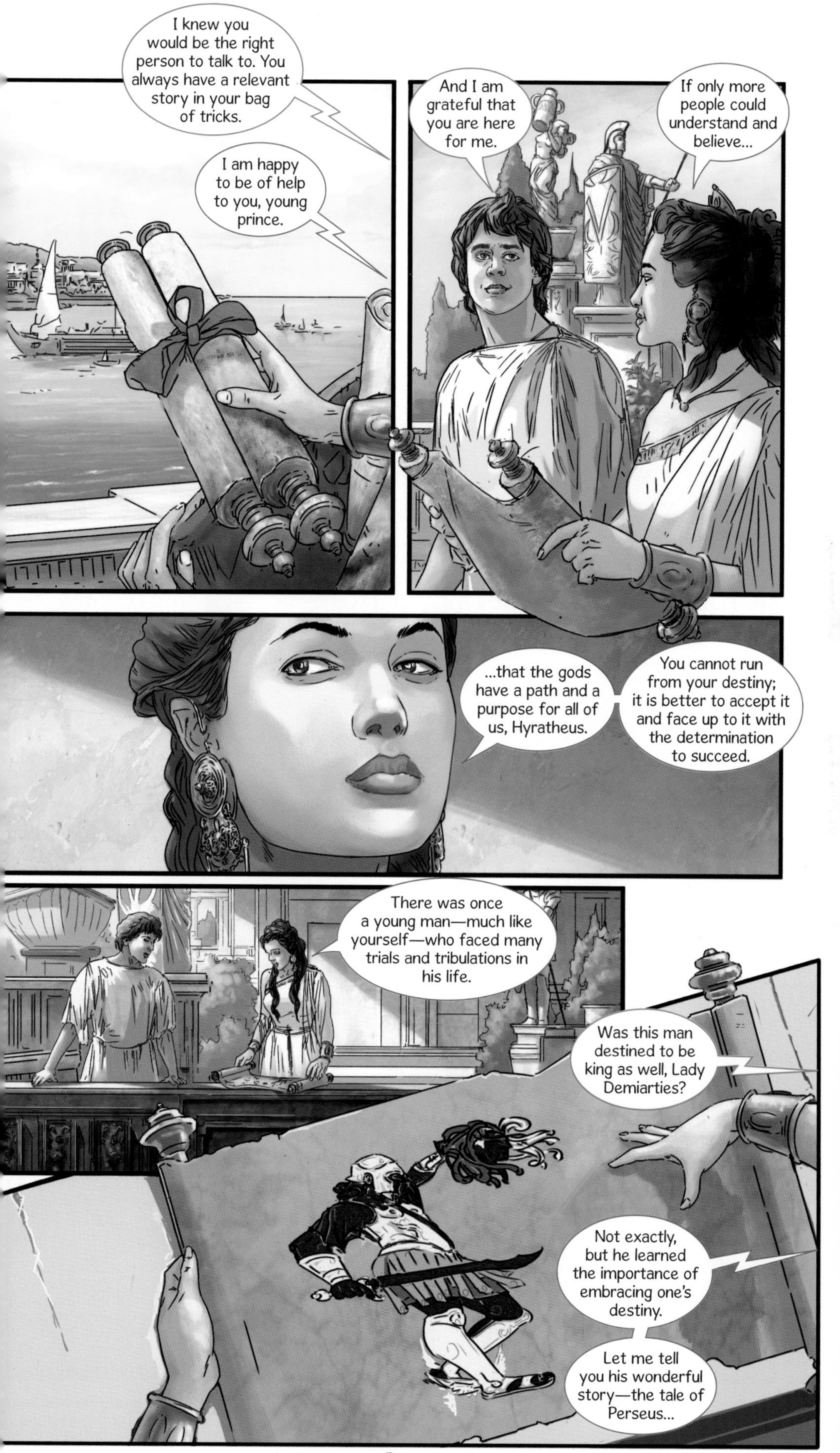
I knew you would be the right person to talk to. You always have a relevant story in your bag of tricks.
I am happy to be of help to you, young prince.
And I am grateful that you are here for me.
If only more people could understand and believe...
...that the gods have a path and a purpose for all of us, Hyratheus.
You cannot run from your destiny; it is better to accept it and face up to it with the determination to succeed.
There was once a young man—much like yourself—who faced many trials and tribulations in his life.
Was this man destined to be king as well, Lady Demiarties?
Not exactly, but he learned the importance of embracing one's destiny.
Let me tell you his wonderful story—the tale of Perseus...

...who was born many years ago in the Kingdom of Argos, a land ruled by Acrisius.

Acrisius loved being king. H[e] loved having servants an[d] slaves. He loved his absolu[te] power and his unlimited wea[lth].

Unfortunately, howe[ver,] he was not a good k[ing.]

He had proven to be uncertain in battle, unlucky in hunt, and was known for his terrible temper.

And his greatest fear was losing [his] power, his wealth, and his kingdo[m.]

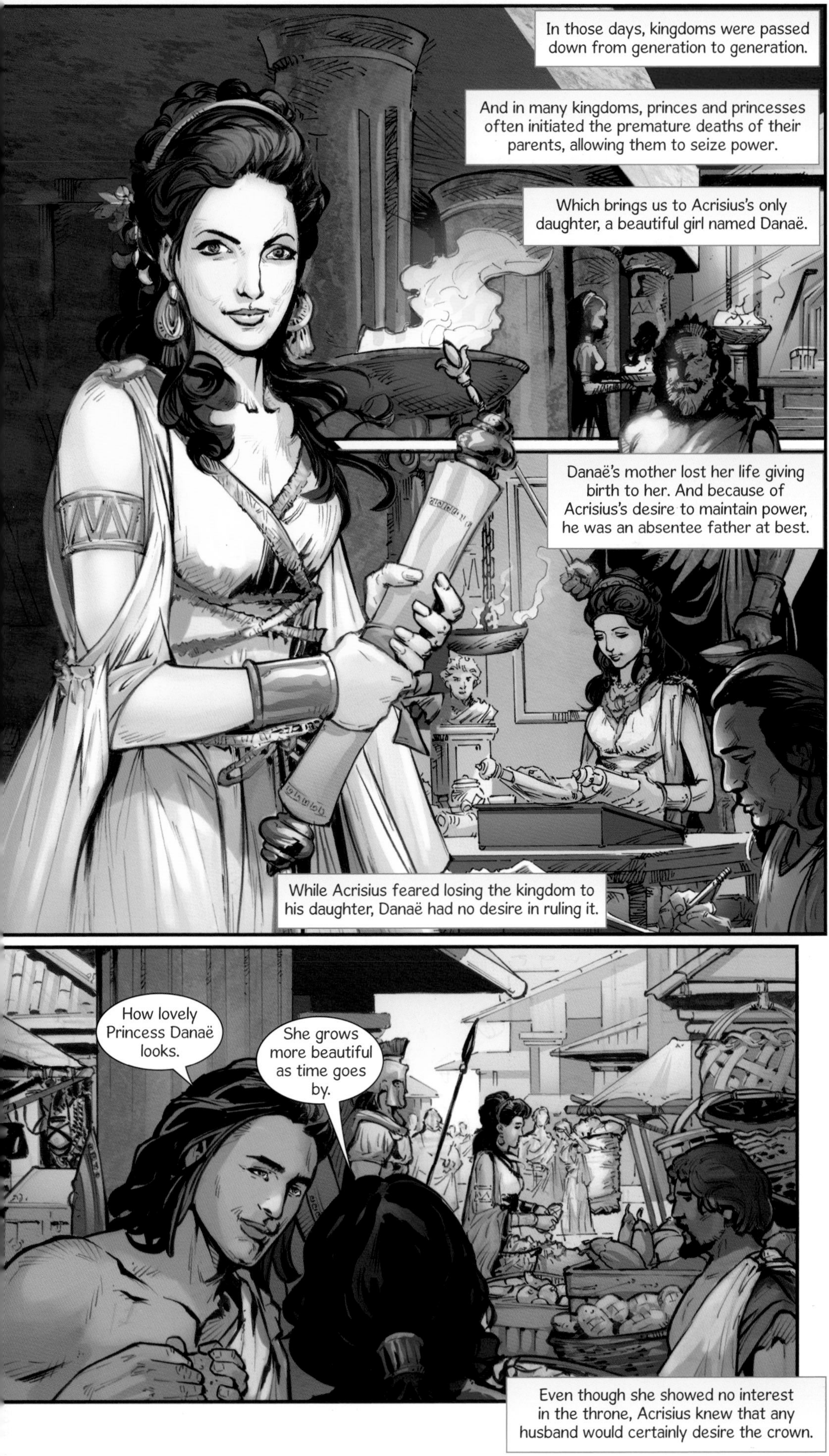
In those days, kingdoms were passed down from generation to generation.
And in many kingdoms, princes and princesses often initiated the premature deaths of their parents, allowing them to seize power.
Which brings us to Acrisius's only daughter, a beautiful girl named Danaë.
Danaë's mother lost her life giving birth to her. And because of Acrisius's desire to maintain power, he was an absentee father at best.
While Acrisius feared losing the kingdom to his daughter, Danaë had no desire in ruling it.
How lovely Princess Danaë looks.
She grows more beautiful as time goes by.
Even though she showed no interest in the throne, Acrisius knew that any husband would certainly desire the crown.

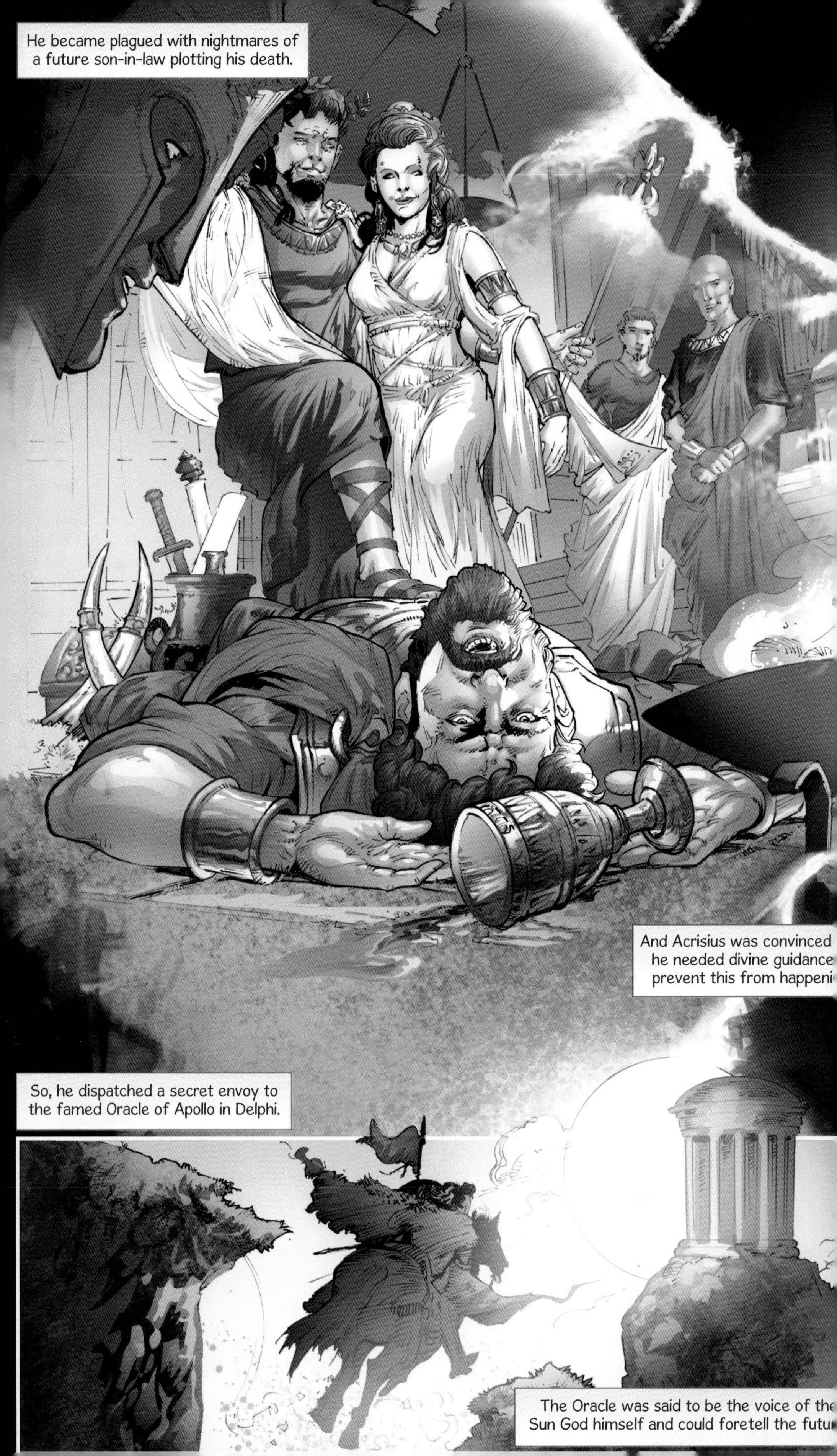
He became plagued with nightmares of a future son-in-law plotting his death.
And Acrisius was convinced he needed divine guidance prevent this from happeni
So, he dispatched a secret envoy to the famed Oracle of Apollo in Delphi.
The Oracle was said to be the voice of the Sun God himself and could foretell the futu

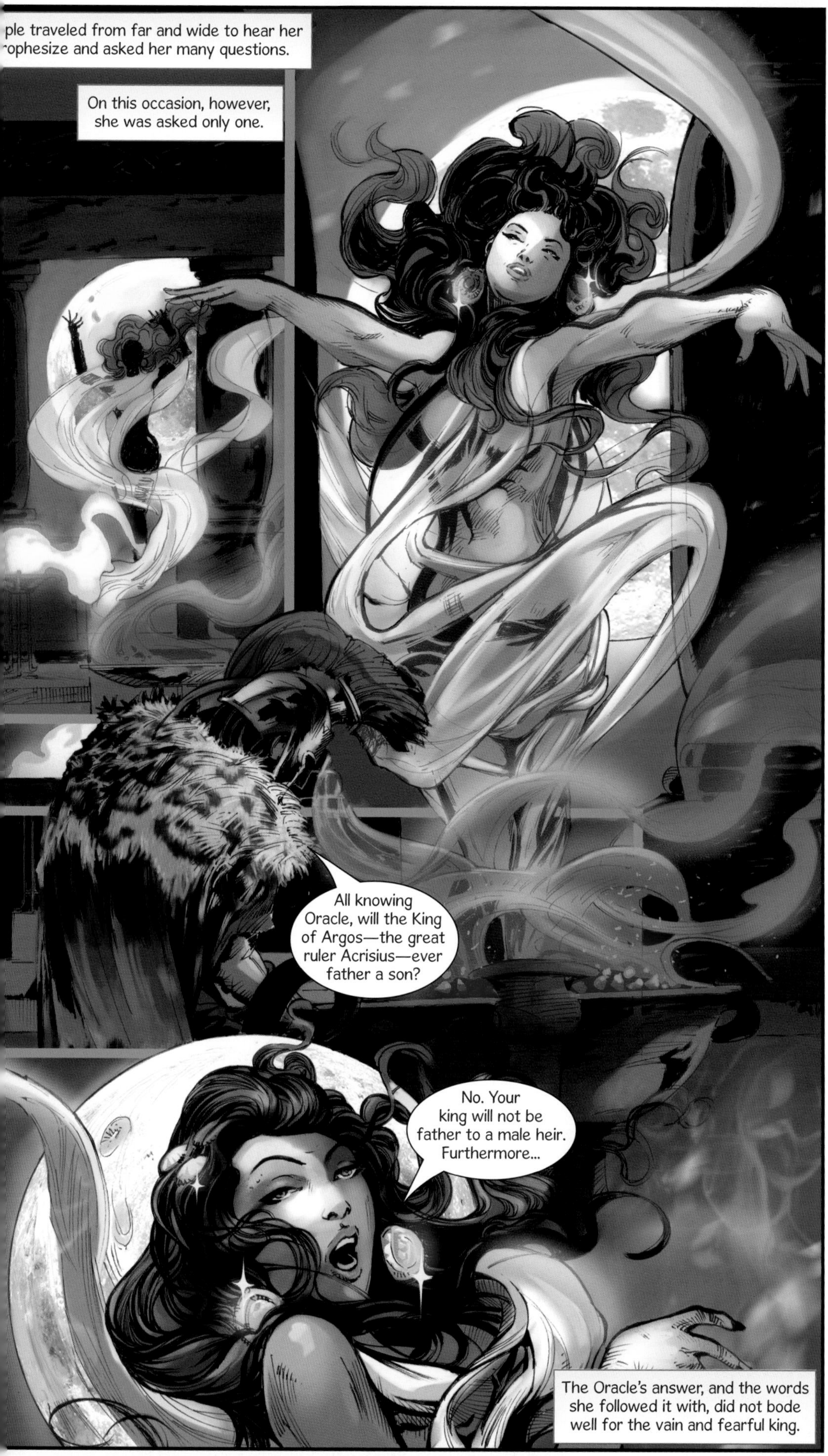
ple traveled from far and wide to hear her
rophesize and asked her many questions.
On this occasion, however, she was asked only one.
All knowing Oracle, will the King of Argos—the great ruler Acrisius—ever father a son?
No. Your king will not be father to a male heir. Furthermore...
The Oracle's answer, and the words she followed it with, did not bode well for the vain and fearful king.

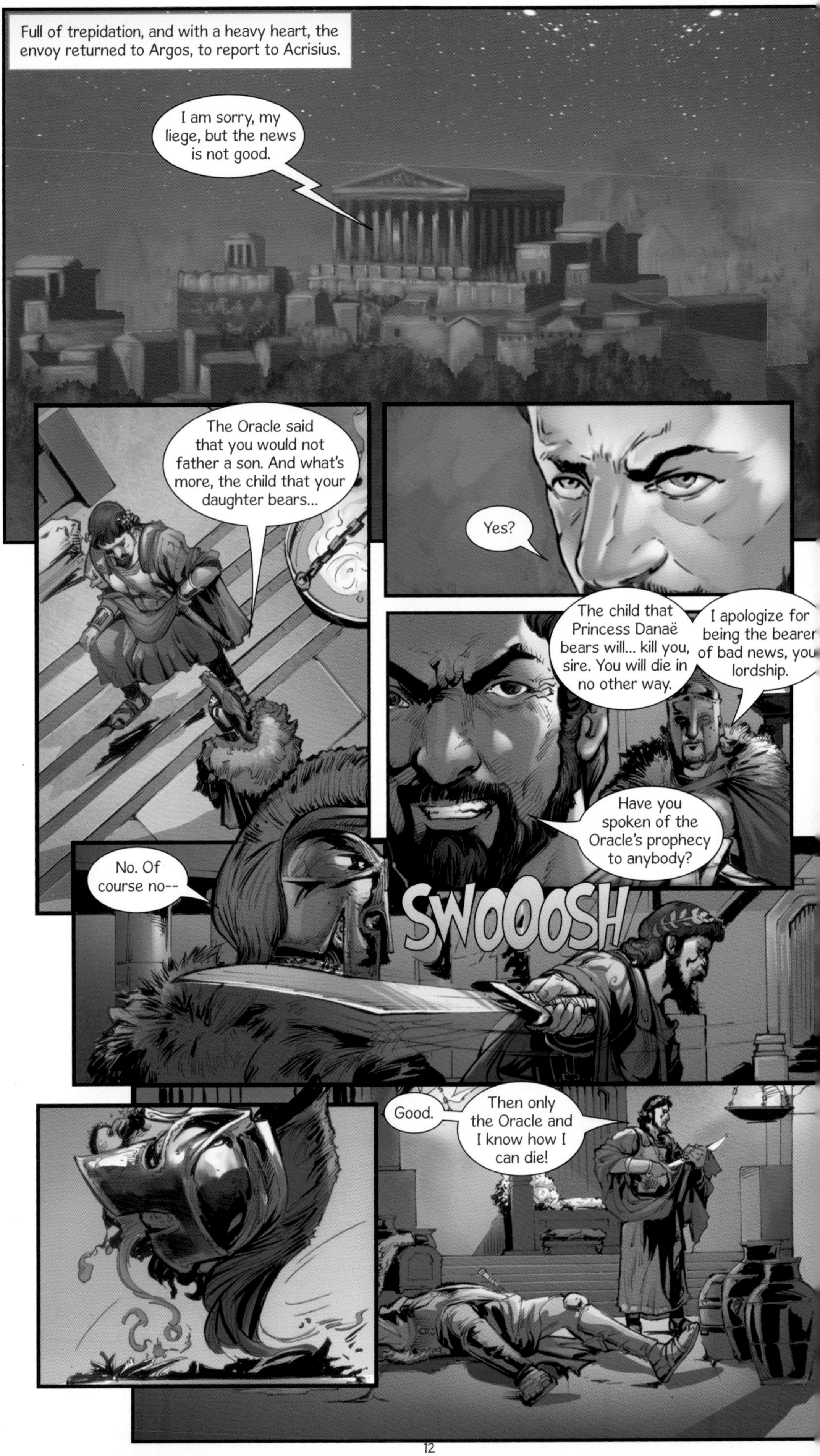
Full of trepidation, and with a heavy heart, the envoy returned to Argos, to report to Acrisius.
I am sorry, my liege, but the news is not good.
The Oracle said that you would not father a son. And what's more, the child that your daughter bears...
Yes?
The child that Princess Danaë bears will... kill you, sire. You will die in no other way.
I apologize for being the bearer of bad news, you lordship.
Have you spoken of the Oracle's prophecy to anybody?
No. Of course no--
SWOOOSH
Good.
Then only the Oracle and I know how I can die!

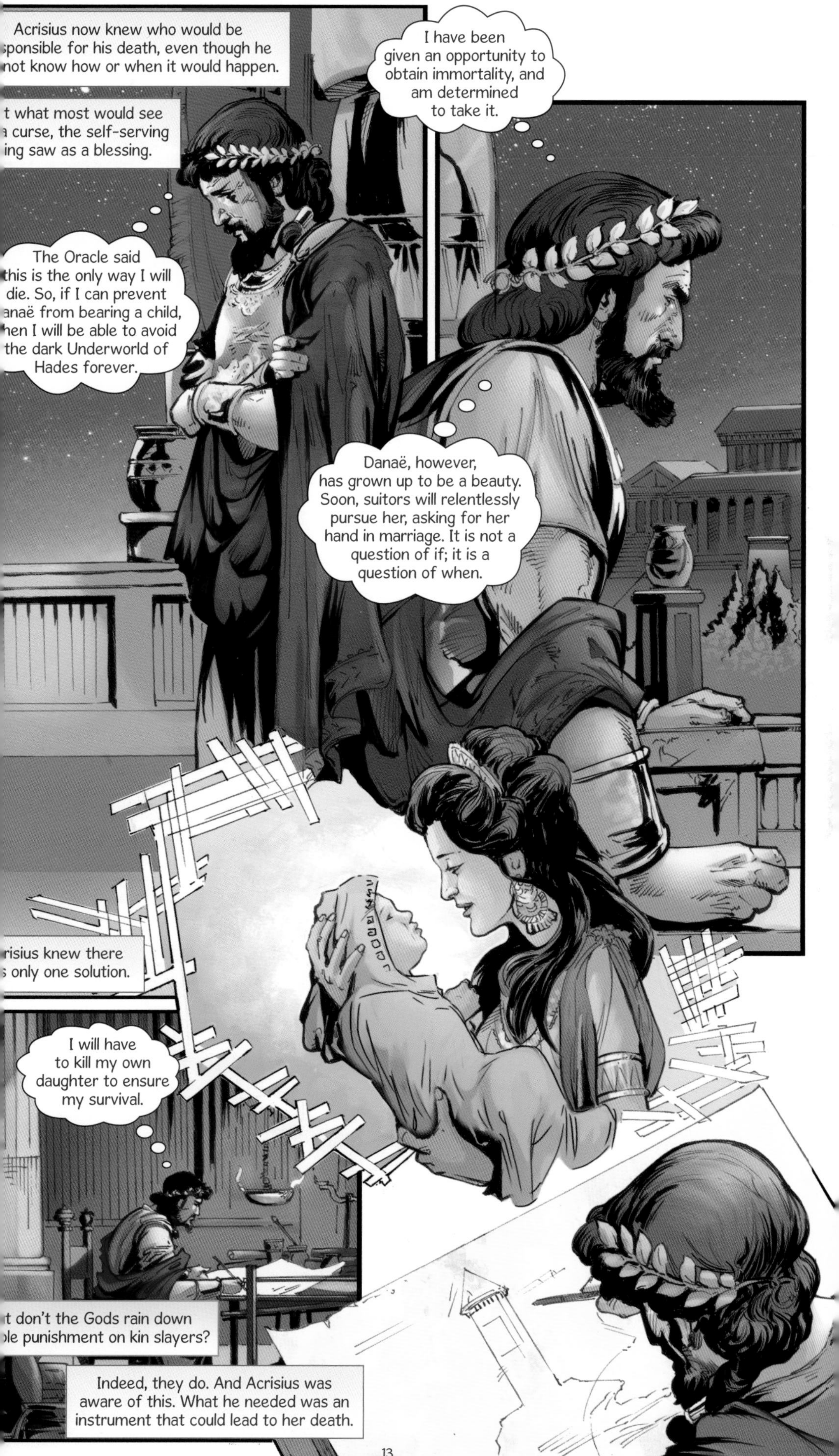

Acrisius now knew who would be
sponsible for his death, even though he
not know how or when it would happen.
t what most would see
a curse, the self-serving
ing saw as a blessing.
The Oracle said this is the only way I will die. So, if I can prevent anaë from bearing a child, hen I will be able to avoid the dark Underworld of Hades forever.
I have been given an opportunity to obtain immortality, and am determined to take it.
Danaë, however, has grown up to be a beauty. Soon, suitors will relentlessly pursue her, asking for her hand in marriage. It is not a question of if; it is a question of when.
risius knew there
s only one solution.
I will have to kill my own daughter to ensure my survival.
t don't the Gods rain down
le punishment on kin slayers?
Indeed, they do. And Acrisius was aware of this. What he needed was an instrument that could lead to her death.

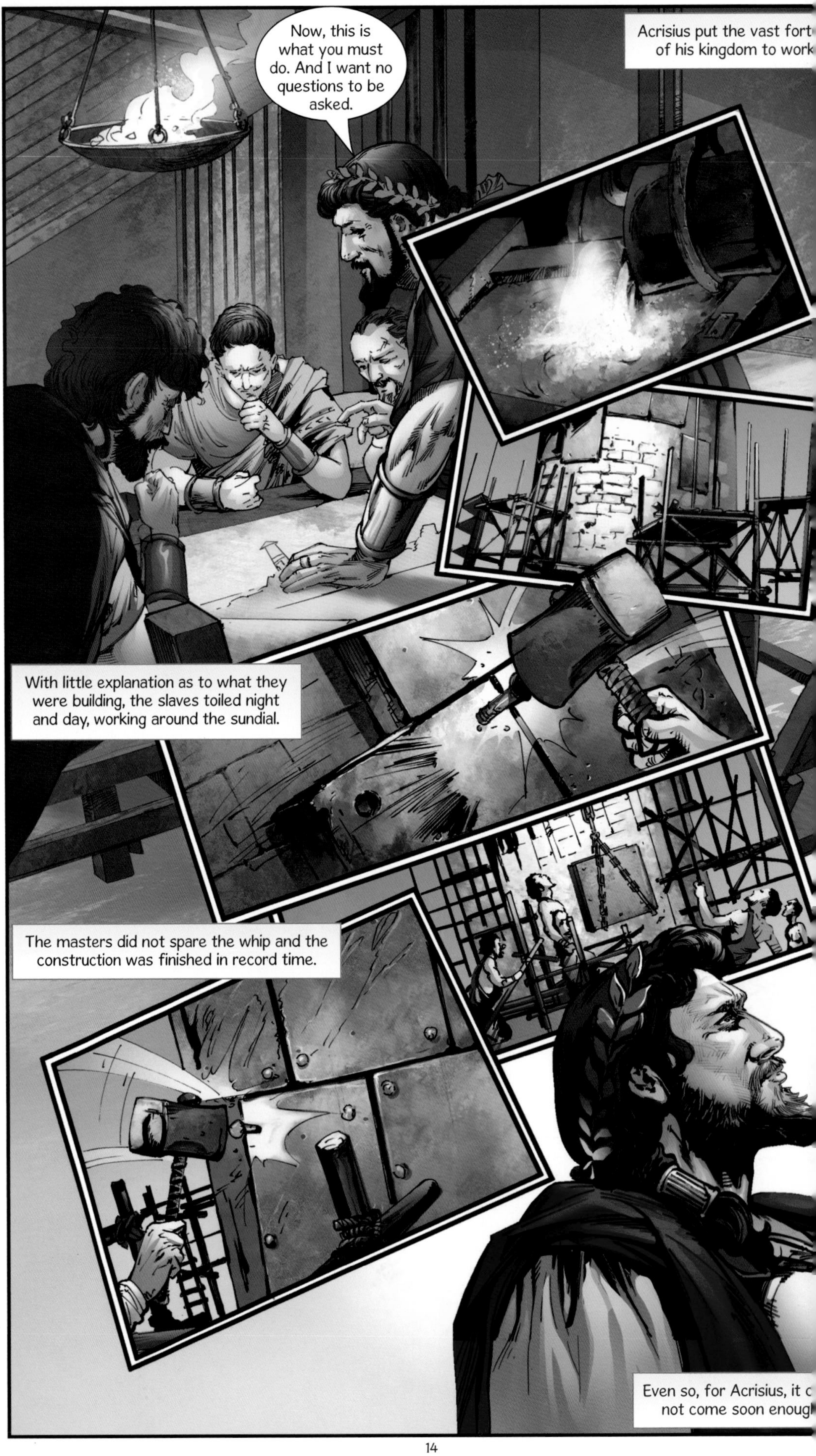
Acrisius put the vast fort
of his kingdom to work
Now, this is what you must do. And I want no questions to be asked.
With little explanation as to what they were building, the slaves toiled night and day, working around the sundial.
The masters did not spare the whip and the construction was finished in record time.
Even so, for Acrisius, it c
not come soon enoug

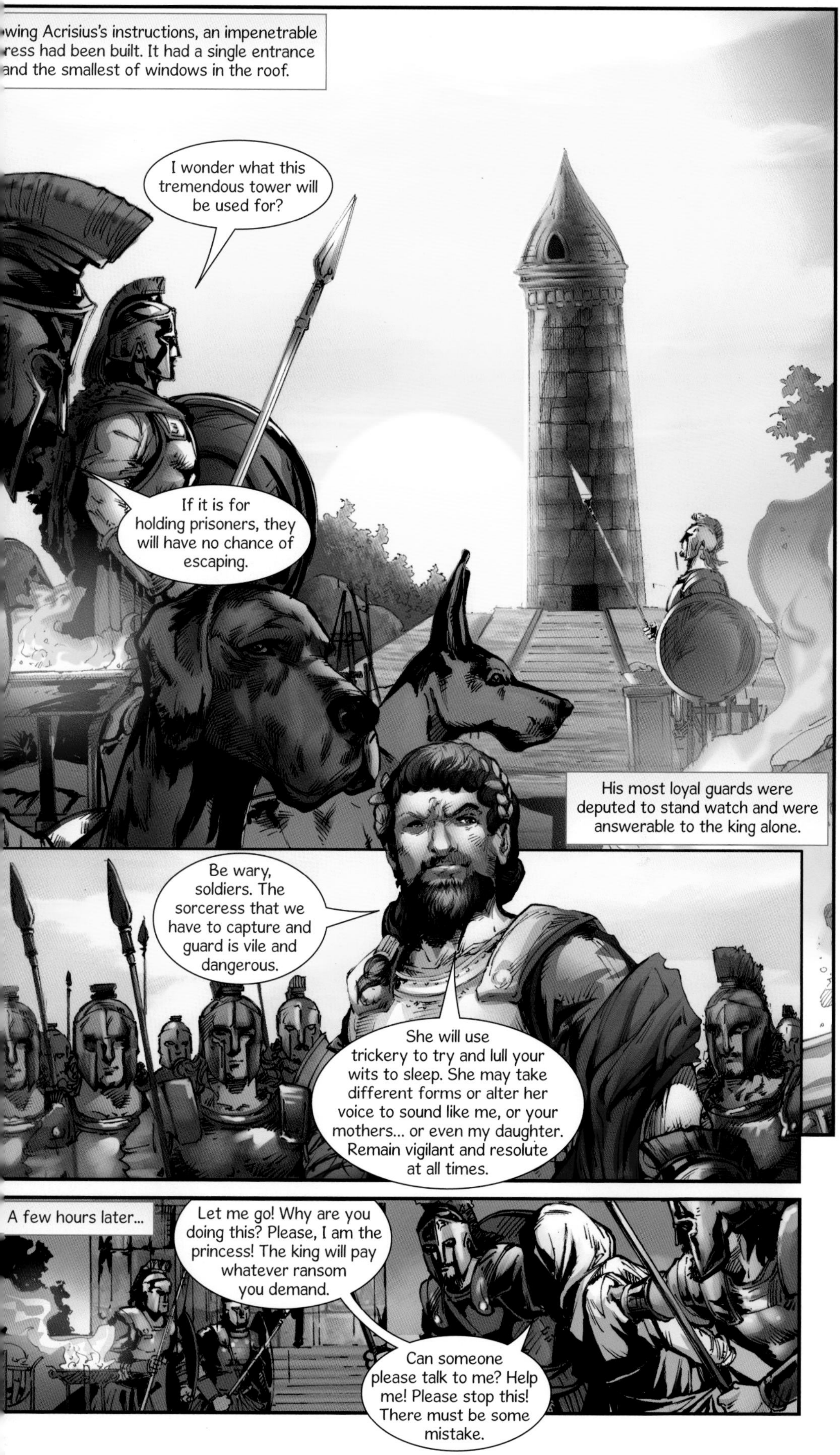

wing Acrisius's instructions, an impenetrable ress had been built. It had a single entrance and the smallest of windows in the roof.
I wonder what this tremendous tower will be used for?
If it is for holding prisoners, they will have no chance of escaping.
His most loyal guards were deputed to stand watch and were answerable to the king alone.
Be wary, soldiers. The sorceress that we have to capture and guard is vile and dangerous.
She will use trickery to try and lull your wits to sleep. She may take different forms or alter her voice to sound like me, or your mothers... or even my daughter. Remain vigilant and resolute at all times.
A few hours later...
Let me go! Why are you doing this? Please, I am the princess! The king will pay whatever ransom you demand.
Can someone please talk to me? Help me! Please stop this! There must be some mistake.

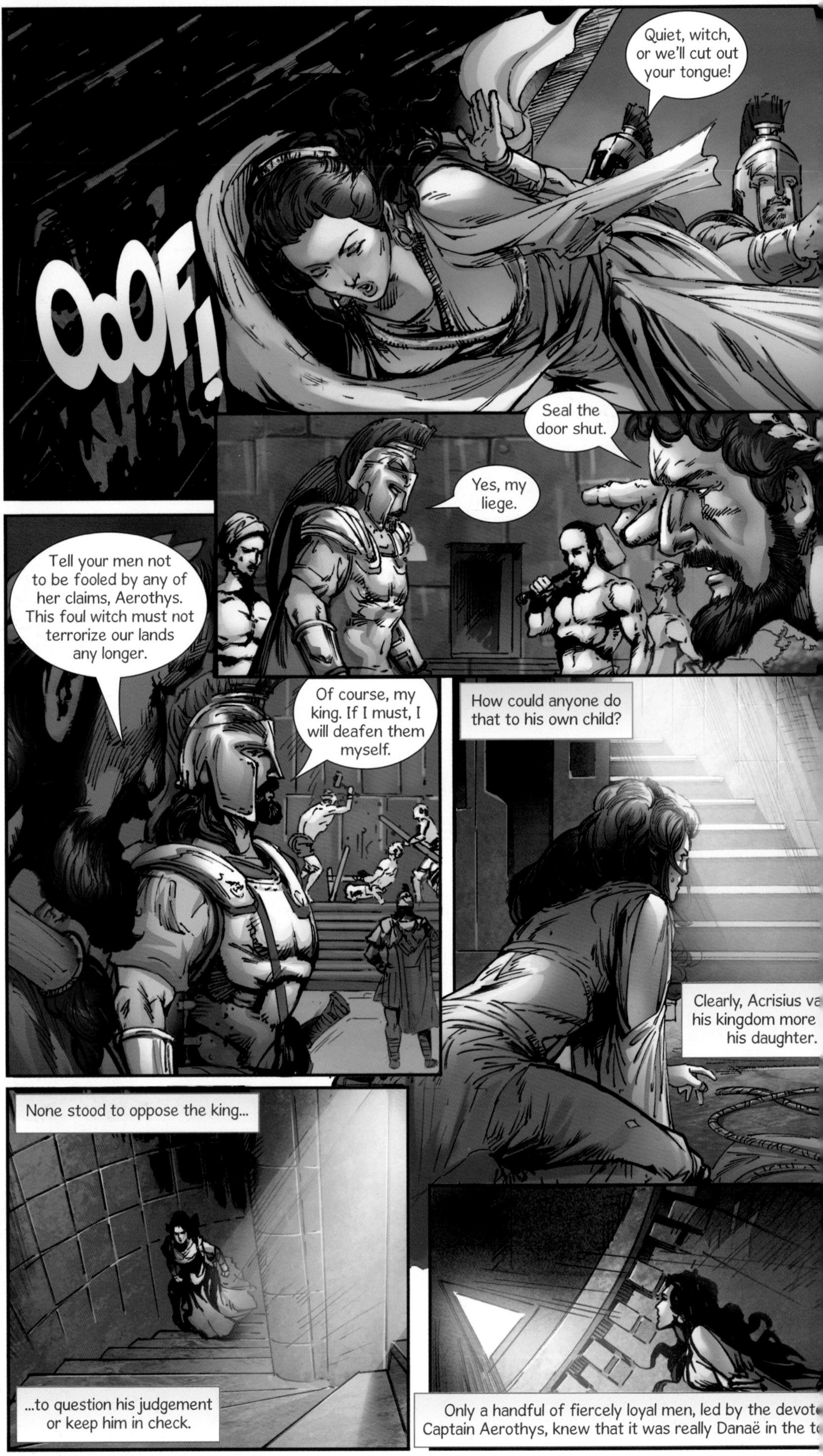

Quiet, witch, or we'll cut out your tongue!
OOOF!
Seal the door shut.
Yes, my liege.
Tell your men not to be fooled by any of her claims, Aerothys. This foul witch must not terrorize our lands any longer.
Of course, my king. If I must, I will deafen them myself.
How could anyone do that to his own child?
Clearly, Acrisius va
his kingdom more
his daughter.
None stood to oppose the king...
...to question his judgement or keep him in check.
Only a handful of fiercely loyal men, led by the devot
Captain Aerothys, knew that it was really Danaë in the t

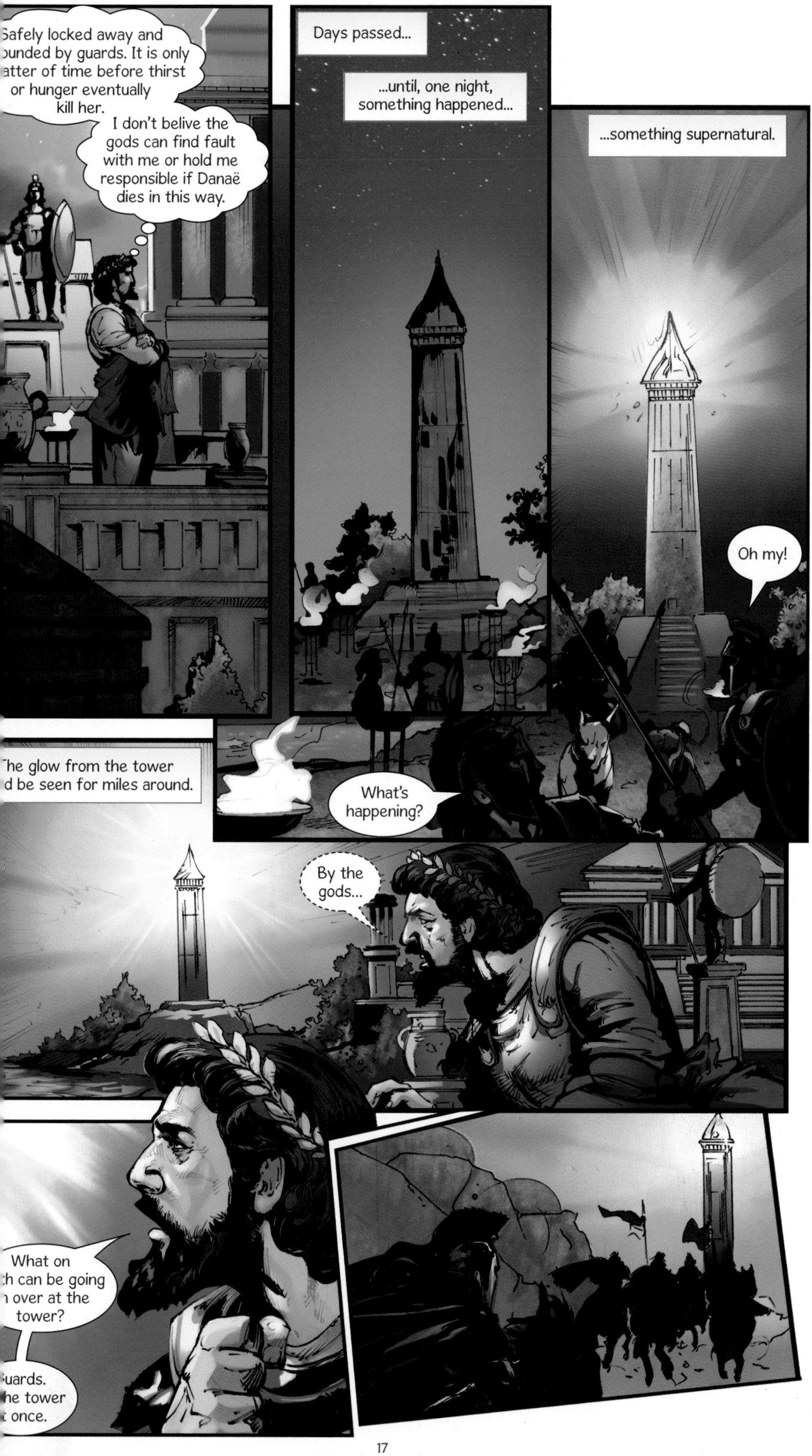

Safely locked away and
ounded by guards. It is only
atter of time before thirst
or hunger eventually
kill her.
I don't belive the
gods can find fault
with me or hold me
responsible if Danaë
dies in this way.
Days passed...
...until, one night,
something happened...
...something supernatural.
Oh my!
What's
happening?
The glow from the tower
d be seen for miles around.
By the
gods...
What on
h can be going
n over at the
tower?
uards.
he tower
t once.

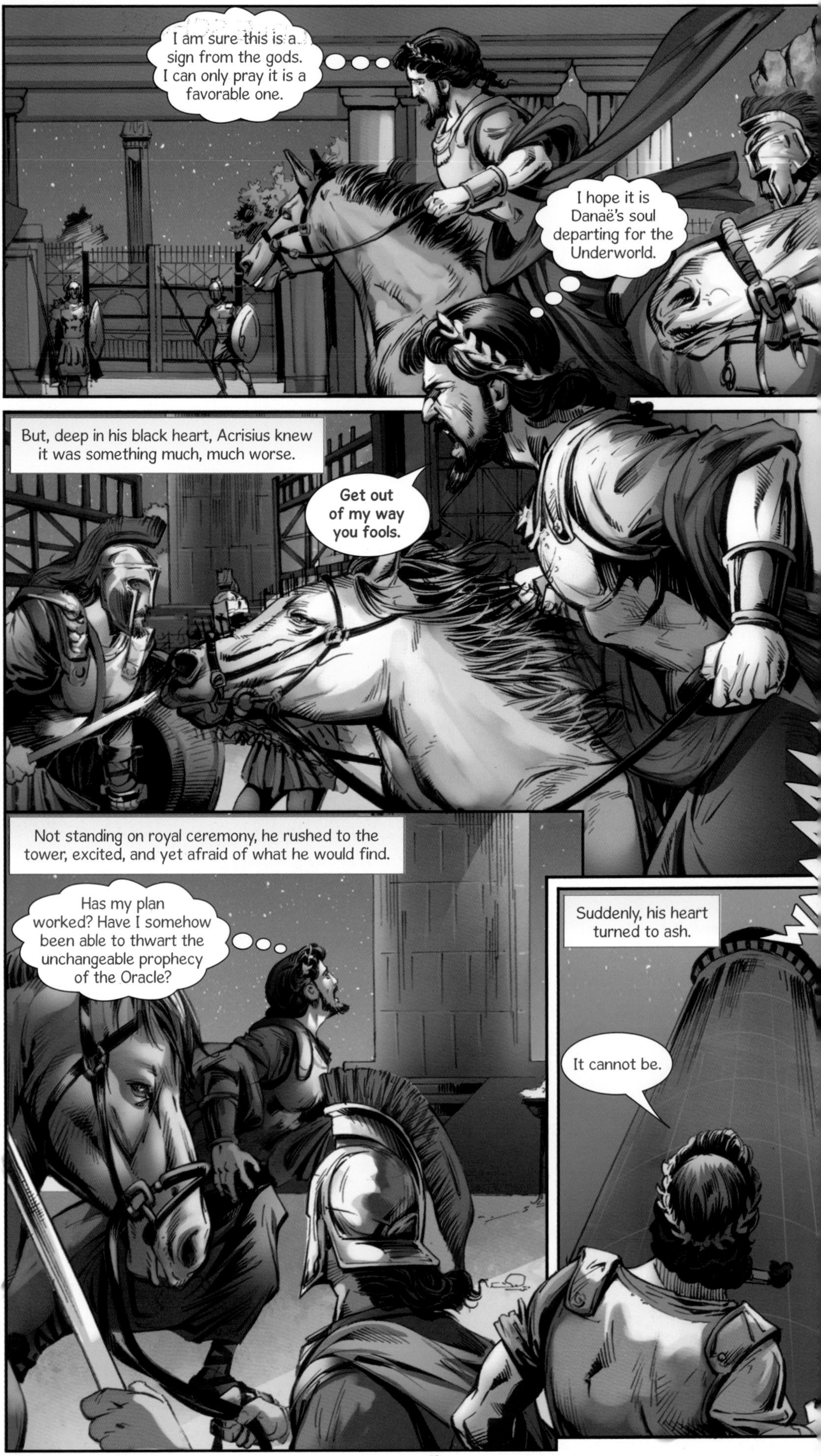
I am sure this is a sign from the gods. I can only pray it is a favorable one.
I hope it is Danaë's soul departing for the Underworld.
But, deep in his black heart, Acrisius knew it was something much, much worse.
Get out of my way you fools.
Not standing on royal ceremony, he rushed to the tower, excited, and yet afraid of what he would find.
Has my plan worked? Have I somehow been able to thwart the unchangeable prophecy of the Oracle?
Suddenly, his heart turned to ash.
It cannot be.

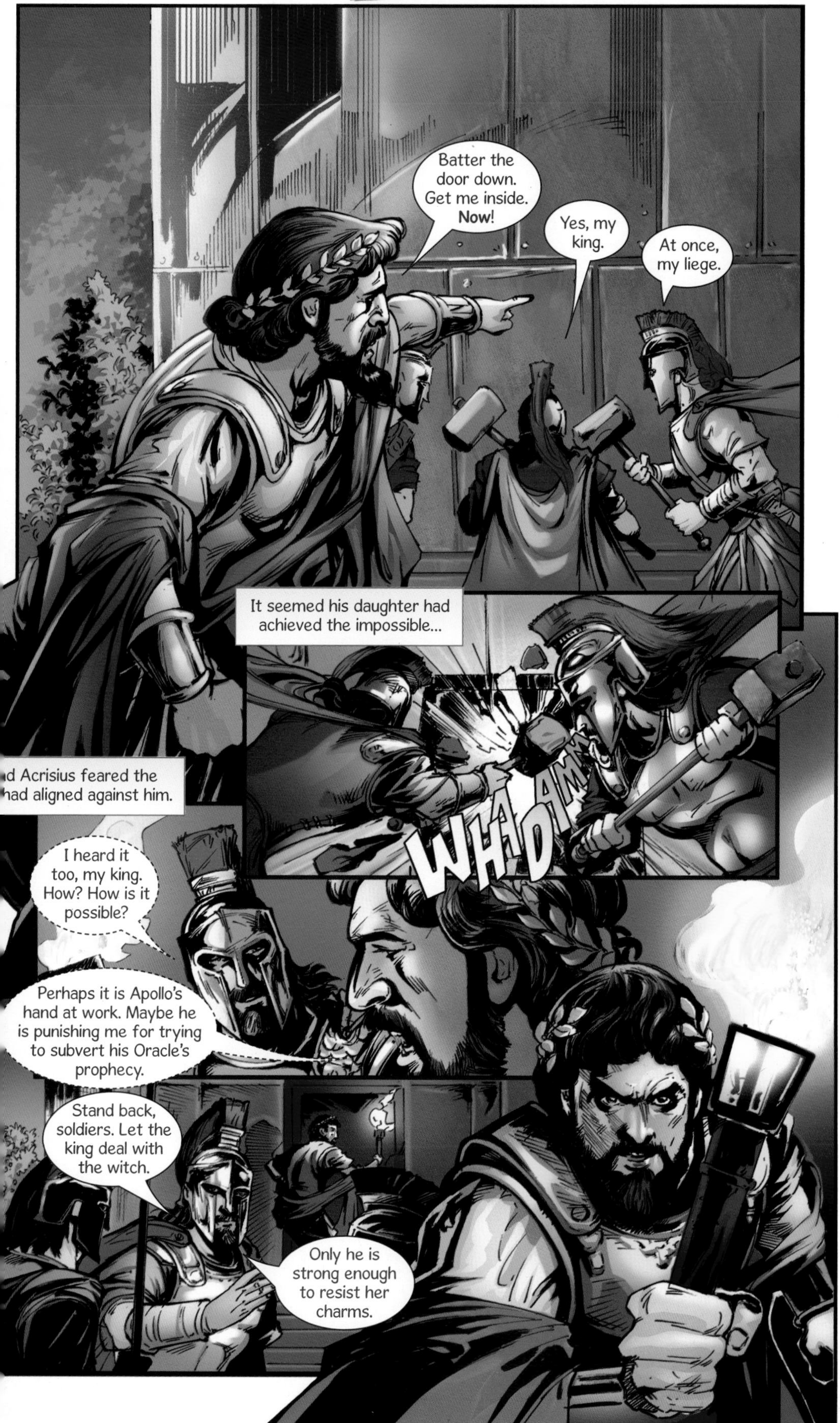
Batter the door down. Get me inside. **Now!**
Yes, my king.
At once, my liege.
It seemed his daughter had achieved the impossible...
d Acrisius feared the
had aligned against him.
I heard it too, my king. How? How is it possible?
Perhaps it is Apollo's hand at work. Maybe he is punishing me for trying to subvert his Oracle's prophecy.
Stand back, soldiers. Let the king deal with the witch.
Only he is strong enough to resist her charms.

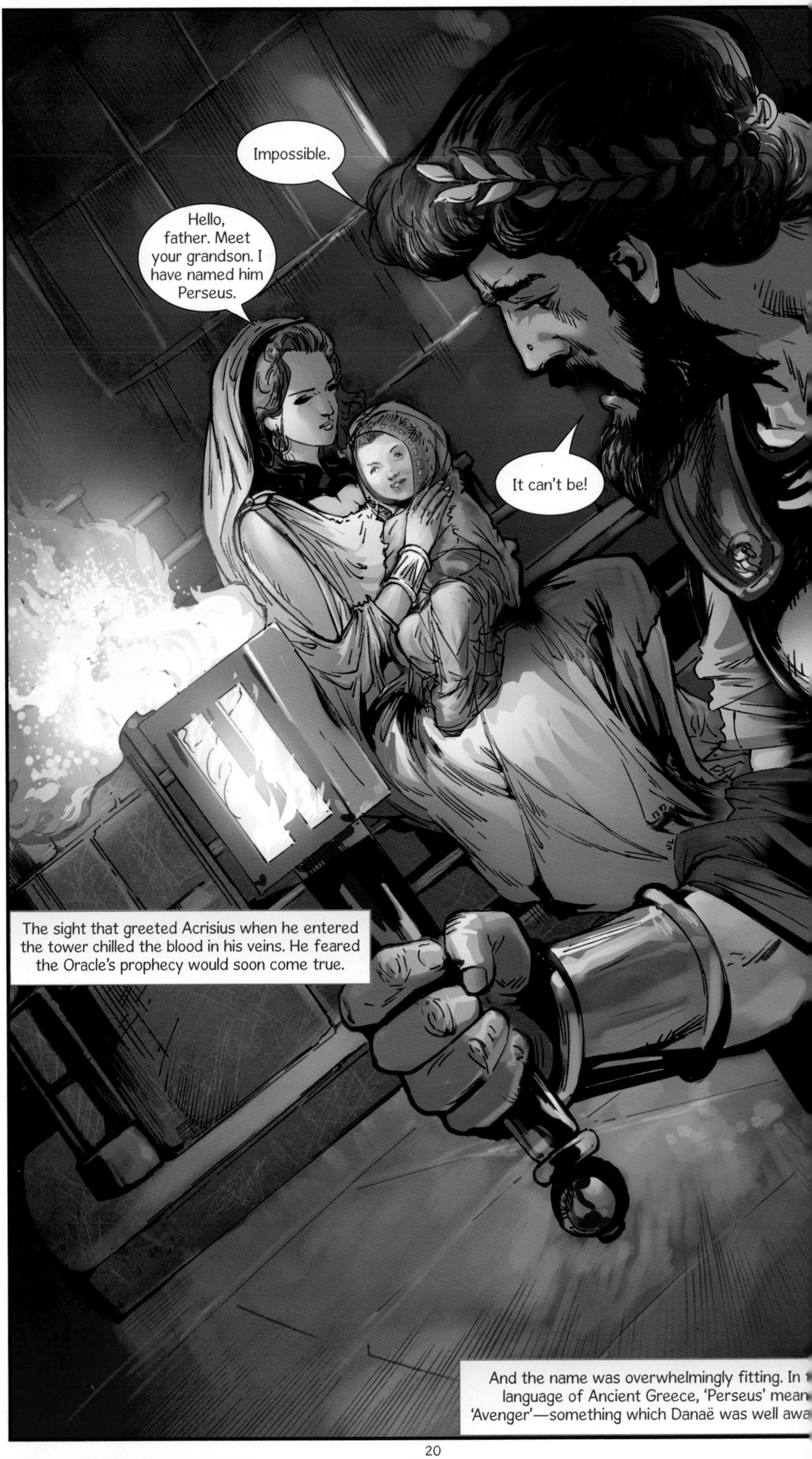
Hello, father. Meet your grandson. I have named him Perseus.
Impossible.
It can't be!
The sight that greeted Acrisius when he entered the tower chilled the blood in his veins. He feared the Oracle's prophecy would soon come true.
And the name was overwhelmingly fitting. In
language of Ancient Greece, 'Perseus' mean
'Avenger'—something which Danaë was well aw

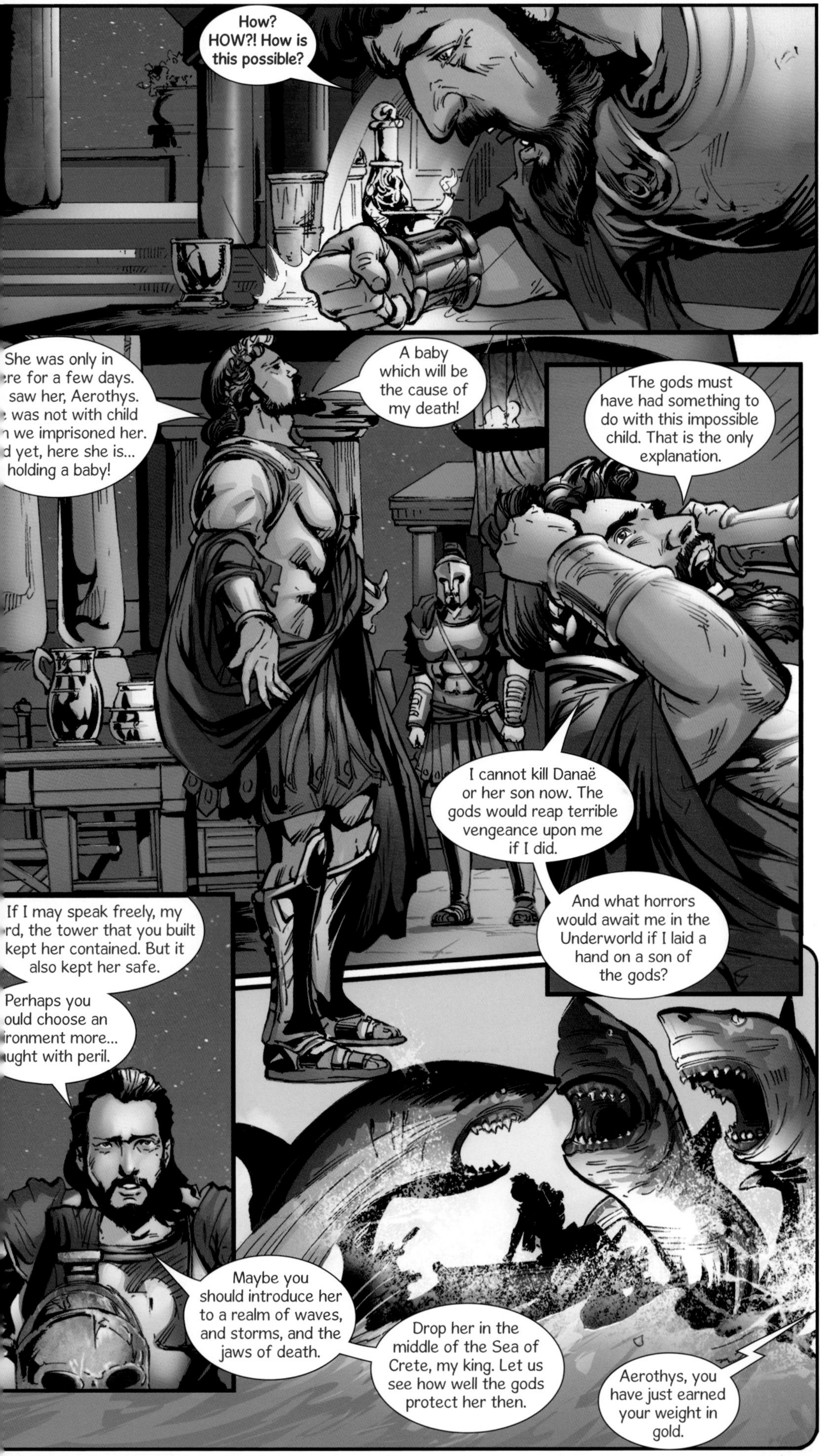
How? HOW?! How is this possible?
She was only in re for a few days. saw her, Aerothys. was not with child n we imprisoned her. d yet, here she is... holding a baby!
A baby which will be the cause of my death!
The gods must have had something to do with this impossible child. That is the only explanation.
I cannot kill Danaë or her son now. The gods would reap terrible vengeance upon me if I did.
And what horrors would await me in the Underworld if I laid a hand on a son of the gods?
If I may speak freely, my rd, the tower that you built kept her contained. But it also kept her safe.
Perhaps you ould choose an ironment more... ught with peril.
Maybe you should introduce her to a realm of waves, and storms, and the jaws of death.
Drop her in the middle of the Sea of Crete, my king. Let us see how well the gods protect her then.
Aerothys, you have just earned your weight in gold.

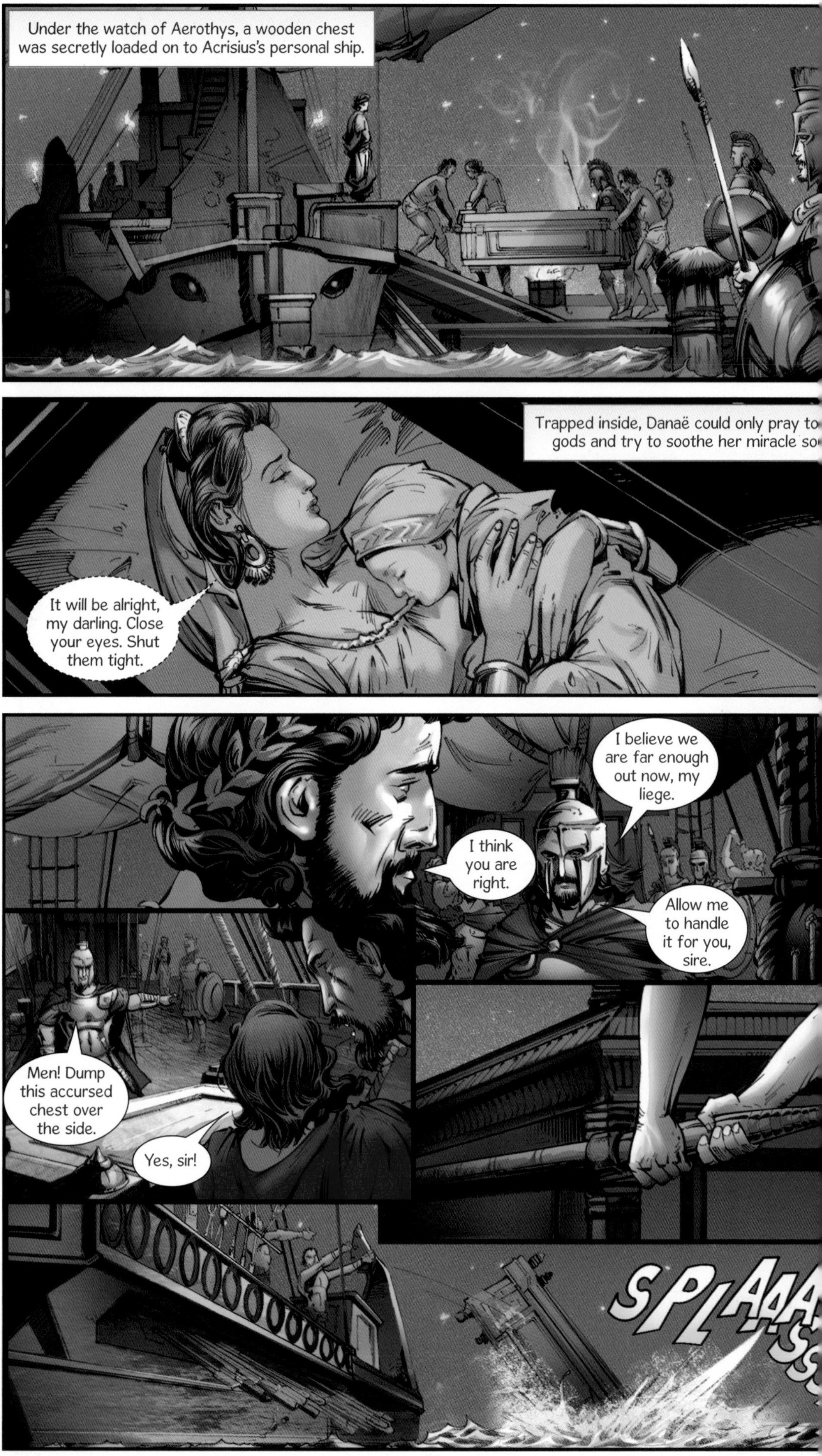
Under the watch of Aerothys, a wooden chest was secretly loaded on to Acrisius's personal ship.
Trapped inside, Danaë could only pray to
gods and try to soothe her miracle so
It will be alright, my darling. Close your eyes. Shut them tight.
I believe we are far enough out now, my liege.
I think you are right.
Allow me to handle it for you, sire.
Men! Dump this accursed chest over the side.
Yes, sir!
SPLAAA
SS

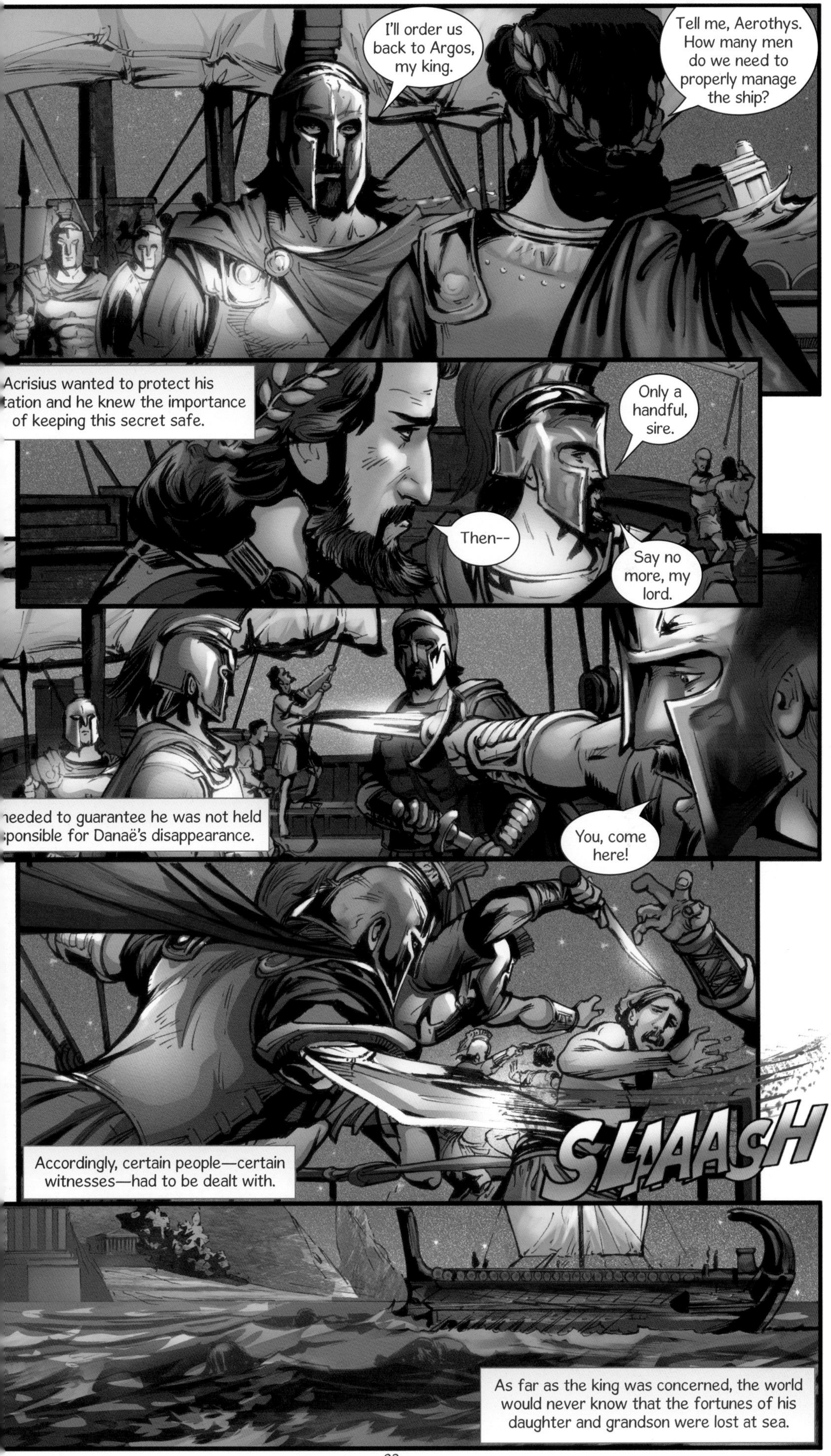
I'll order us back to Argos, my king.
Tell me, Aerothys. How many men do we need to properly manage the ship?
Acrisius wanted to protect his tation and he knew the importance of keeping this secret safe.
Only a handful, sire.
Then--
Say no more, my lord.
ieeded to guarantee he was not held sponsible for Danaë's disappearance.
You, come here!
SLAASH
Accordingly, certain people—certain witnesses—had to be dealt with.
As far as the king was concerned, the world would never know that the fortunes of his daughter and grandson were lost at sea.

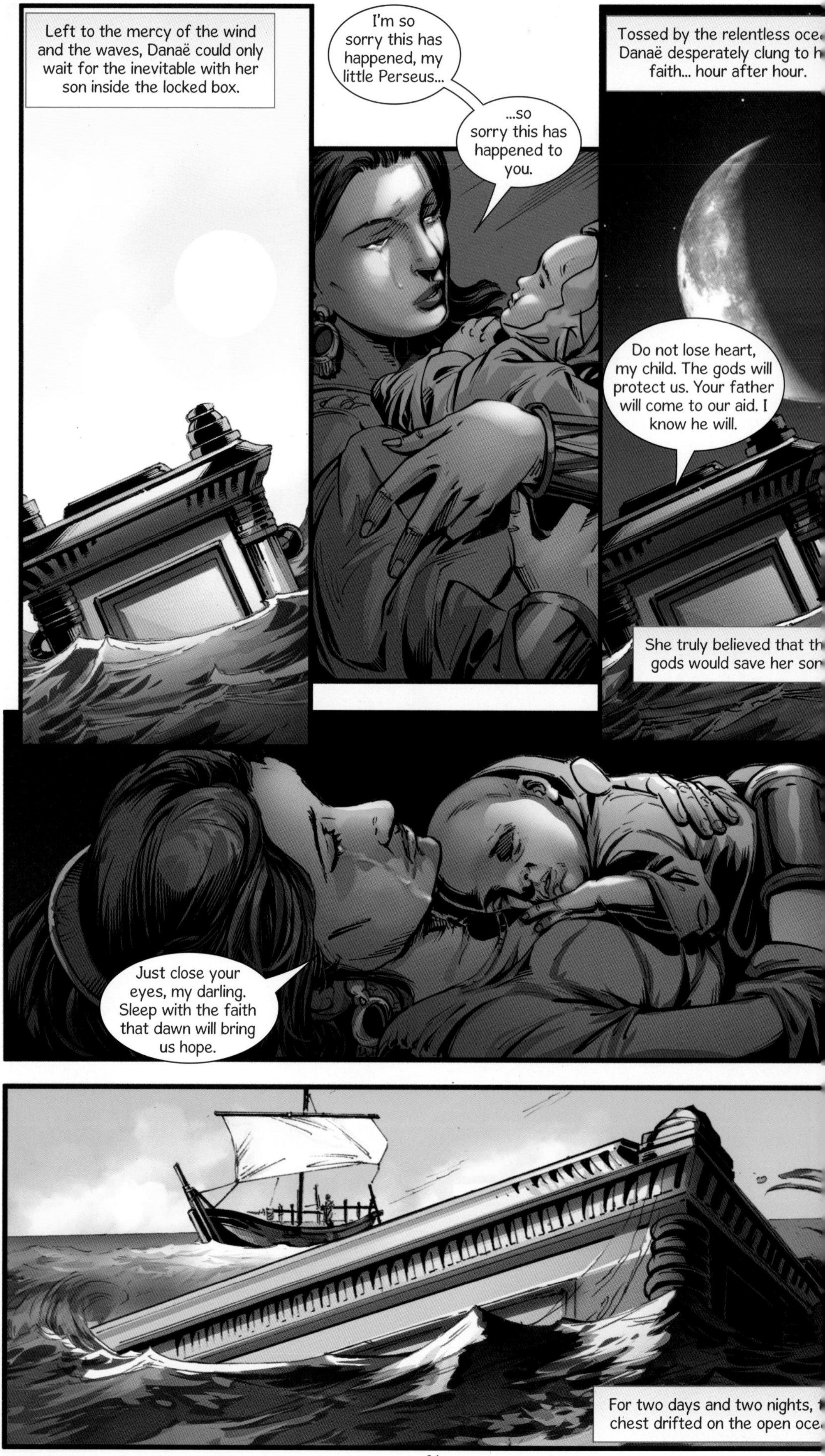
Left to the mercy of the wind and the waves, Danaë could only wait for the inevitable with her son inside the locked box.
I'm so sorry this has happened, my little Perseus...
...so sorry this has happened to you.
Tossed by the relentless oce
Danaë desperately clung to h
faith... hour after hour.
Do not lose heart, my child. The gods will protect us. Your father will come to our aid. I know he will.
She truly believed that th
gods would save her so
Just close your eyes, my darling. Sleep with the faith that dawn will bring us hope.
For two days and two nights,
chest drifted on the open oce

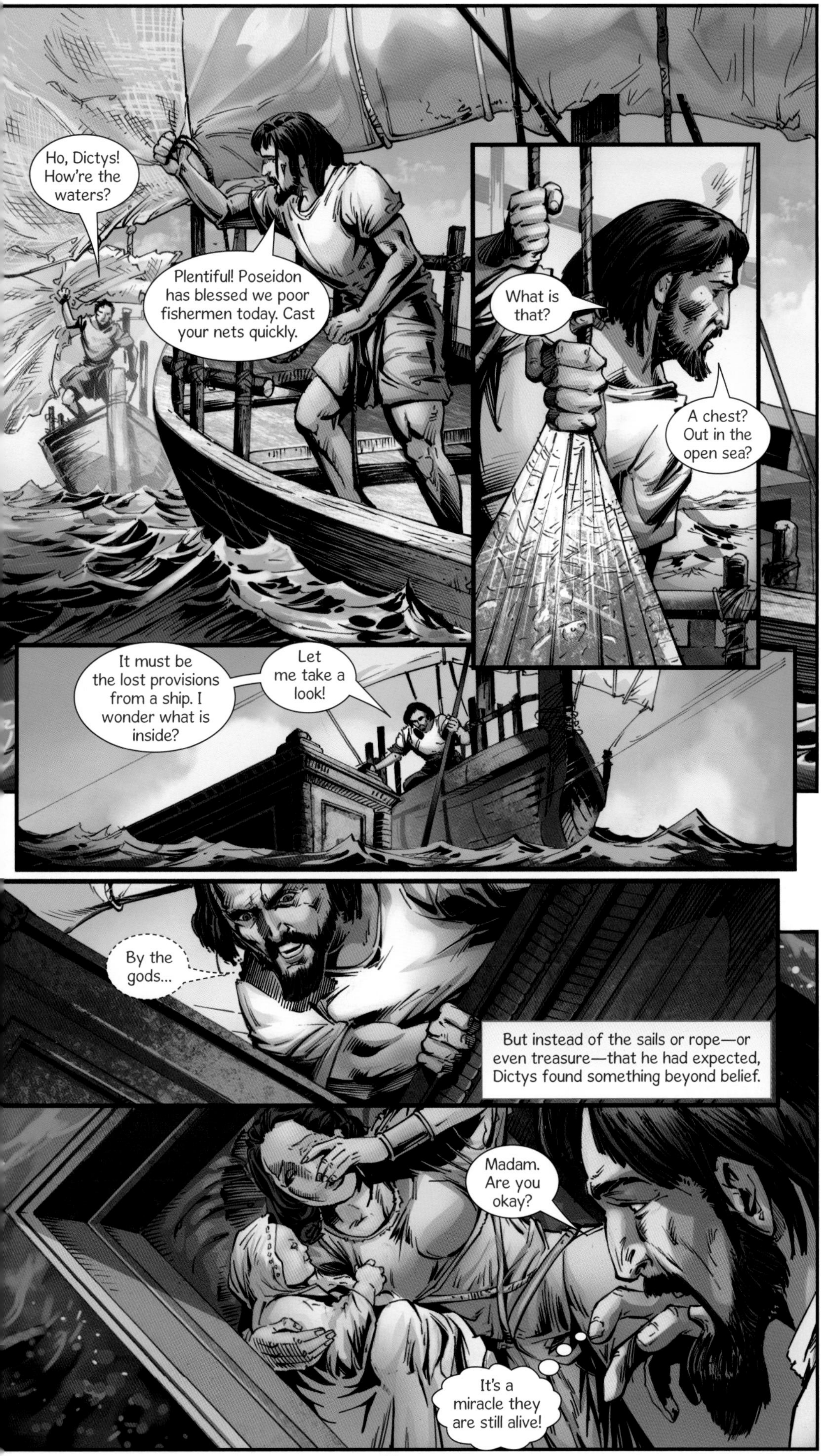
Ho, Dictys! How're the waters?
Plentiful! Poseidon has blessed we poor fishermen today. Cast your nets quickly.
What is that?
A chest? Out in the open sea?
It must be the lost provisions from a ship. I wonder what is inside?
Let me take a look!
By the gods...
But instead of the sails or rope—or even treasure—that he had expected, Dictys found something beyond belief.
Madam. Are you okay?
It's a miracle they are still alive!

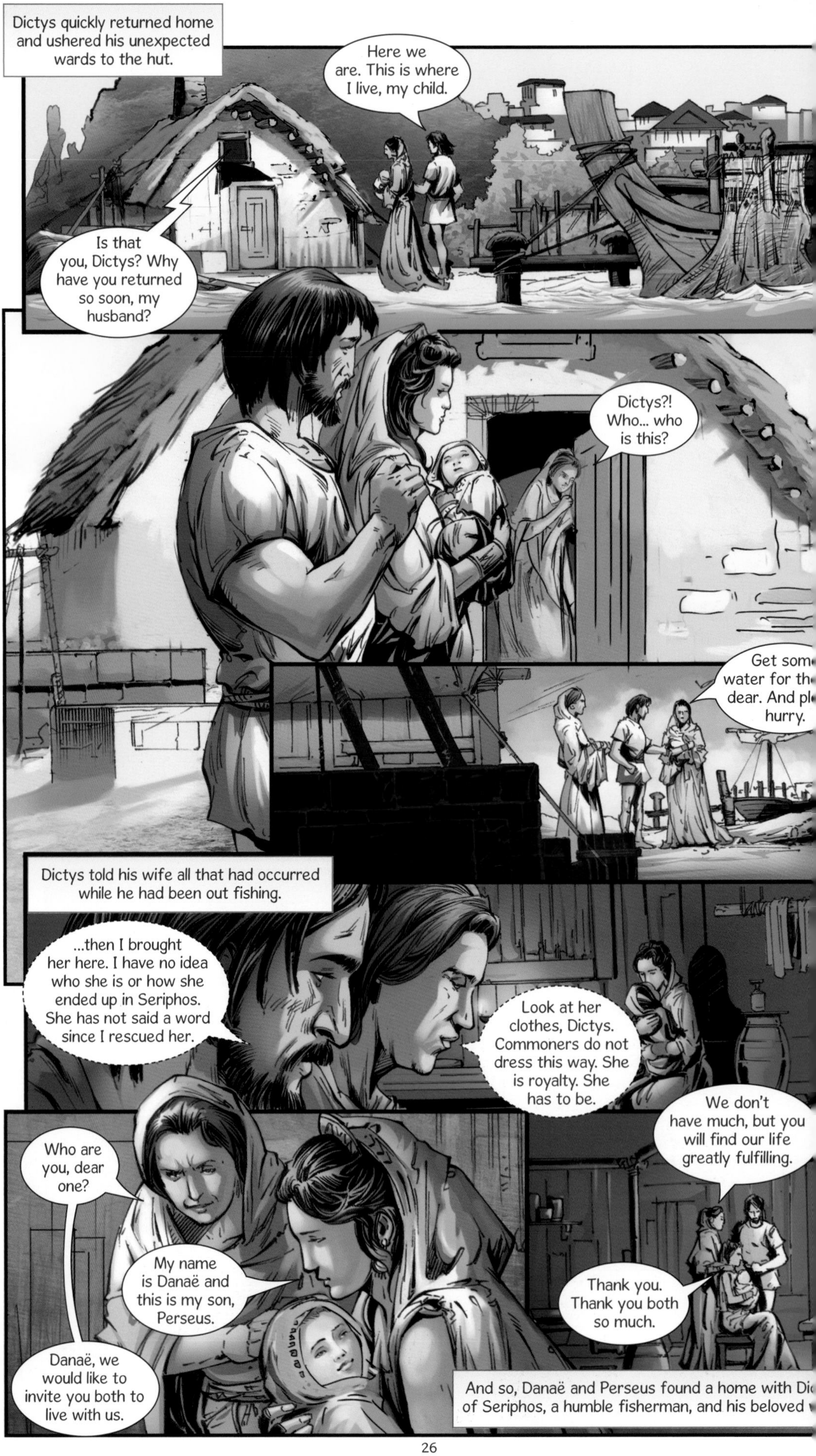

Dictys quickly returned home and ushered his unexpected wards to the hut.
Here we are. This is where I live, my child.
Is that you, Dictys? Why have you returned so soon, my husband?
Dictys?! Who... who is this?
Get som water for th dear. And pl hurry.
Dictys told his wife all that had occurred while he had been out fishing.
...then I brought her here. I have no idea who she is or how she ended up in Seriphos. She has not said a word since I rescued her.
Look at her clothes, Dictys. Commoners do not dress this way. She is royalty. She has to be.
Who are you, dear one?
My name is Danaë and this is my son, Perseus.
Danaë, we would like to invite you both to live with us.
We don't have much, but you will find our life greatly fulfilling.
Thank you. Thank you both so much.
And so, Danaë and Perseus found a home with Di of Seriphos, a humble fisherman, and his beloved

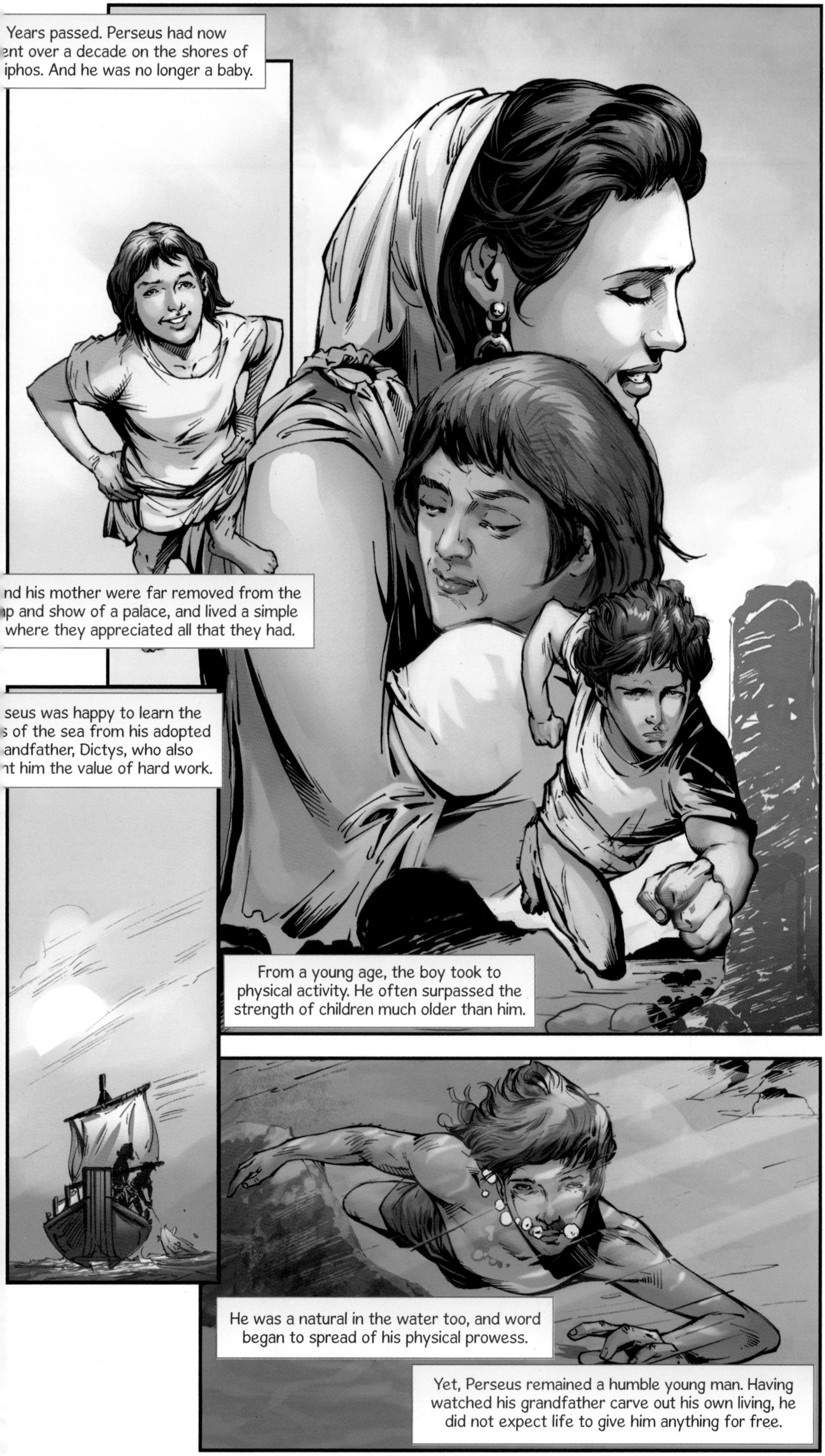
Years passed. Perseus had now
ent over a decade on the shores of
iphos. And he was no longer a baby.
nd his mother were far removed from the
p and show of a palace, and lived a simple
where they appreciated all that they had.
seus was happy to learn the
s of the sea from his adopted
andfather, Dictys, who also
nt him the value of hard work.
From a young age, the boy took to physical activity. He often surpassed the strength of children much older than him.
He was a natural in the water too, and word began to spread of his physical prowess.
Yet, Perseus remained a humble young man. Having watched his grandfather carve out his own living, he did not expect life to give him anything for free.

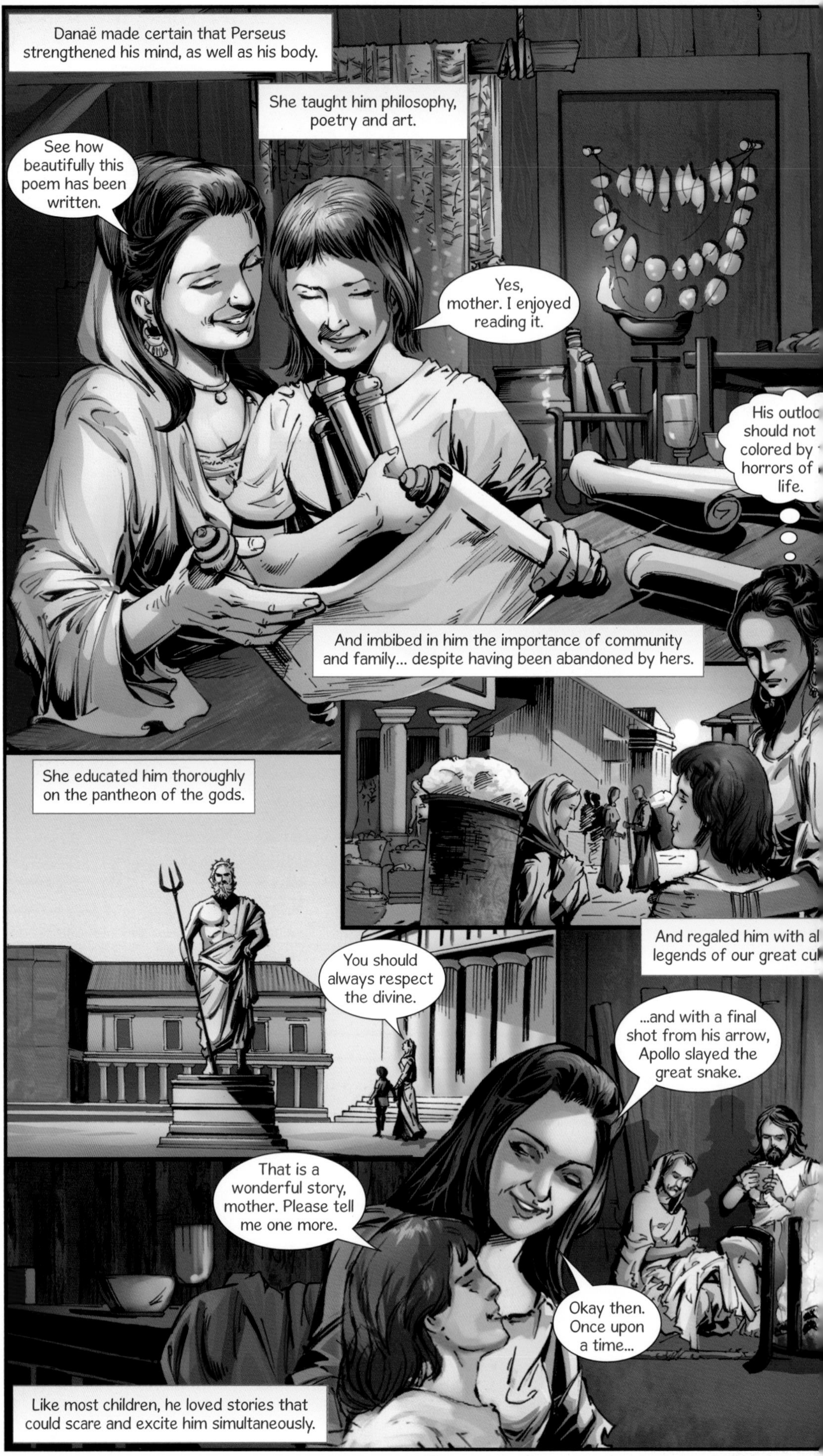

Danaë made certain that Perseus strengthened his mind, as well as his body.
She taught him philosophy, poetry and art.
See how beautifully this poem has been written.
Yes, mother. I enjoyed reading it.
His outloo should not colored by horrors of life.
And imbibed in him the importance of community and family... despite having been abandoned by hers.
She educated him thoroughly on the pantheon of the gods.
You should always respect the divine.
And regaled him with al legends of our great cu
...and with a final shot from his arrow, Apollo slayed the great snake.
That is a wonderful story, mother. Please tell me one more.
Okay then. Once upon a time...
Like most children, he loved stories that could scare and excite him simultaneously.

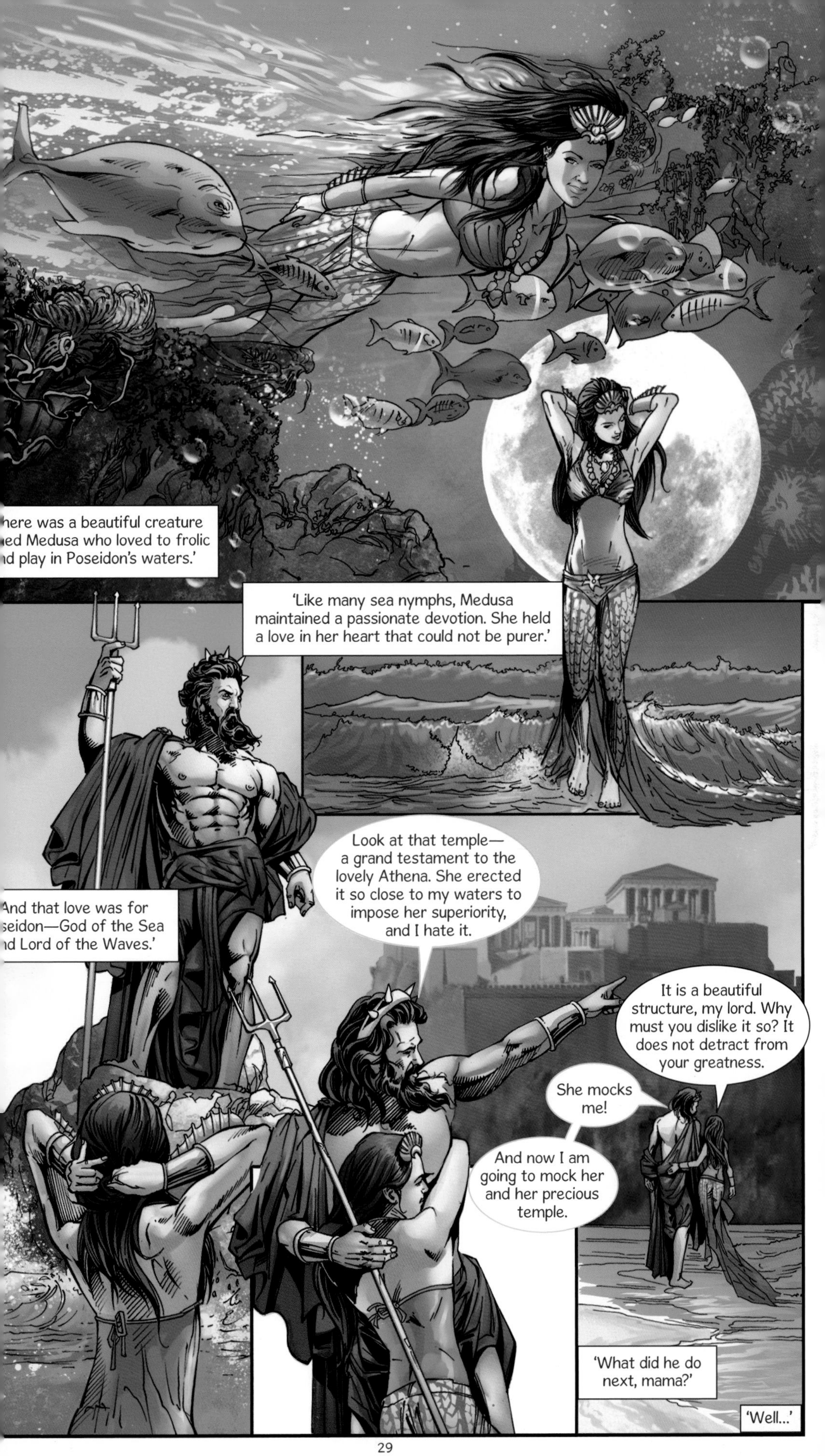
here was a beautiful creature
ed Medusa who loved to frolic
d play in Poseidon's waters.'
'Like many sea nymphs, Medusa maintained a passionate devotion. She held a love in her heart that could not be purer.'
And that love was for
seidon—God of the Sea
d Lord of the Waves.'
Look at that temple— a grand testament to the lovely Athena. She erected it so close to my waters to impose her superiority, and I hate it.
It is a beautiful structure, my lord. Why must you dislike it so? It does not detract from your greatness.
She mocks me!
And now I am going to mock her and her precious temple.
'What did he do next, mama?'
'Well...'

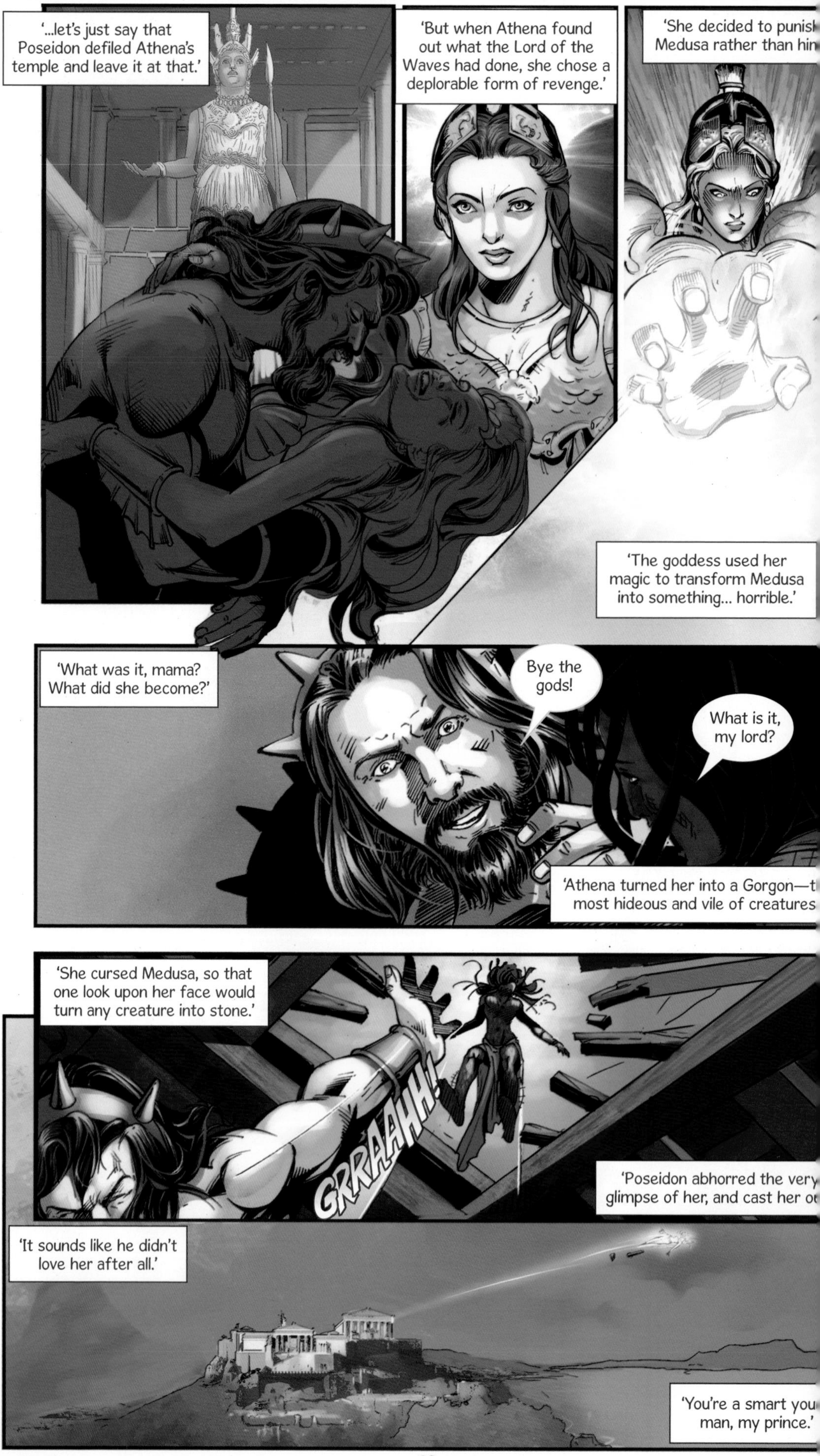

'...let's just say that Poseidon defiled Athena's temple and leave it at that.'
'But when Athena found out what the Lord of the Waves had done, she chose a deplorable form of revenge.'
'She decided to punis Medusa rather than hi
'The goddess used her magic to transform Medusa into something... horrible.'
'What was it, mama? What did she become?'
Bye the gods!
What is it, my lord?
'Athena turned her into a Gorgon—t most hideous and vile of creatures
'She cursed Medusa, so that one look upon her face would turn any creature into stone.'
GRRAAHH!
'Poseidon abhorred the ver glimpse of her, and cast her o
'It sounds like he didn't love her after all.'
'You're a smart you man, my prince.'

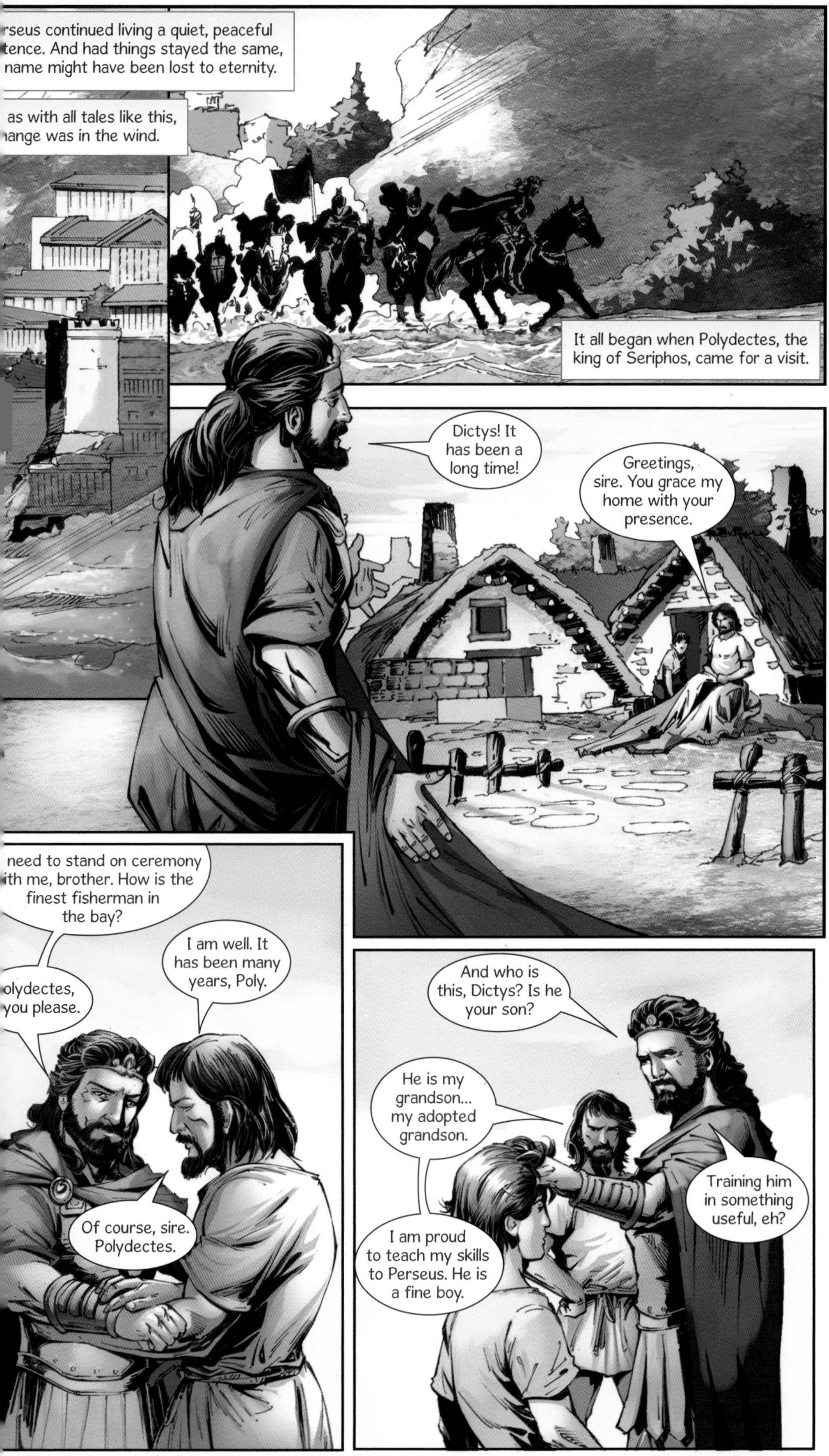

rseus continued living a quiet, peaceful tence. And had things stayed the same, name might have been lost to eternity.
as with all tales like this, ıange was in the wind.
It all began when Polydectes, the king of Seriphos, came for a visit.
Dictys! It has been a long time!
Greetings, sire. You grace my home with your presence.
need to stand on ceremony ith me, brother. How is the finest fisherman in the bay?
I am well. It has been many years, Poly.
olydectes, you please.
Of course, sire. Polydectes.
And who is this, Dictys? Is he your son?
He is my grandson... my adopted grandson.
Training him in something useful, eh?
I am proud to teach my skills to Perseus. He is a fine boy.

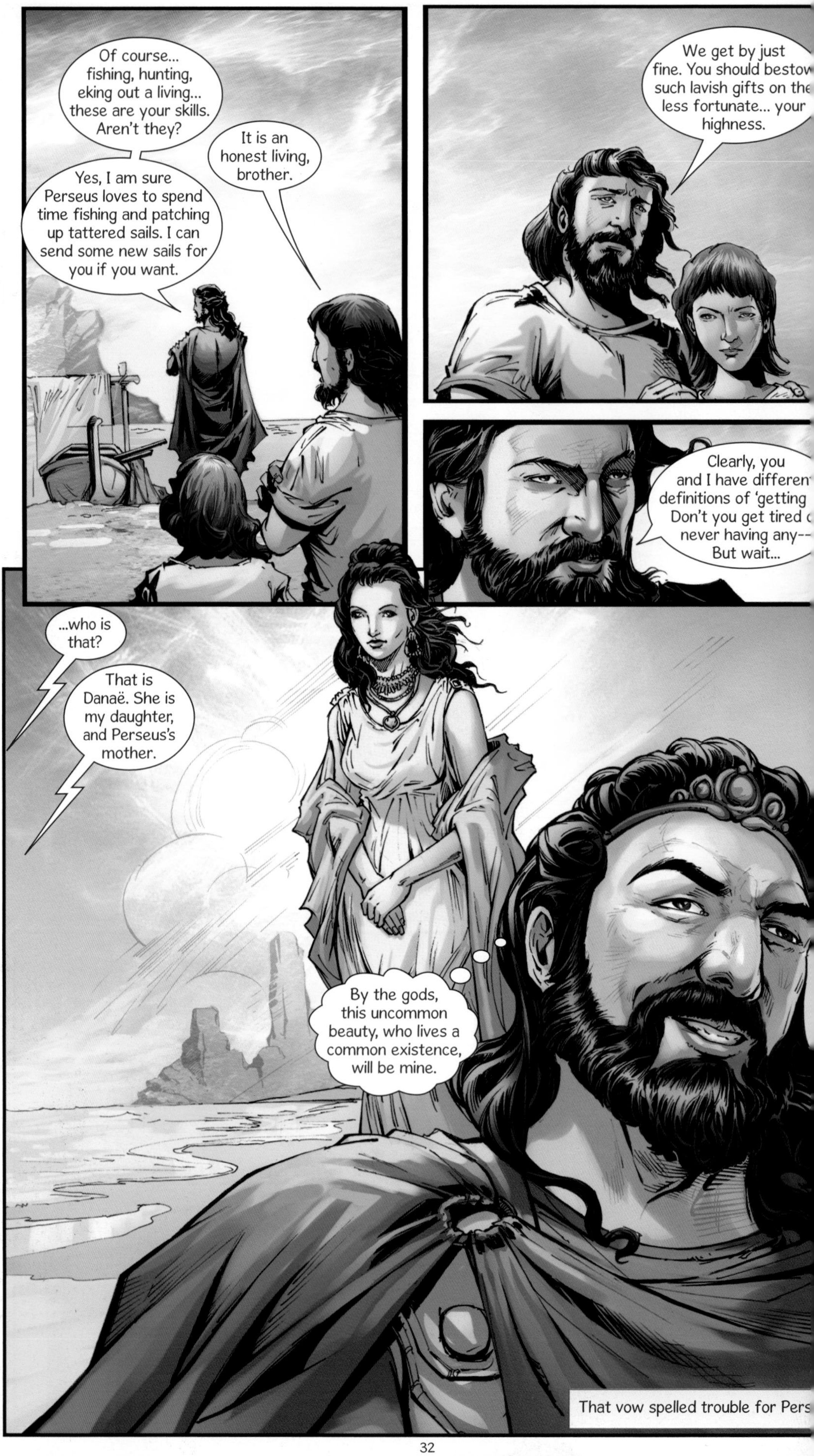
Of course... fishing, hunting, eking out a living... these are your skills. Aren't they?
Yes, I am sure Perseus loves to spend time fishing and patching up tattered sails. I can send some new sails for you if you want.
It is an honest living, brother.
We get by just fine. You should bestow such lavish gifts on the less fortunate... your highness.
Clearly, you and I have differen definitions of 'getting Don't you get tired never having any-- But wait...
...who is that?
That is Danaë. She is my daughter, and Perseus's mother.
By the gods, this uncommon beauty, who lives a common existence, will be mine.
That vow spelled trouble for Pers

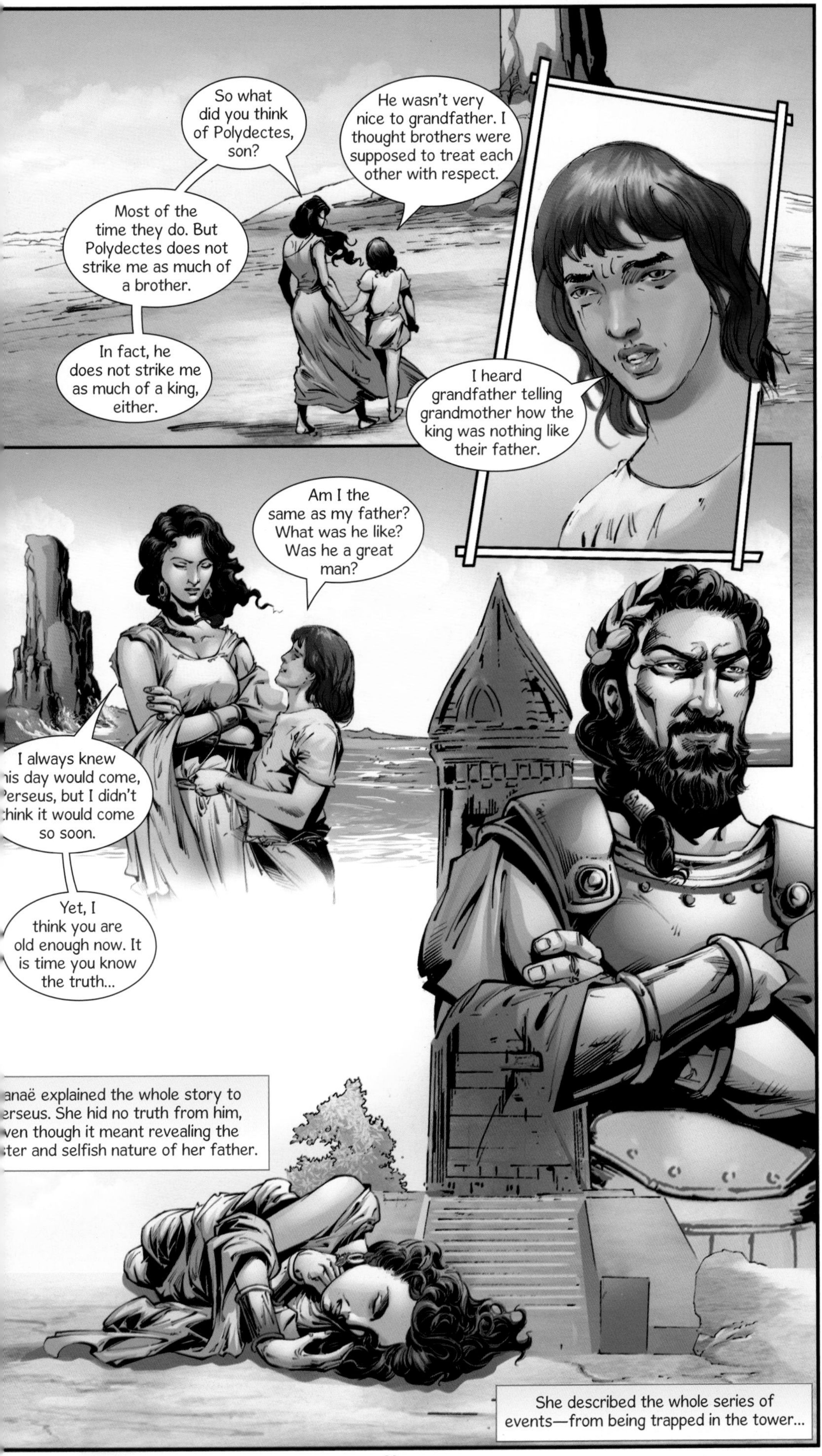

So what did you think of Polydectes, son?
He wasn't very nice to grandfather. I thought brothers were supposed to treat each other with respect.
Most of the time they do. But Polydectes does not strike me as much of a brother.
In fact, he does not strike me as much of a king, either.
I heard grandfather telling grandmother how the king was nothing like their father.
Am I the same as my father? What was he like? Was he a great man?
I always knew his day would come, Perseus, but I didn't think it would come so soon.
Yet, I think you are old enough now. It is time you know the truth...
anaë explained the whole story to erseus. She hid no truth from him, ven though it meant revealing the ster and selfish nature of her father.
She described the whole series of events—from being trapped in the tower...

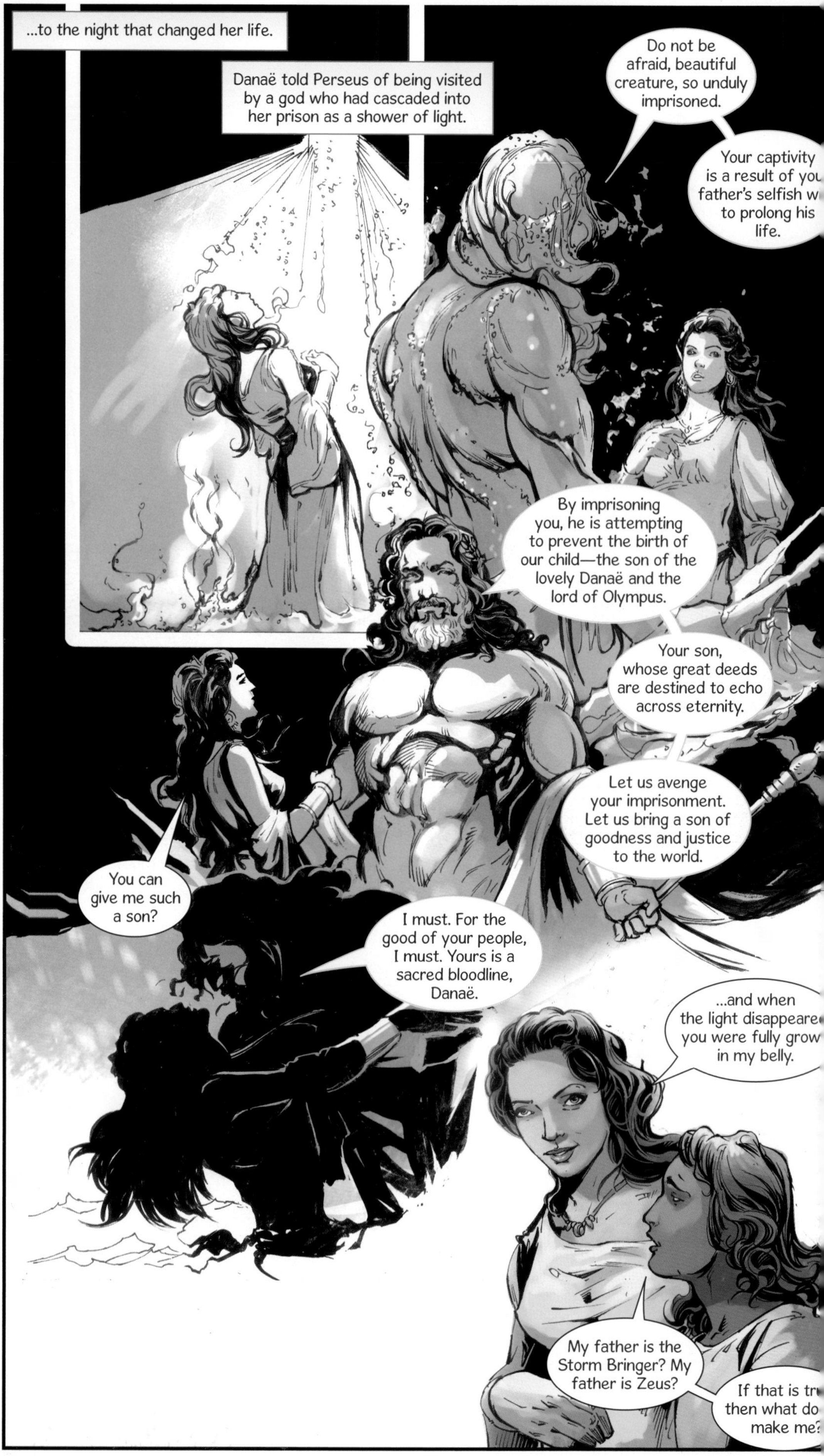
...to the night that changed her life.
Danaë told Perseus of being visited by a god who had cascaded into her prison as a shower of light.
Do not be afraid, beautiful creature, so unduly imprisoned.
Your captivity is a result of you father's selfish w to prolong his life.
By imprisoning you, he is attempting to prevent the birth of our child—the son of the lovely Danaë and the lord of Olympus.
Your son, whose great deeds are destined to echo across eternity.
Let us avenge your imprisonment. Let us bring a son of goodness and justice to the world.
You can give me such a son?
I must. For the good of your people, I must. Yours is a sacred bloodline, Danaë.
...and when the light disappeare you were fully grow in my belly.
My father is the Storm Bringer? My father is Zeus?
If that is tr then what do make me?

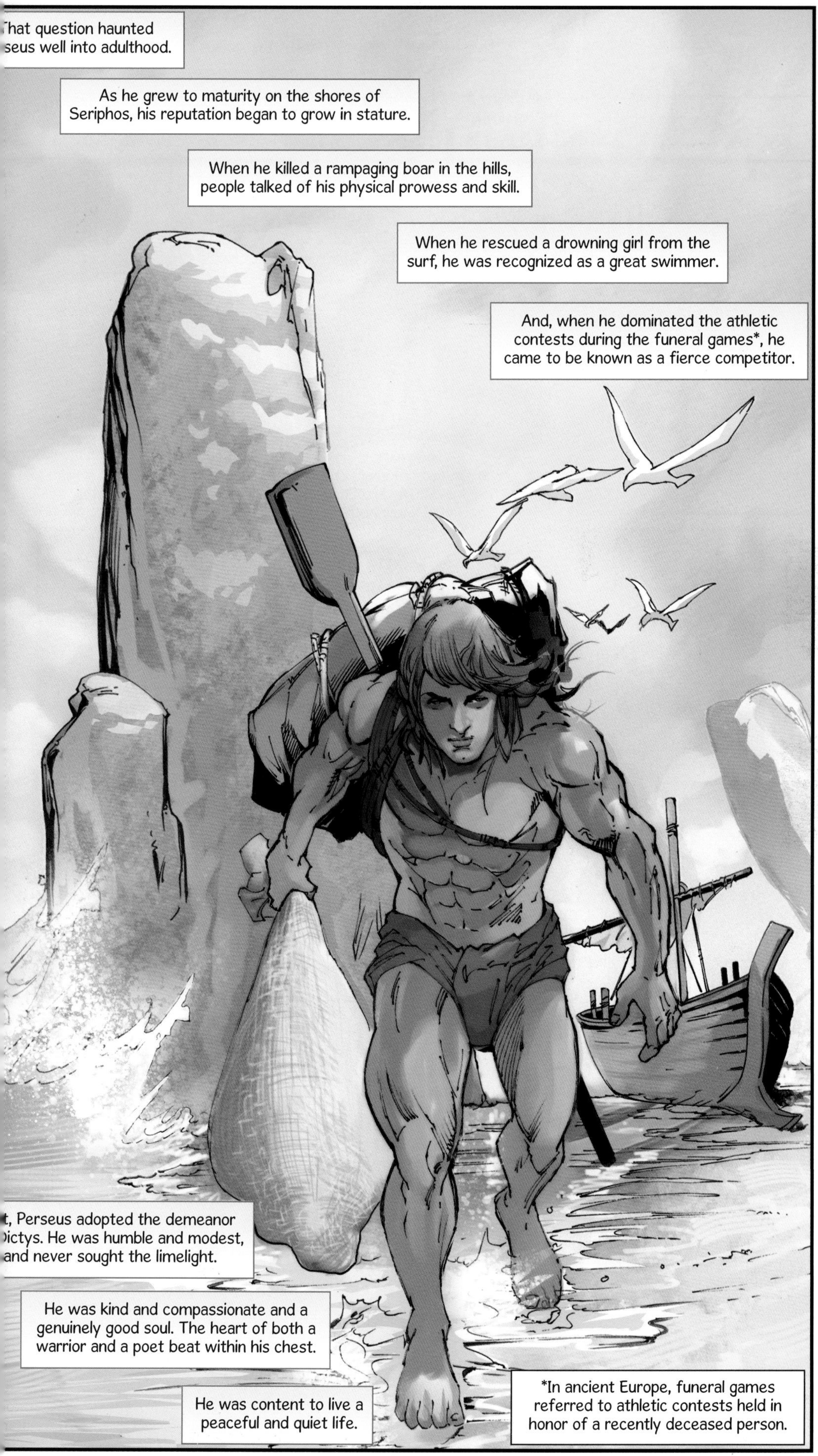
That question haunted
seus well into adulthood.
As he grew to maturity on the shores of Seriphos, his reputation began to grow in stature.
When he killed a rampaging boar in the hills, people talked of his physical prowess and skill.
When he rescued a drowning girl from the surf, he was recognized as a great swimmer.
And, when he dominated the athletic contests during the funeral games*, he came to be known as a fierce competitor.
t, Perseus adopted the demeanor
ictys. He was humble and modest,
and never sought the limelight.
He was kind and compassionate and a genuinely good soul. The heart of both a warrior and a poet beat within his chest.
He was content to live a peaceful and quiet life.
*In ancient Europe, funeral games referred to athletic contests held in honor of a recently deceased person.

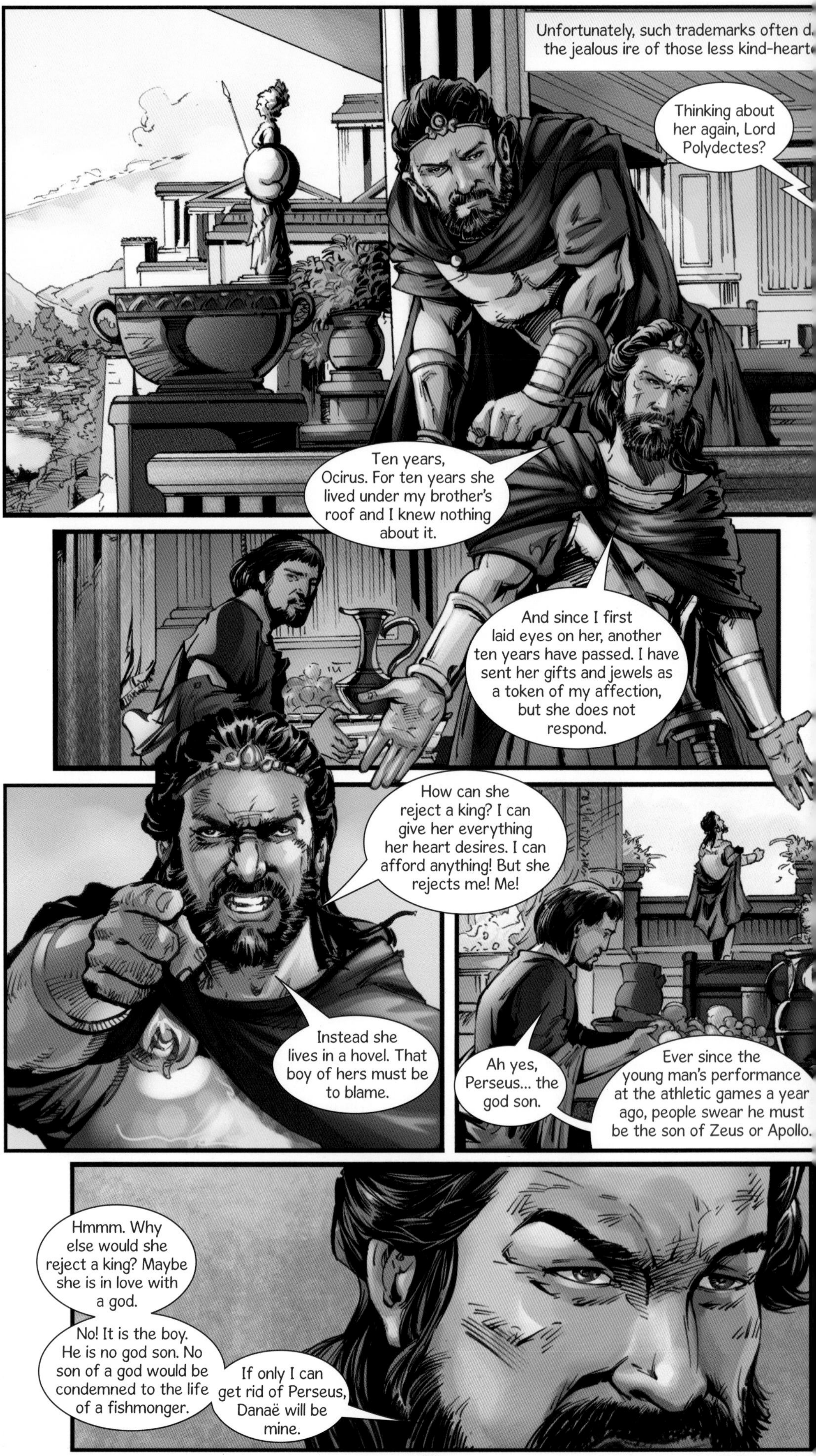
Unfortunately, such trademarks often d
the jealous ire of those less kind-heart
Thinking about her again, Lord Polydectes?
Ten years, Ocirus. For ten years she lived under my brother's roof and I knew nothing about it.
And since I first laid eyes on her, another ten years have passed. I have sent her gifts and jewels as a token of my affection, but she does not respond.
How can she reject a king? I can give her everything her heart desires. I can afford anything! But she rejects me! Me!
Instead she lives in a hovel. That boy of hers must be to blame.
Ah yes, Perseus... the god son.
Ever since the young man's performance at the athletic games a year ago, people swear he must be the son of Zeus or Apollo.
Hmmm. Why else would she reject a king? Maybe she is in love with a god.
No! It is the boy. He is no god son. No son of a god would be condemned to the life of a fishmonger.
If only I can get rid of Perseus, Danaë will be mine.

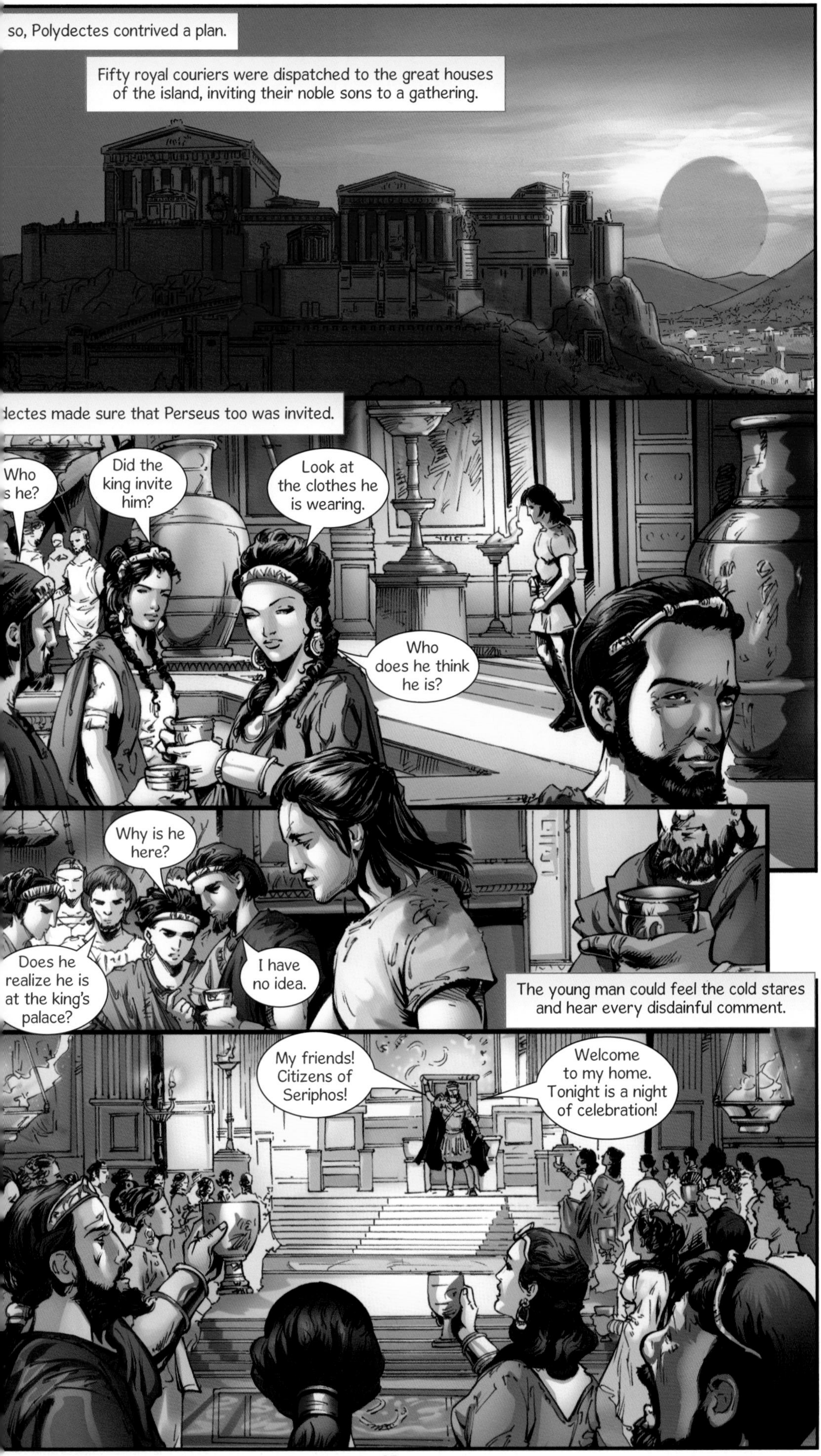
so, Polydectes contrived a plan.
Fifty royal couriers were dispatched to the great houses of the island, inviting their noble sons to a gathering.
lectes made sure that Perseus too was invited.
Who s he?
Did the king invite him?
Look at the clothes he is wearing.
Who does he think he is?
Why is he here?
Does he realize he is at the king's palace?
I have no idea.
The young man could feel the cold stares and hear every disdainful comment.
My friends! Citizens of Seriphos!
Welcome to my home. Tonight is a night of celebration!

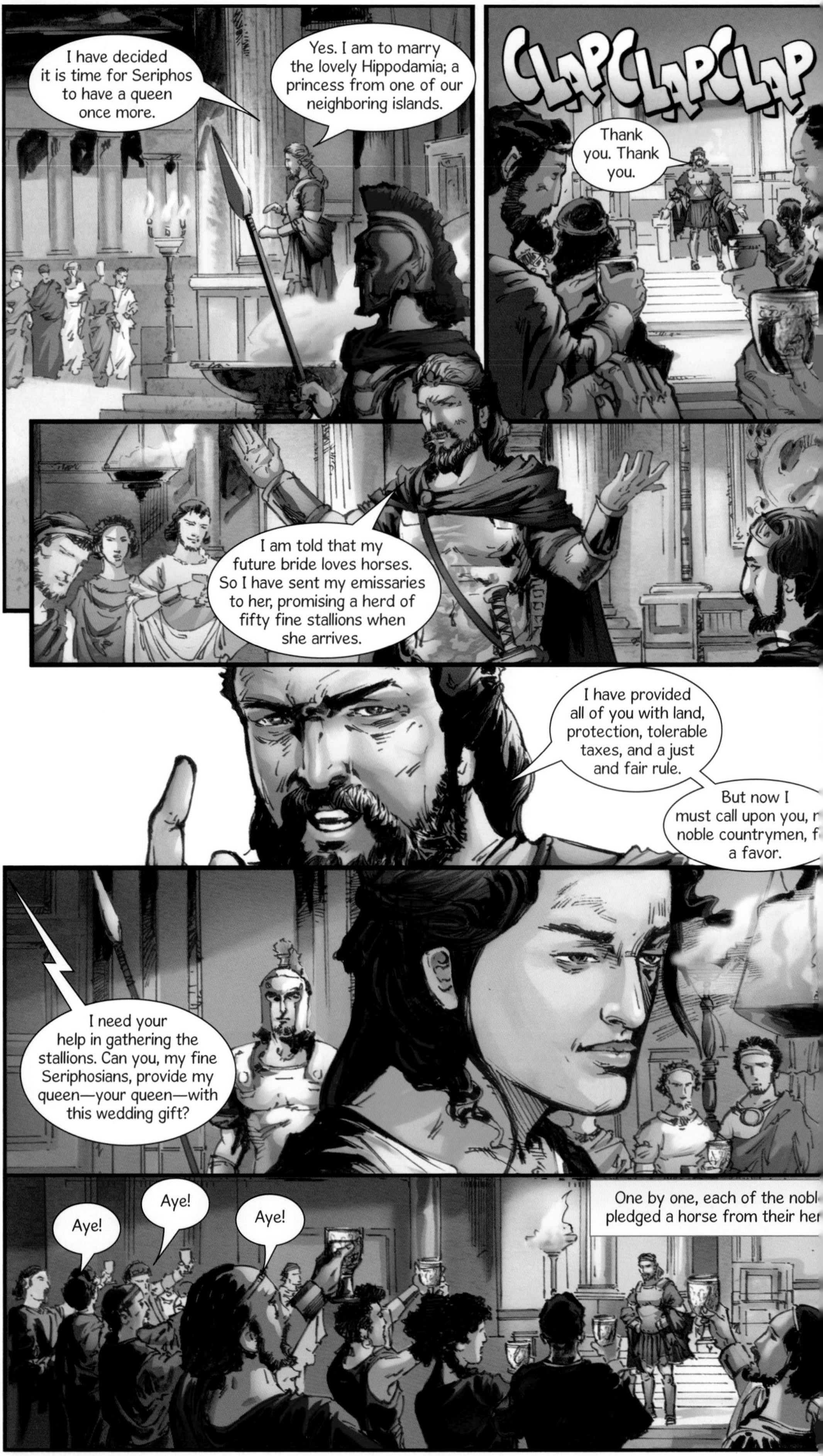

I have decided it is time for Seriphos to have a queen once more.
Yes. I am to marry the lovely Hippodamia; a princess from one of our neighboring islands.
CLAPCLAPCLAP
Thank you. Thank you.
I am told that my future bride loves horses. So I have sent my emissaries to her, promising a herd of fifty fine stallions when she arrives.
I have provided all of you with land, protection, tolerable taxes, and a just and fair rule.
But now I must call upon you, noble countrymen, a favor.
I need your help in gathering the stallions. Can you, my fine Seriphosians, provide my queen—your queen—with this wedding gift?
Aye!
Aye!
Aye!
One by one, each of the nobl pledged a horse from their her

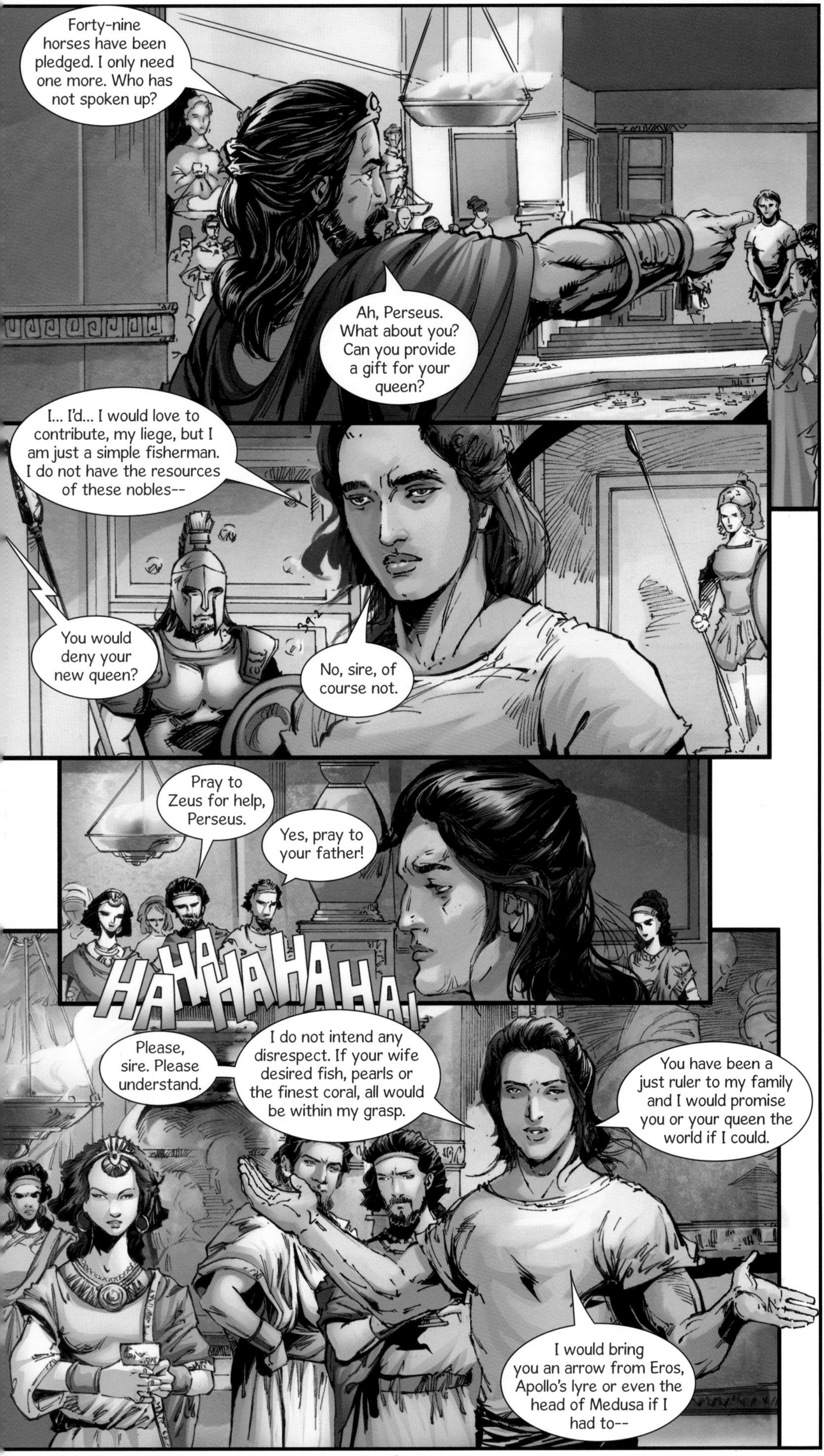
Forty-nine horses have been pledged. I only need one more. Who has not spoken up?
Ah, Perseus. What about you? Can you provide a gift for your queen?
I... I'd... I would love to contribute, my liege, but I am just a simple fisherman. I do not have the resources of these nobles--
You would deny your new queen?
No, sire, of course not.
Pray to Zeus for help, Perseus.
Yes, pray to your father!
HAHAHAHAHA!
Please, sire. Please understand.
I do not intend any disrespect. If your wife desired fish, pearls or the finest coral, all would be within my grasp.
You have been a just ruler to my family and I would promise you or your queen the world if I could.
I would bring you an arrow from Eros, Apollo's lyre or even the head of Medusa if I had to--

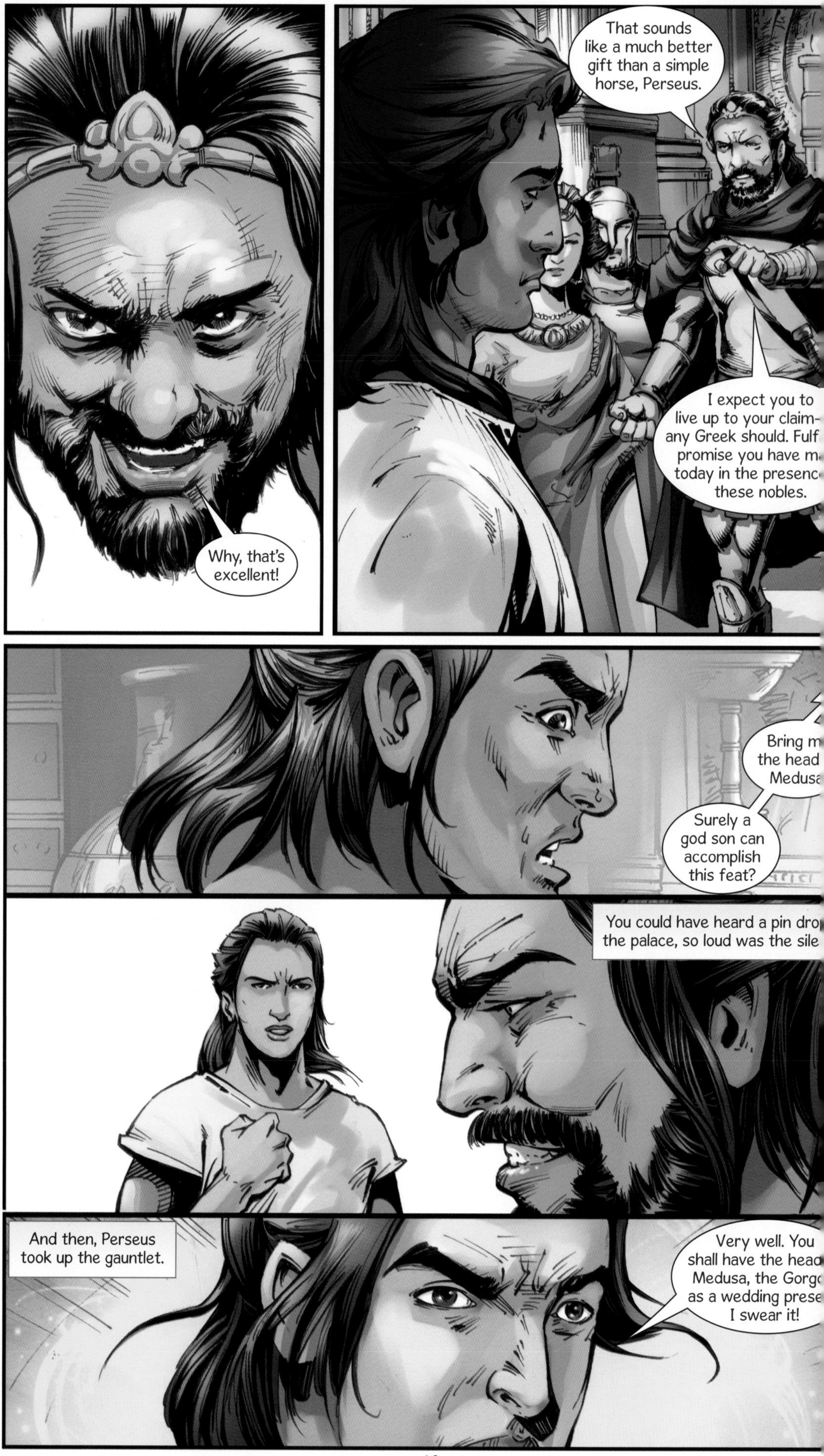
Why, that's excellent!
That sounds like a much better gift than a simple horse, Perseus.
I expect you to live up to your claim- any Greek should. Fulf promise you have m today in the presenc these nobles.
Bring m the head Medusa
Surely a god son can accomplish this feat?
You could have heard a pin dro the palace, so loud was the sile
And then, Perseus took up the gauntlet.
Very well. You shall have the head Medusa, the Gorg as a wedding prese I swear it!

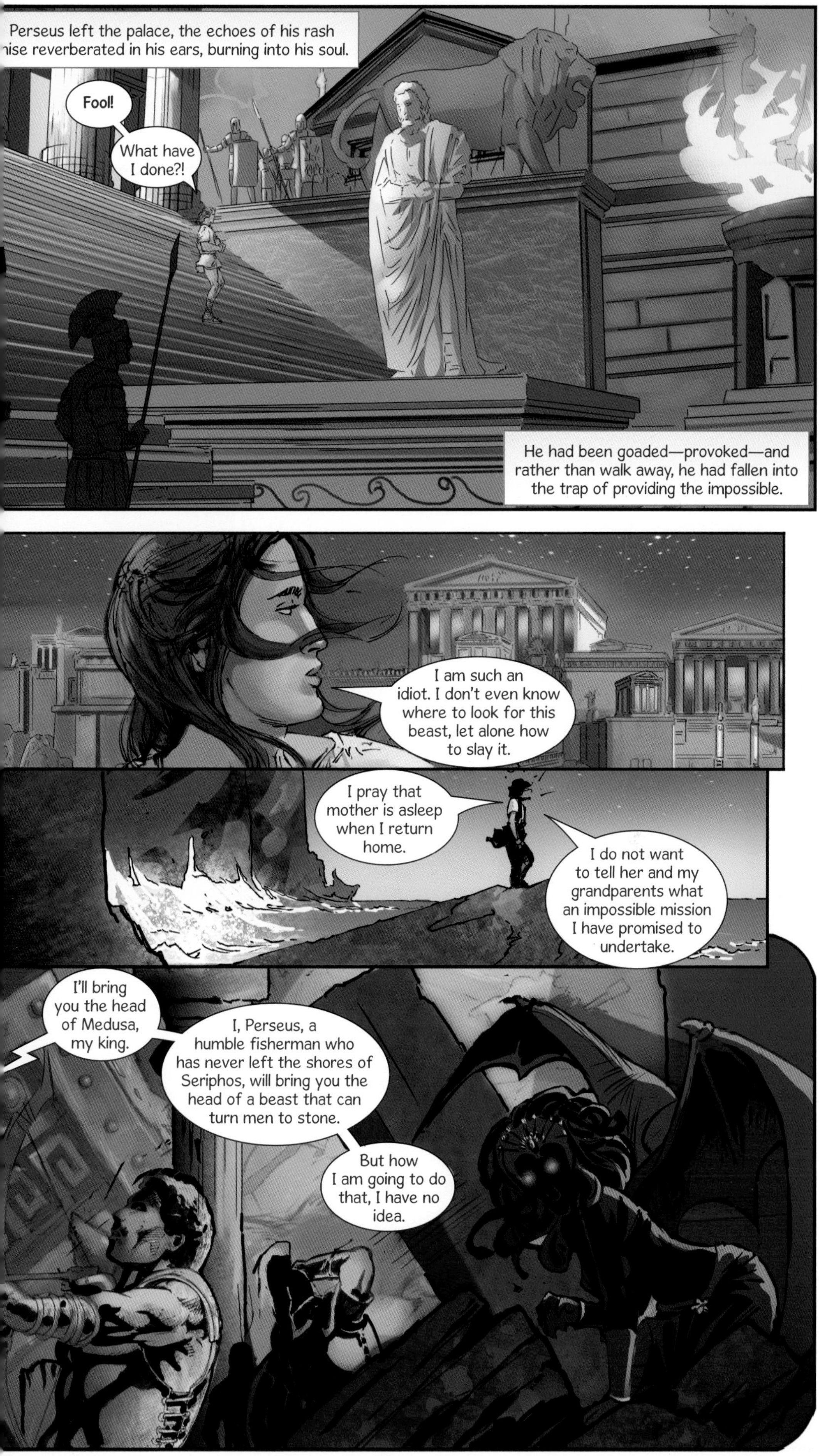

Perseus left the palace, the echoes of his rash
ise reverberated in his ears, burning into his soul.
Fool!
What have I done?!
He had been goaded—provoked—and rather than walk away, he had fallen into the trap of providing the impossible.
I am such an idiot. I don't even know where to look for this beast, let alone how to slay it.
I pray that mother is asleep when I return home.
I do not want to tell her and my grandparents what an impossible mission I have promised to undertake.
I'll bring you the head of Medusa, my king.
I, Perseus, a humble fisherman who has never left the shores of Seriphos, will bring you the head of a beast that can turn men to stone.
But how I am going to do that, I have no idea.

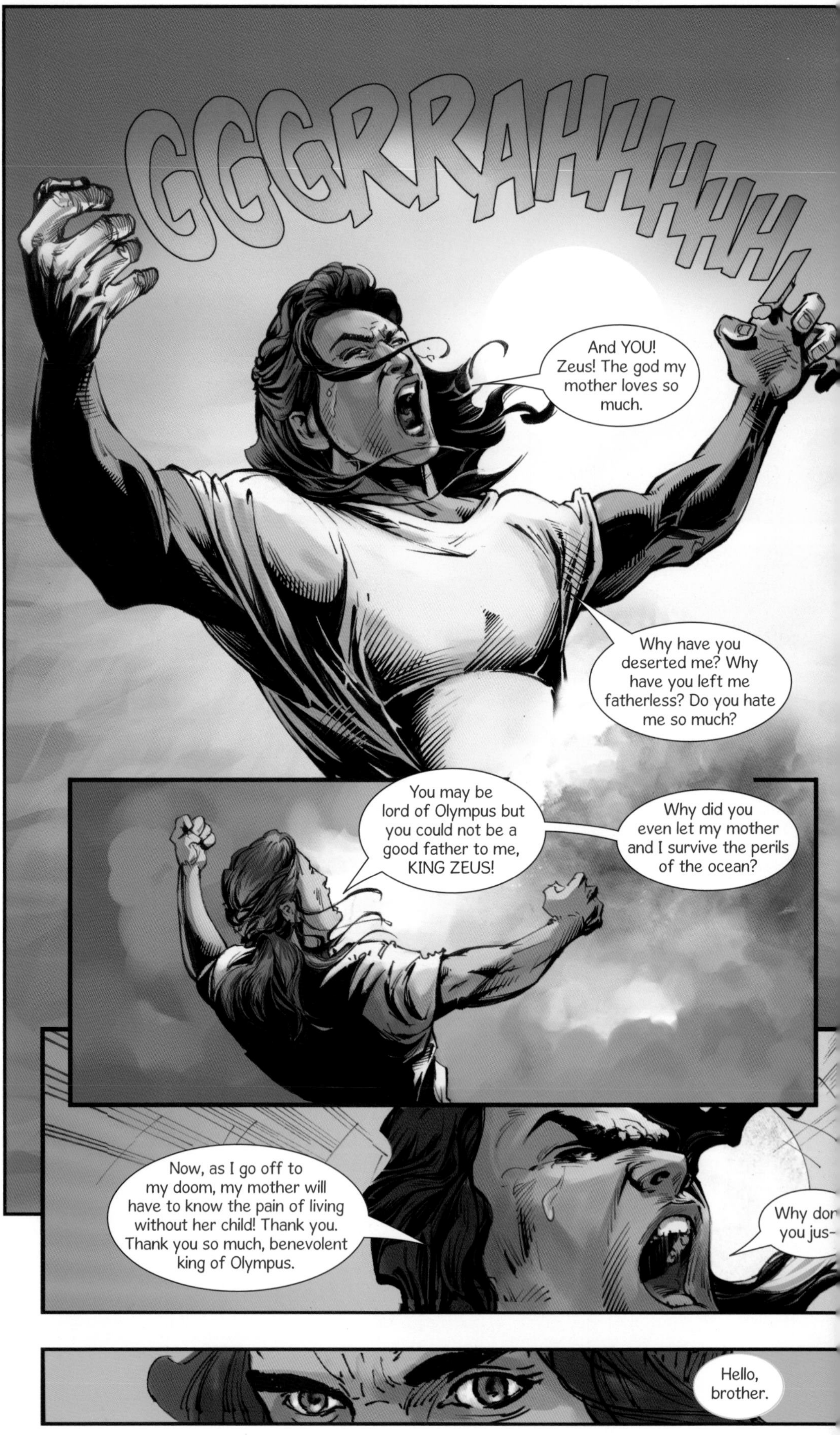
GGGRRAHHHHH!
And YOU! Zeus! The god my mother loves so much.
Why have you deserted me? Why have you left me fatherless? Do you hate me so much?
You may be lord of Olympus but you could not be a good father to me, KING ZEUS!
Why did you even let my mother and I survive the perils of the ocean?
Now, as I go off to my doom, my mother will have to know the pain of living without her child! Thank you. Thank you so much, benevolent king of Olympus.
Why don you jus-
Hello, brother.

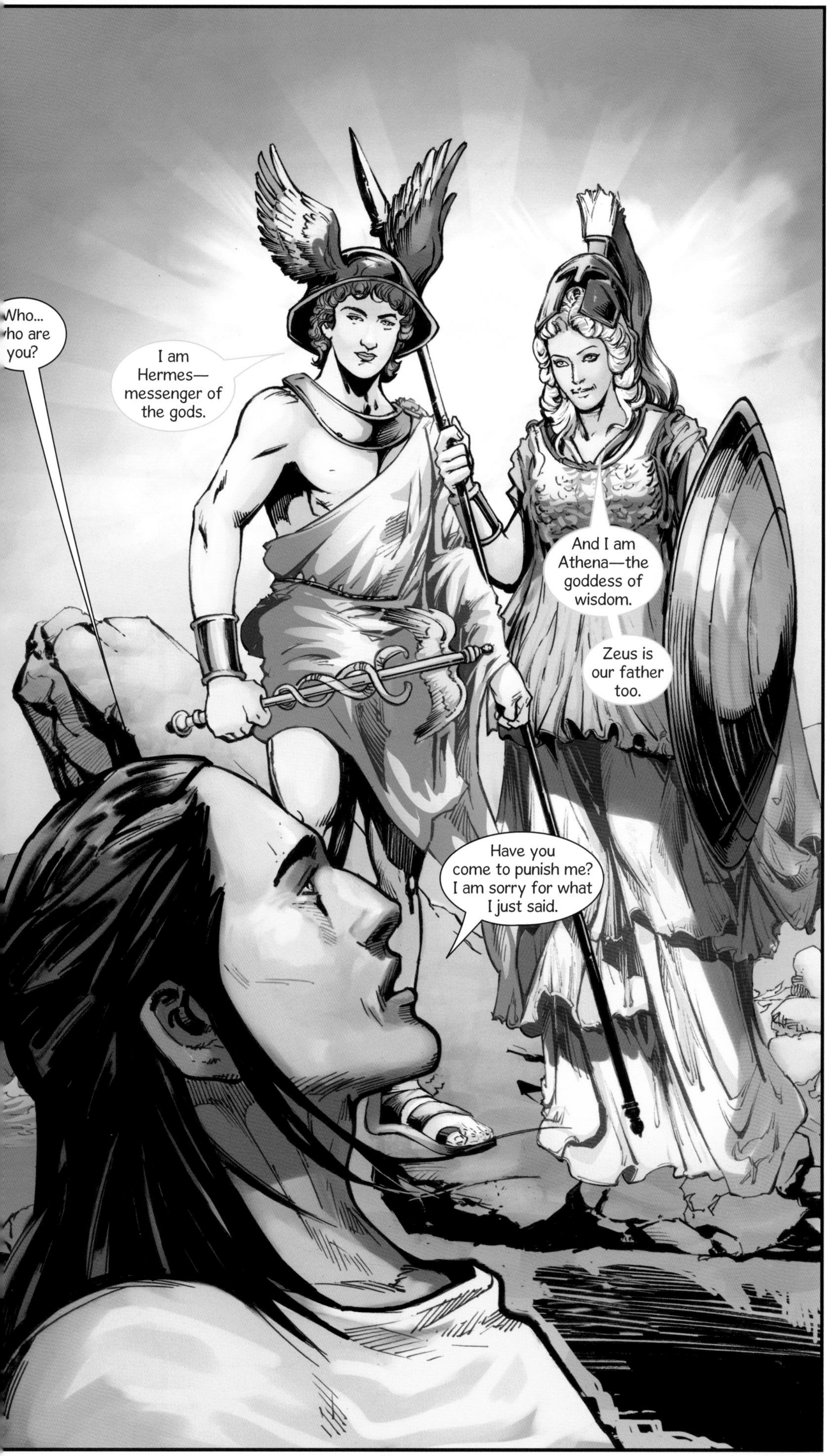
Who... who are you?
I am Hermes—messenger of the gods.
And I am Athena—the goddess of wisdom.
Zeus is our father too.
Have you come to punish me? I am sorry for what I just said.

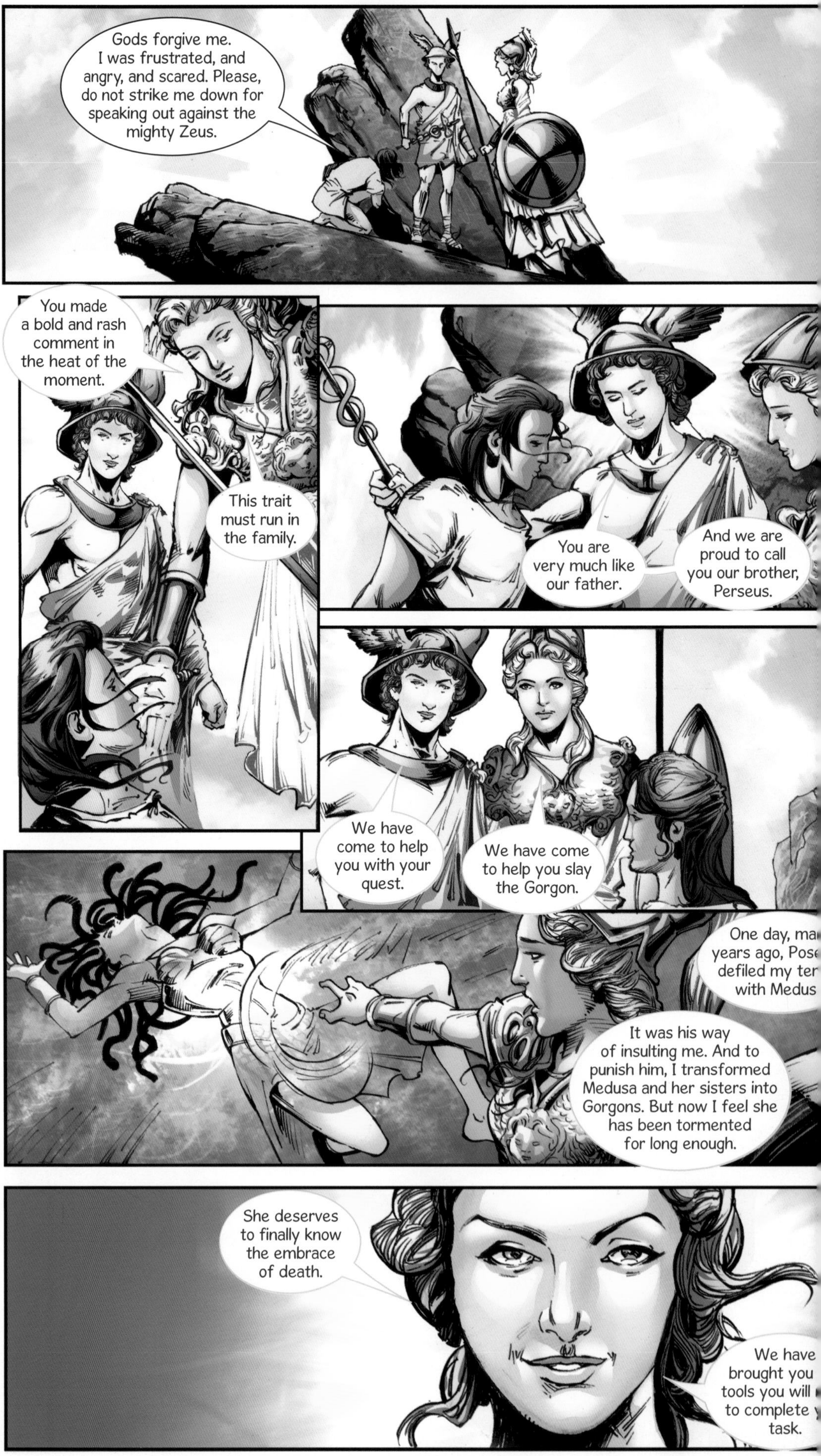

Gods forgive me. I was frustrated, and angry, and scared. Please, do not strike me down for speaking out against the mighty Zeus.
You made a bold and rash comment in the heat of the moment.
This trait must run in the family.
You are very much like our father.
And we are proud to call you our brother, Perseus.
We have come to help you with your quest.
We have come to help you slay the Gorgon.
It was his way of insulting me. And to punish him, I transformed Medusa and her sisters into Gorgons. But now I feel she has been tormented for long enough.
She deserves to finally know the embrace of death.

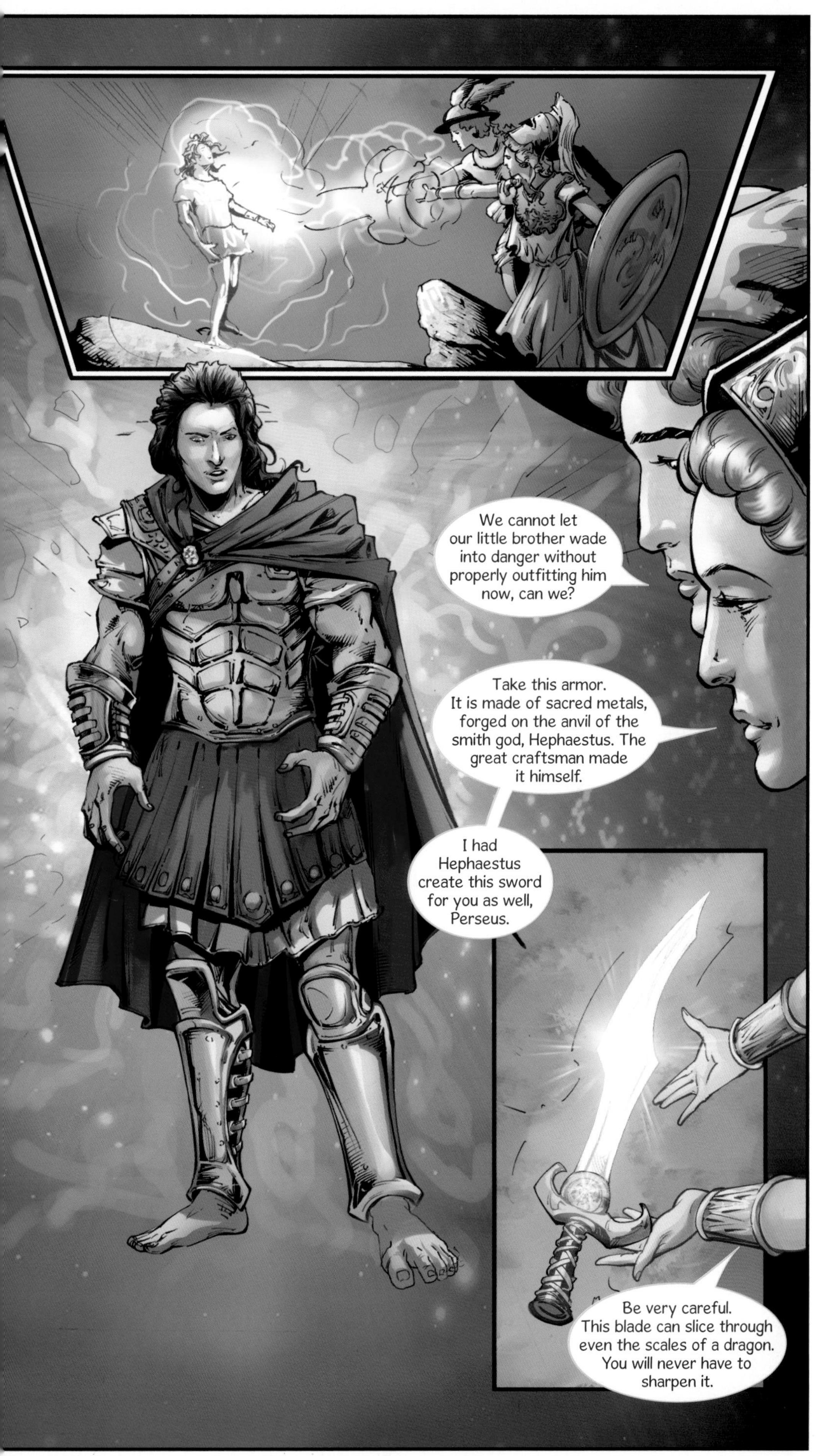
We cannot let our little brother wade into danger without properly outfitting him now, can we?
Take this armor. It is made of sacred metals, forged on the anvil of the smith god, Hephaestus. The great craftsman made it himself.
I had Hephaestus create this sword for you as well, Perseus.
Be very careful. This blade can slice through even the scales of a dragon. You will never have to sharpen it.

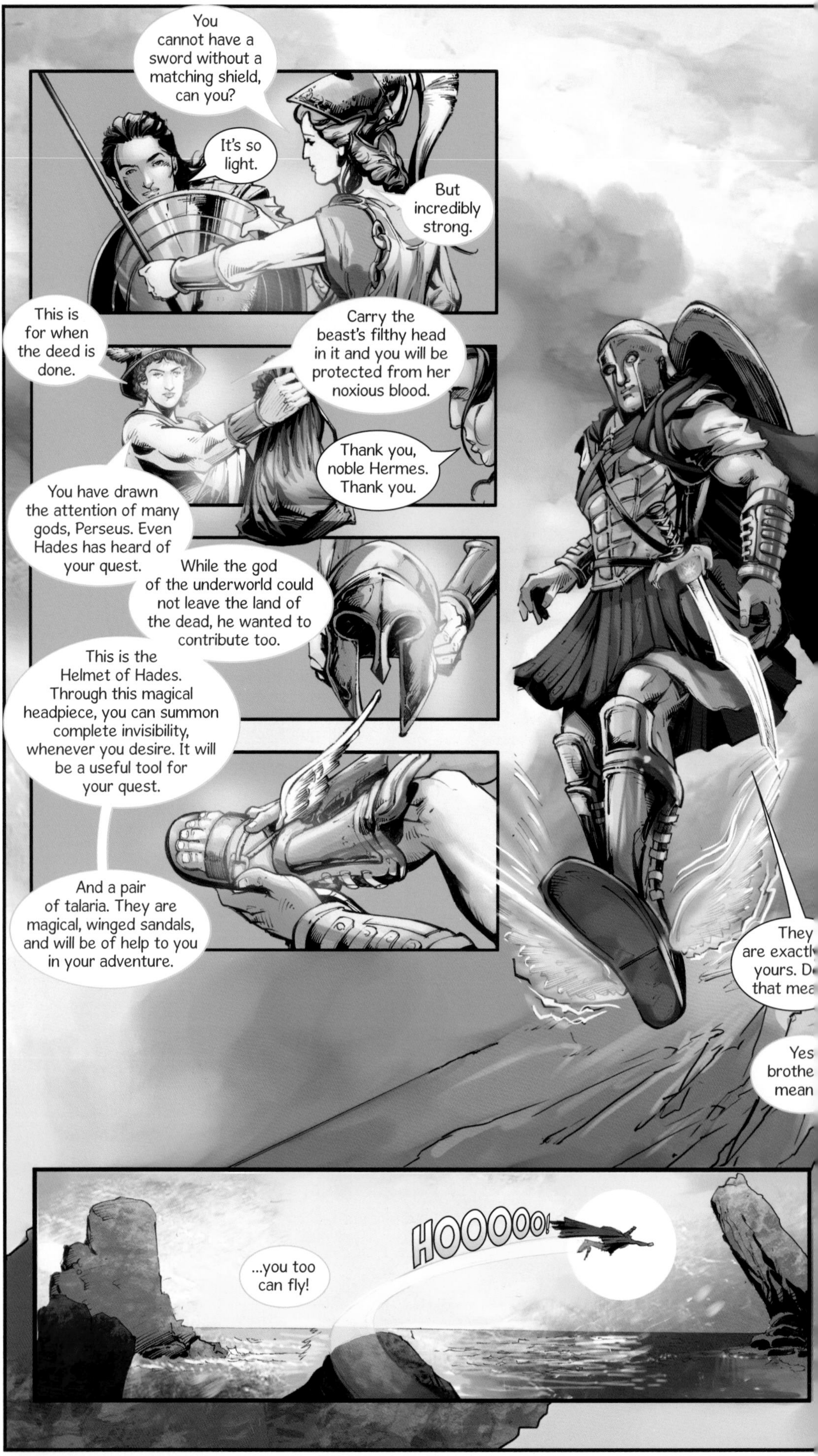
You cannot have a sword without a matching shield, can you?
It's so light.
But incredibly strong.
This is for when the deed is done.
Carry the beast's filthy head in it and you will be protected from her noxious blood.
Thank you, noble Hermes. Thank you.
You have drawn the attention of many gods, Perseus. Even Hades has heard of your quest.
While the god of the underworld could not leave the land of the dead, he wanted to contribute too.
This is the Helmet of Hades. Through this magical headpiece, you can summon complete invisibility, whenever you desire. It will be a useful tool for your quest.
And a pair of talaria. They are magical, winged sandals, and will be of help to you in your adventure.
They are exactl yours. D that mea
Yes brothe mean
HOOOOO!
...you too can fly!

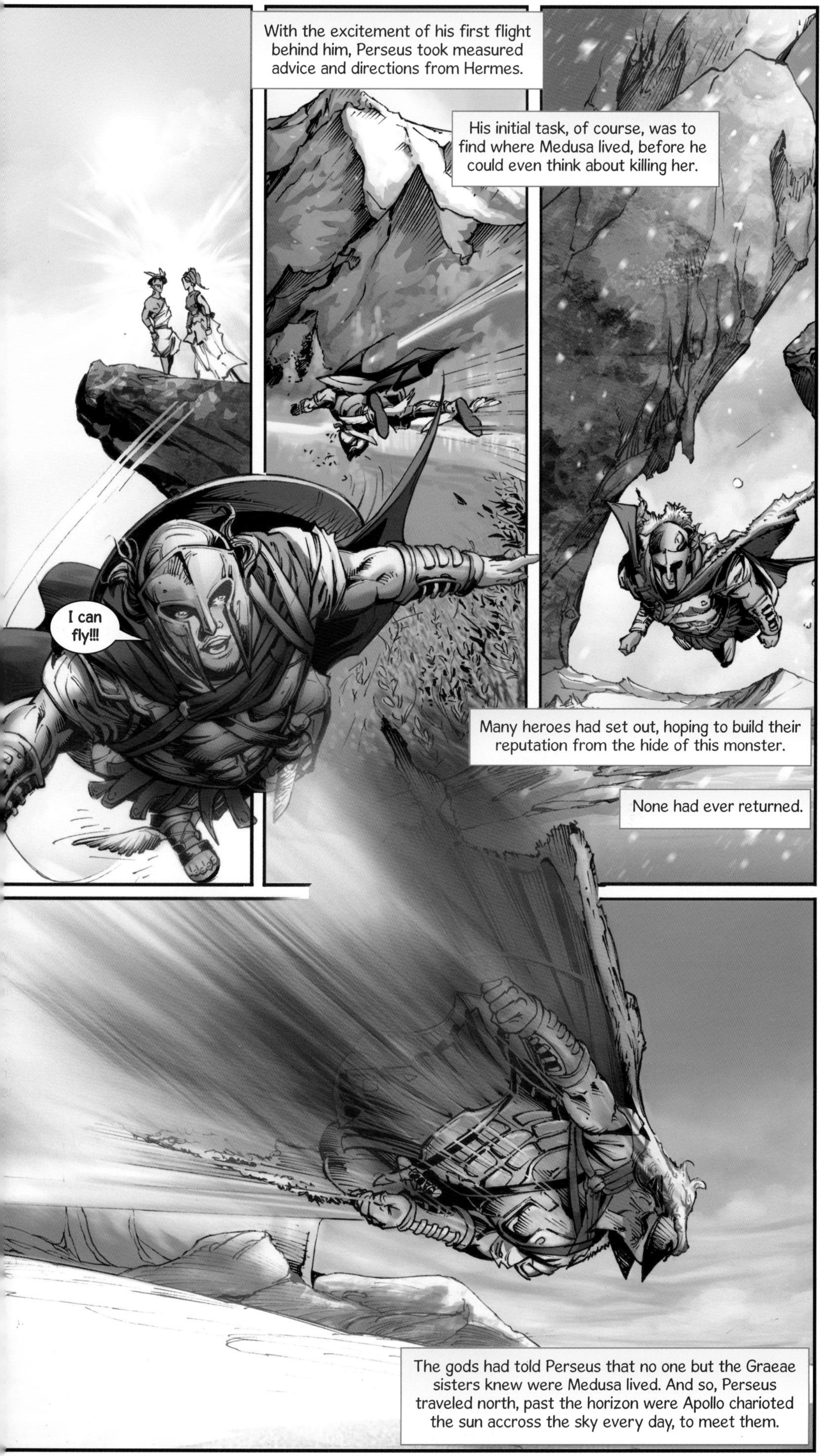
With the excitement of his first flight behind him, Perseus took measured advice and directions from Hermes.
I can fly!!!
His initial task, of course, was to find where Medusa lived, before he could even think about killing her.
Many heroes had set out, hoping to build their reputation from the hide of this monster.
None had ever returned.
The gods had told Perseus that no one but the Graeae sisters knew were Medusa lived. And so, Perseus traveled north, past the horizon were Apollo charioted the sun accross the sky every day, to meet them.

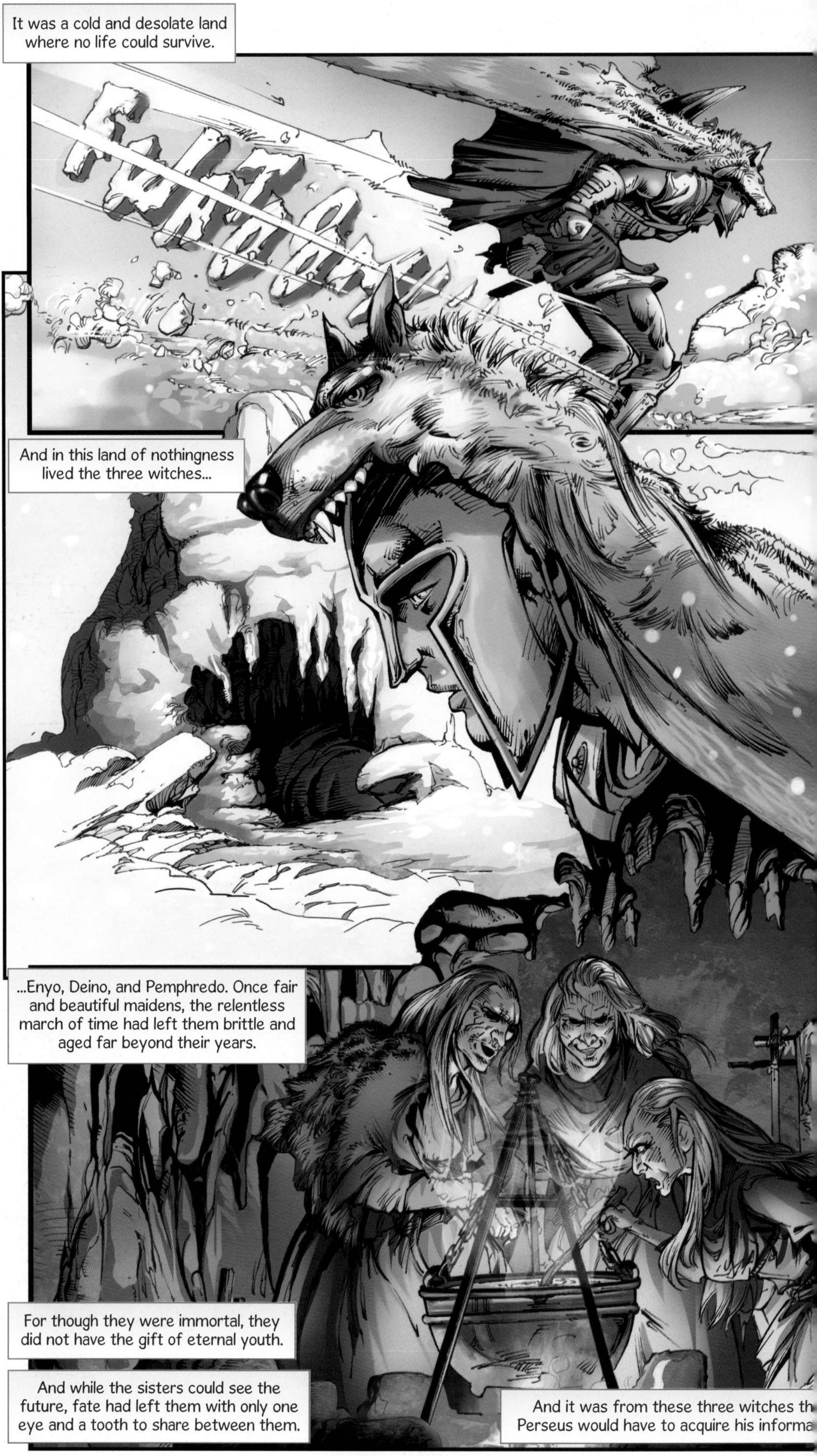
It was a cold and desolate land where no life could survive.
And in this land of nothingness lived the three witches...
...Enyo, Deino, and Pemphredo. Once fair and beautiful maidens, the relentless march of time had left them brittle and aged far beyond their years.
For though they were immortal, they did not have the gift of eternal youth.
And while the sisters could see the future, fate had left them with only one eye and a tooth to share between them.
And it was from these three witches th
Perseus would have to acquire his informa

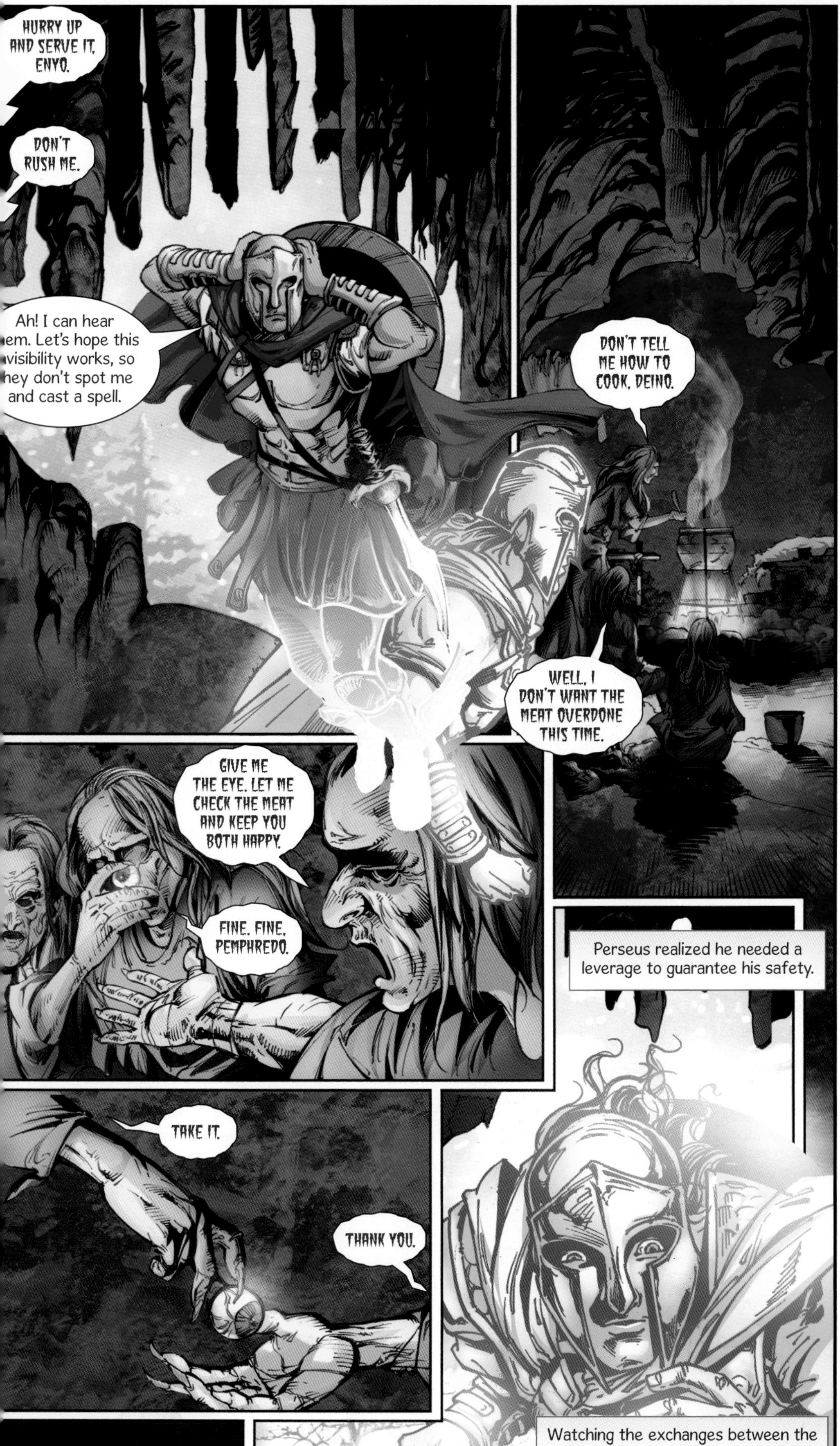
HURRY UP AND SERVE IT, ENYO.
DON'T RUSH ME.
Ah! I can hear em. Let's hope this visibility works, so hey don't spot me and cast a spell.
DON'T TELL ME HOW TO COOK, DEINO.
WELL, I DON'T WANT THE MEAT OVERDONE THIS TIME.
GIVE ME THE EYE. LET ME CHECK THE MEAT AND KEEP YOU BOTH HAPPY.
FINE. FINE, PEMPHREDO.
Perseus realized he needed a leverage to guarantee his safety.
TAKE IT.
THANK YOU.
Watching the exchanges between the sisters, he spotted his opportunity.

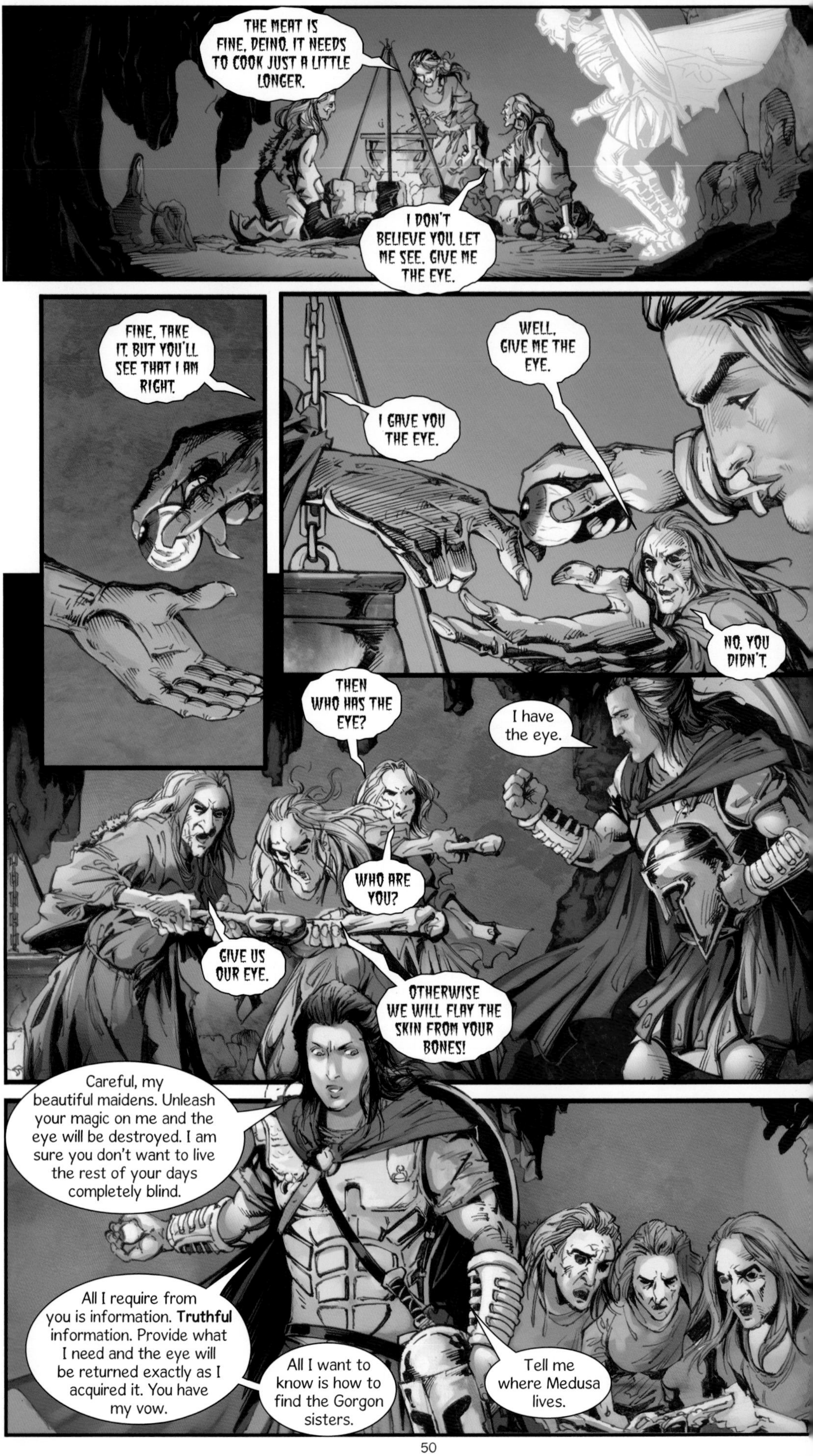

THE MEAT IS FINE, DEINO. IT NEEDS TO COOK JUST A LITTLE LONGER.
I DON'T BELIEVE YOU. LET ME SEE. GIVE ME THE EYE.
FINE, TAKE IT. BUT YOU'LL SEE THAT I AM RIGHT.
I GAVE YOU THE EYE.
WELL, GIVE ME THE EYE.
NO, YOU DIDN'T.
THEN WHO HAS THE EYE?
I have the eye.
WHO ARE YOU?
GIVE US OUR EYE.
OTHERWISE WE WILL FLAY THE SKIN FROM YOUR BONES!
Careful, my beautiful maidens. Unleash your magic on me and the eye will be destroyed. I am sure you don't want to live the rest of your days completely blind.
All I require from you is information. **Truthful** information. Provide what I need and the eye will be returned exactly as I acquired it. You have my vow.
All I want to know is how to find the Gorgon sisters.
Tell me where Medusa lives.

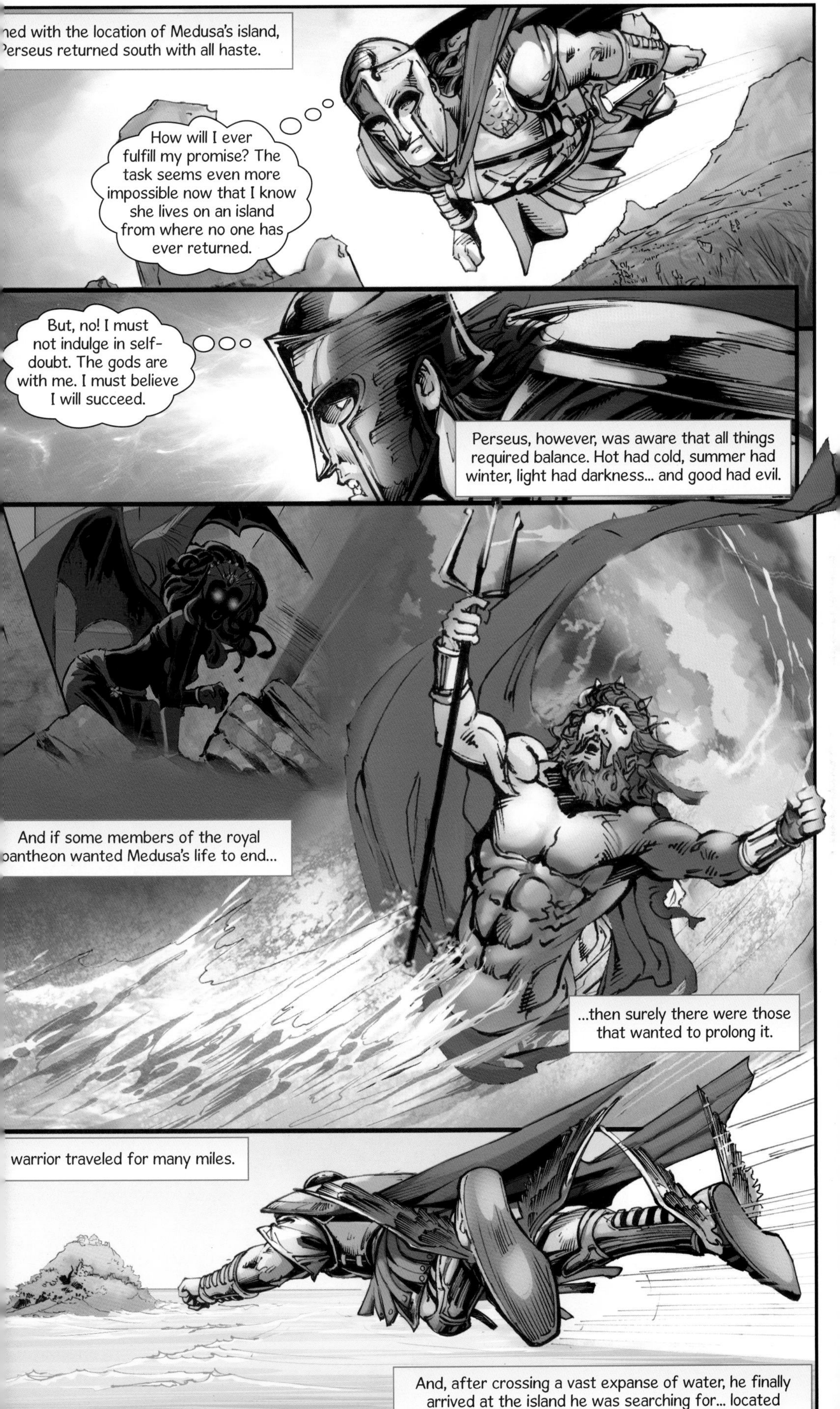

ned with the location of Medusa's island, Perseus returned south with all haste.
How will I ever fulfill my promise? The task seems even more impossible now that I know she lives on an island from where no one has ever returned.
But, no! I must not indulge in self-doubt. The gods are with me. I must believe I will succeed.
Perseus, however, was aware that all things required balance. Hot had cold, summer had winter, light had darkness... and good had evil.
And if some members of the royal pantheon wanted Medusa's life to end...
...then surely there were those that wanted to prolong it.
warrior traveled for many miles.
And, after crossing a vast expanse of water, he finally arrived at the island he was searching for... located precisely where the Graeae sisters had said it would be.

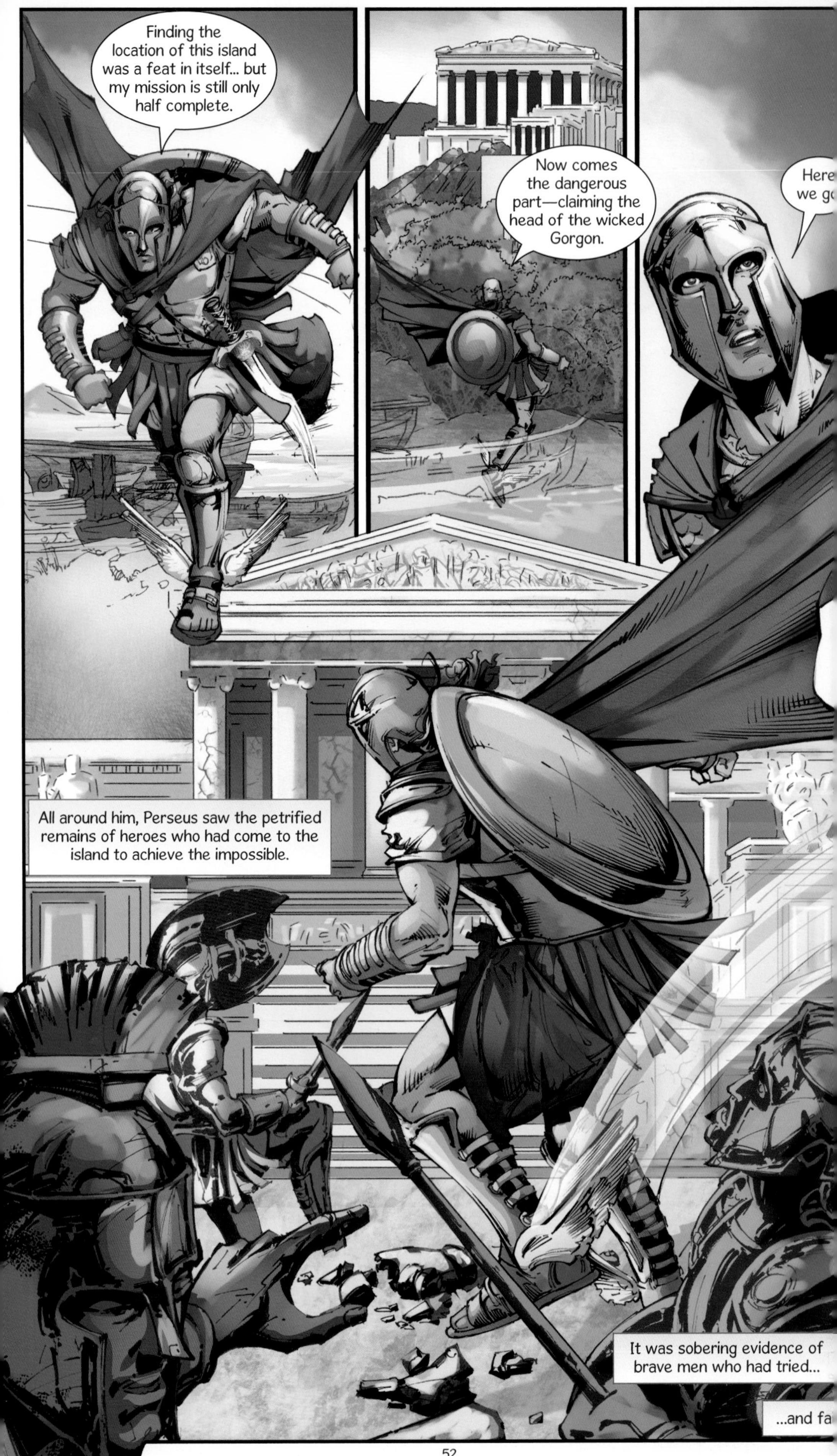
Finding the location of this island was a feat in itself... but my mission is still only half complete.
Now comes the dangerous part—claiming the head of the wicked Gorgon.
Here we
All around him, Perseus saw the petrified remains of heroes who had come to the island to achieve the impossible.
It was sobering evidence of brave men who had tried...
...and

So many men! All who have come here to claim fortune and glory.

And they have all perished.

I have the gifts from Hermes and Athena, but they are still just items.

They are only as effective as the person wielding them. No matter how sharp, a sword is useless in unskilled hands.

He could feel his hair standing on end and cold sweat trickling down his back.

I must not let fear overpower me. I must believe in myself and use my gifts wisely.

People say that the petrifying gaze of the Gorgon is her most lethal weapon. Anyone who looks at her turns to stone.

I must act smartly. I will use the shield as a mirror, and walk backward to safeguard my life from the hideous monster's stare.

This will give me the chance to attack first.

Quiet now.

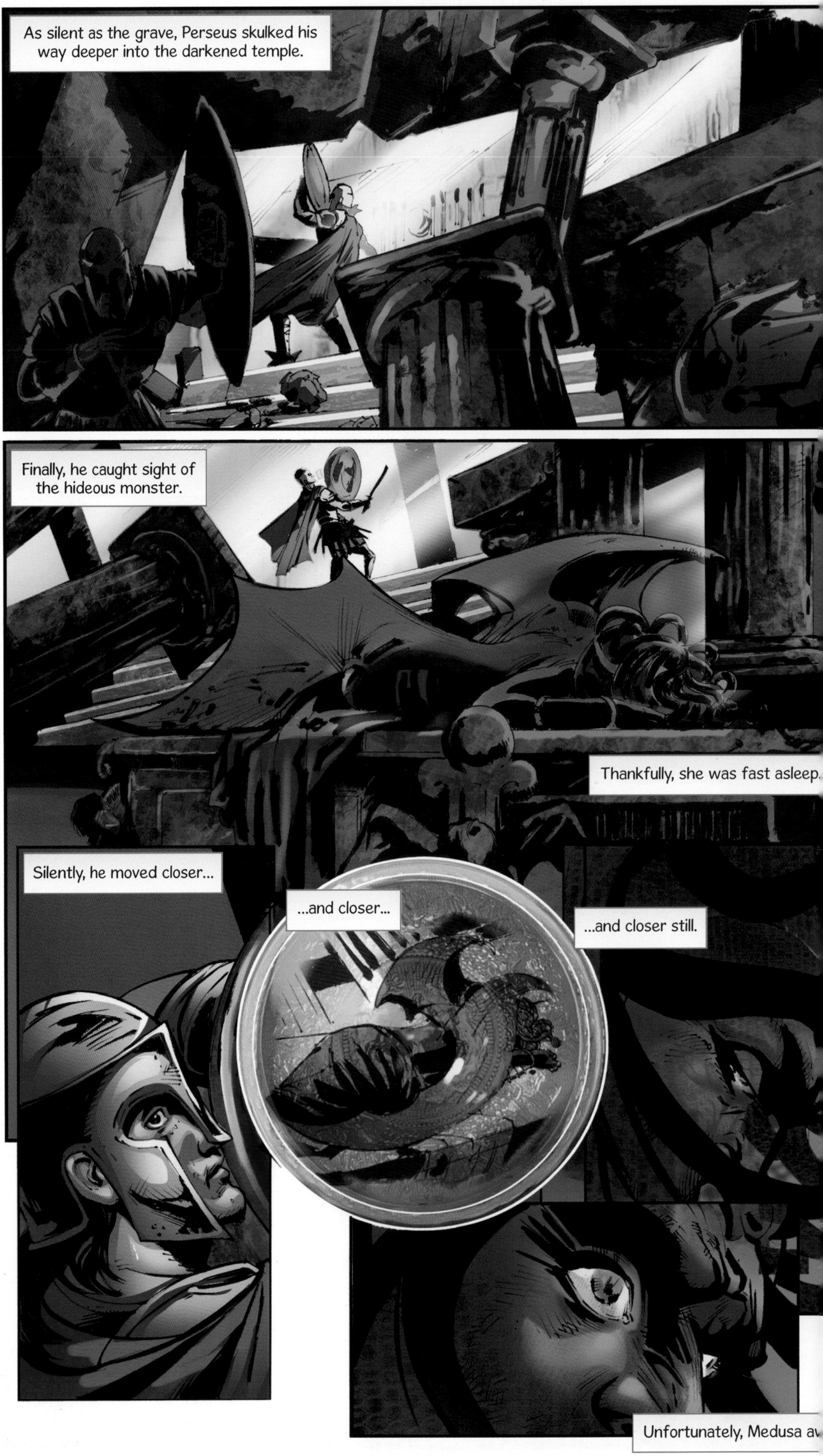
As silent as the grave, Perseus skulked his way deeper into the darkened temple.
Finally, he caught sight of the hideous monster.
Thankfully, she was fast asleep.
Silently, he moved closer...
...and closer...
...and closer still.
Unfortunately, Medusa av

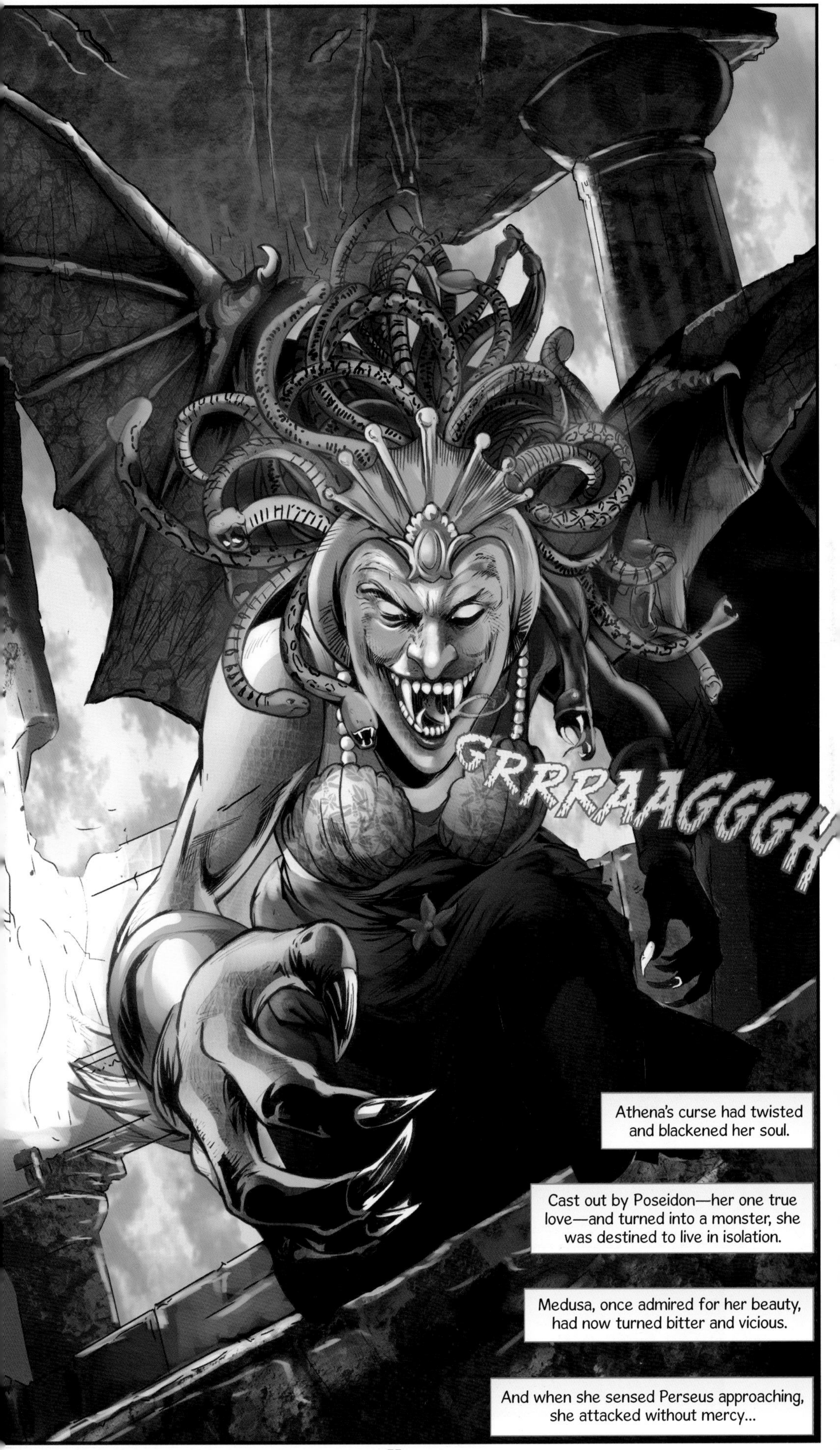
GRRRAAGGGH
Athena's curse had twisted and blackened her soul.
Cast out by Poseidon—her one true love—and turned into a monster, she was destined to live in isolation.
Medusa, once admired for her beauty, had now turned bitter and vicious.
And when she sensed Perseus approaching, she attacked without mercy...

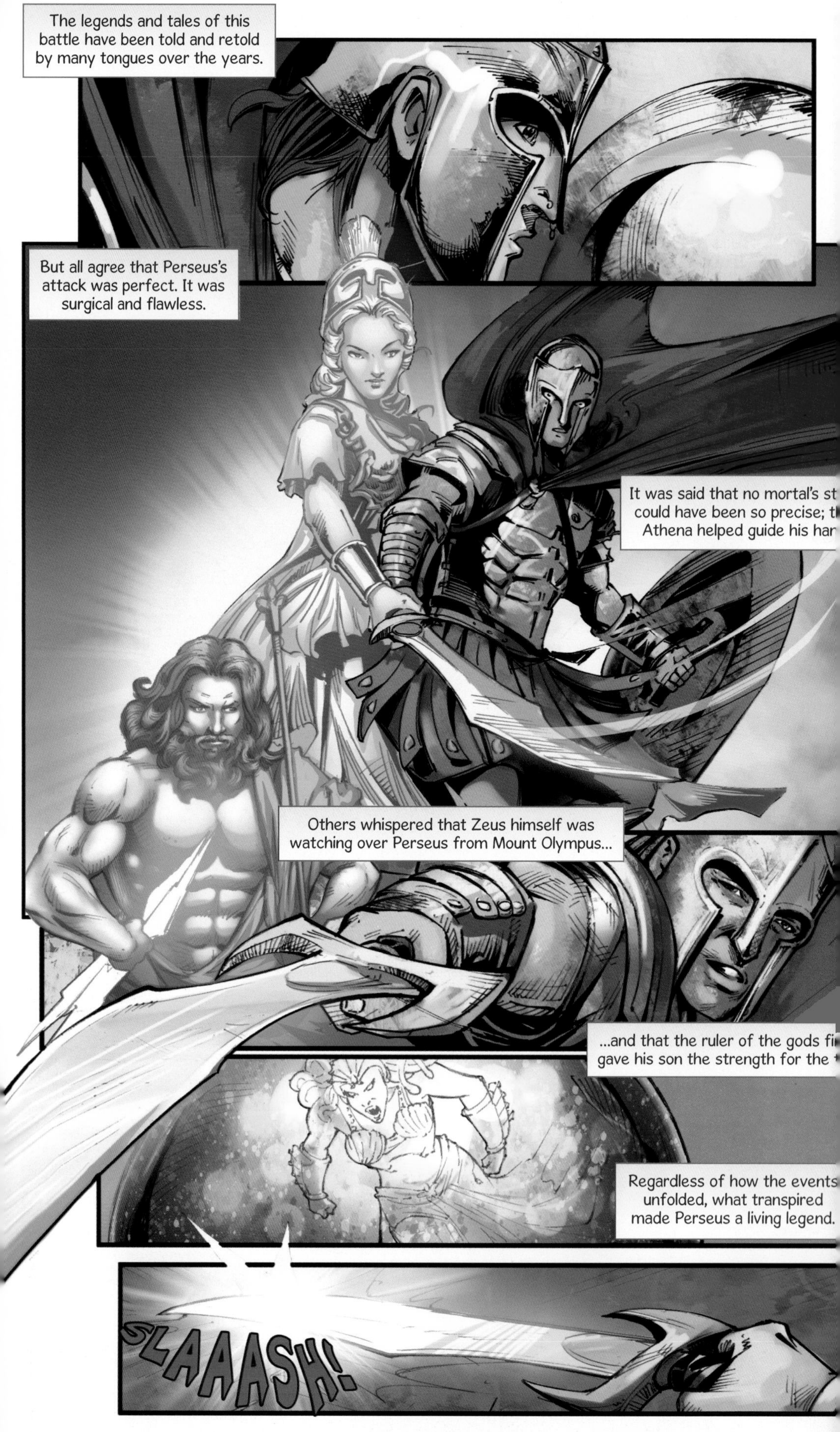
The legends and tales of this battle have been told and retold by many tongues over the years.
But all agree that Perseus's attack was perfect. It was surgical and flawless.
It was said that no mortal's st could have been so precise; t Athena helped guide his har
Others whispered that Zeus himself was watching over Perseus from Mount Olympus...
...and that the ruler of the gods fi gave his son the strength for the
Regardless of how the events unfolded, what transpired made Perseus a living legend.
SLAAASH!

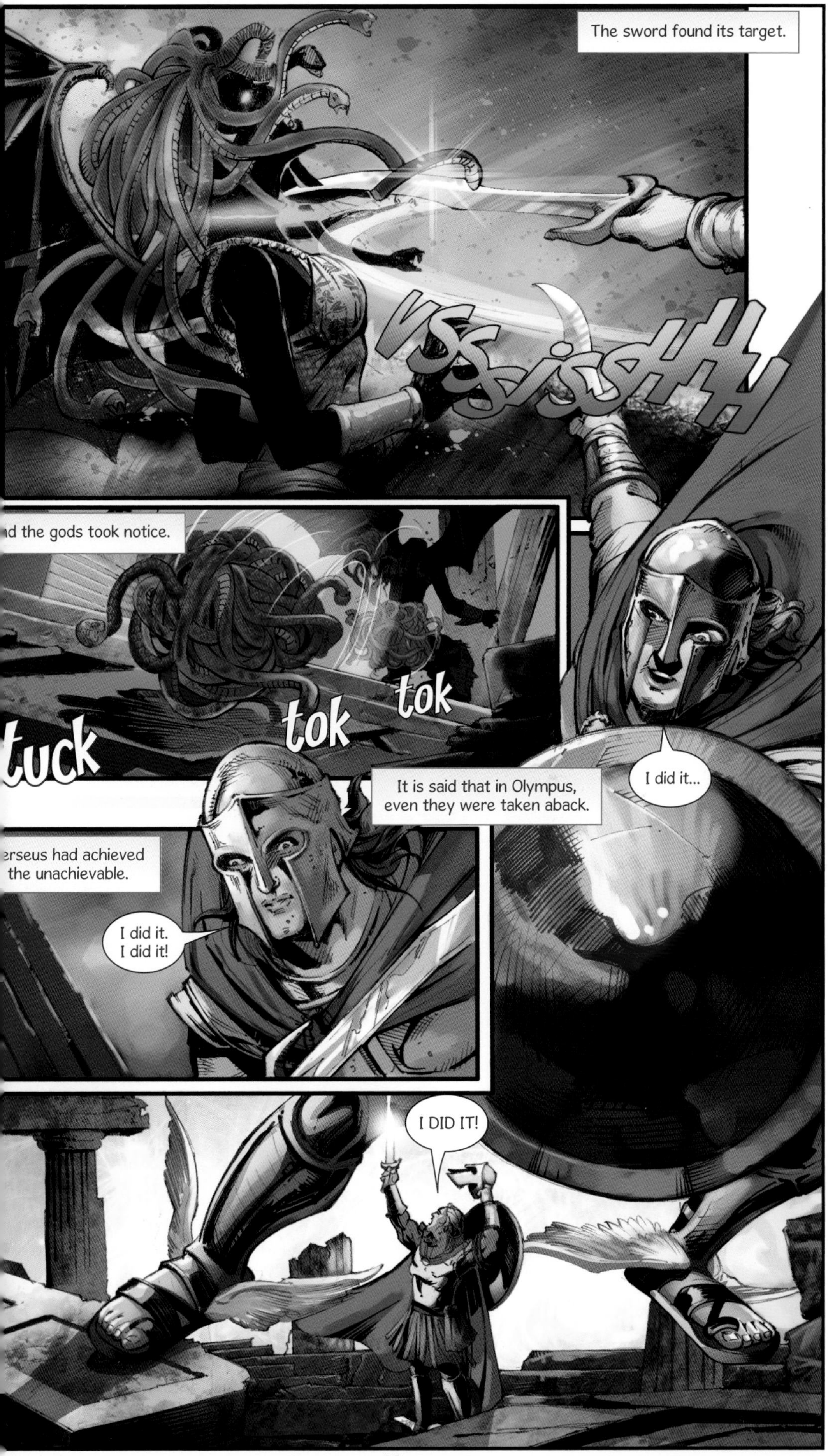
The sword found its target.
VSSSISHHH
...d the gods took notice.
tuck
tok
tok
It is said that in Olympus, even they were taken aback.
I did it...
...erseus had achieved the unachievable.
I did it. I did it!
I DID IT!

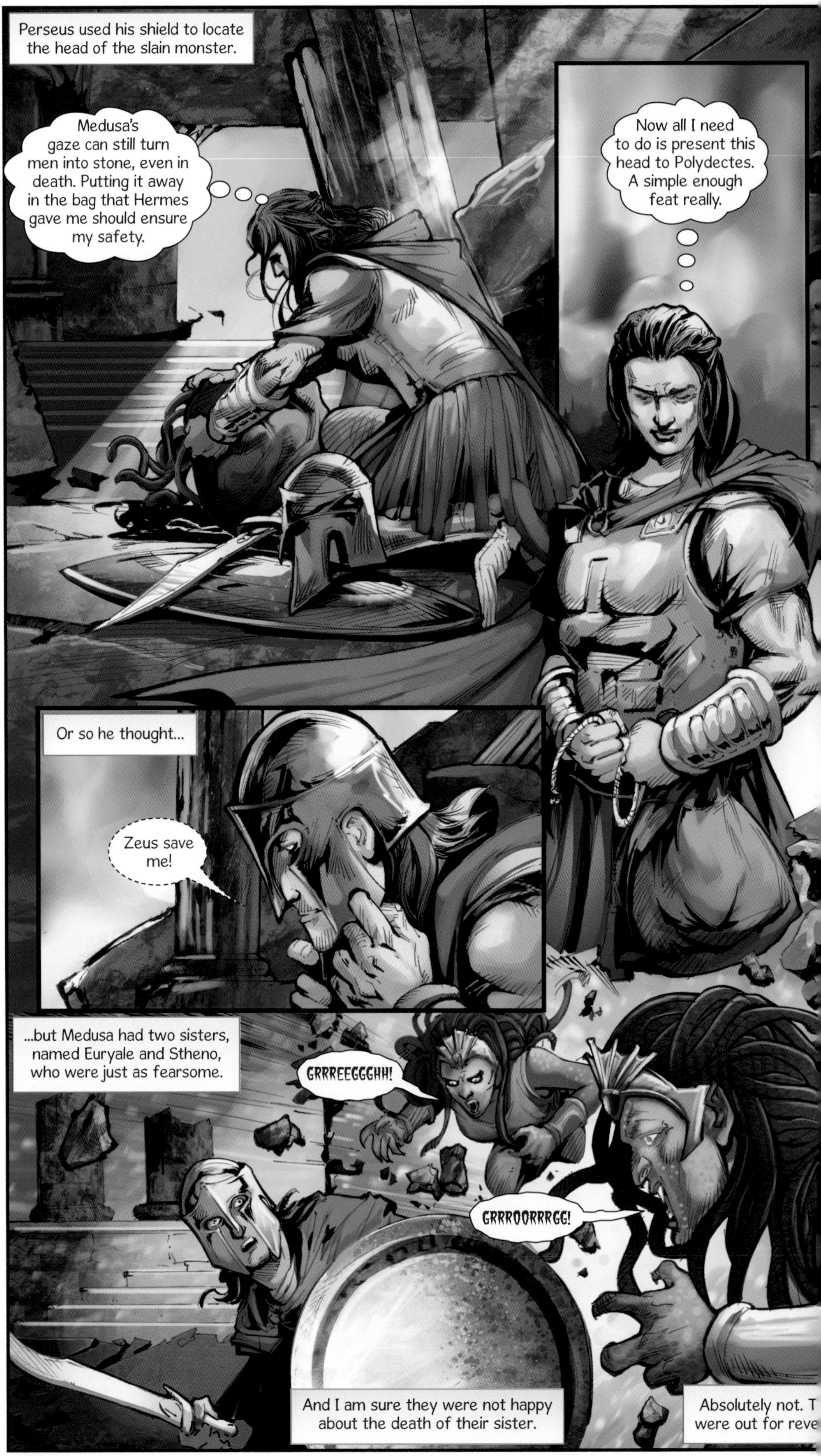
Perseus used his shield to locate the head of the slain monster.
Medusa's gaze can still turn men into stone, even in death. Putting it away in the bag that Hermes gave me should ensure my safety.
Now all I need to do is present this head to Polydectes. A simple enough feat really.
Or so he thought...
Zeus save me!
...but Medusa had two sisters, named Euryale and Stheno, who were just as fearsome.
GRRREEGGGHH!
GRRROORRRGG!
And I am sure they were not happy about the death of their sister.
Absolutely not. T
were out for reve

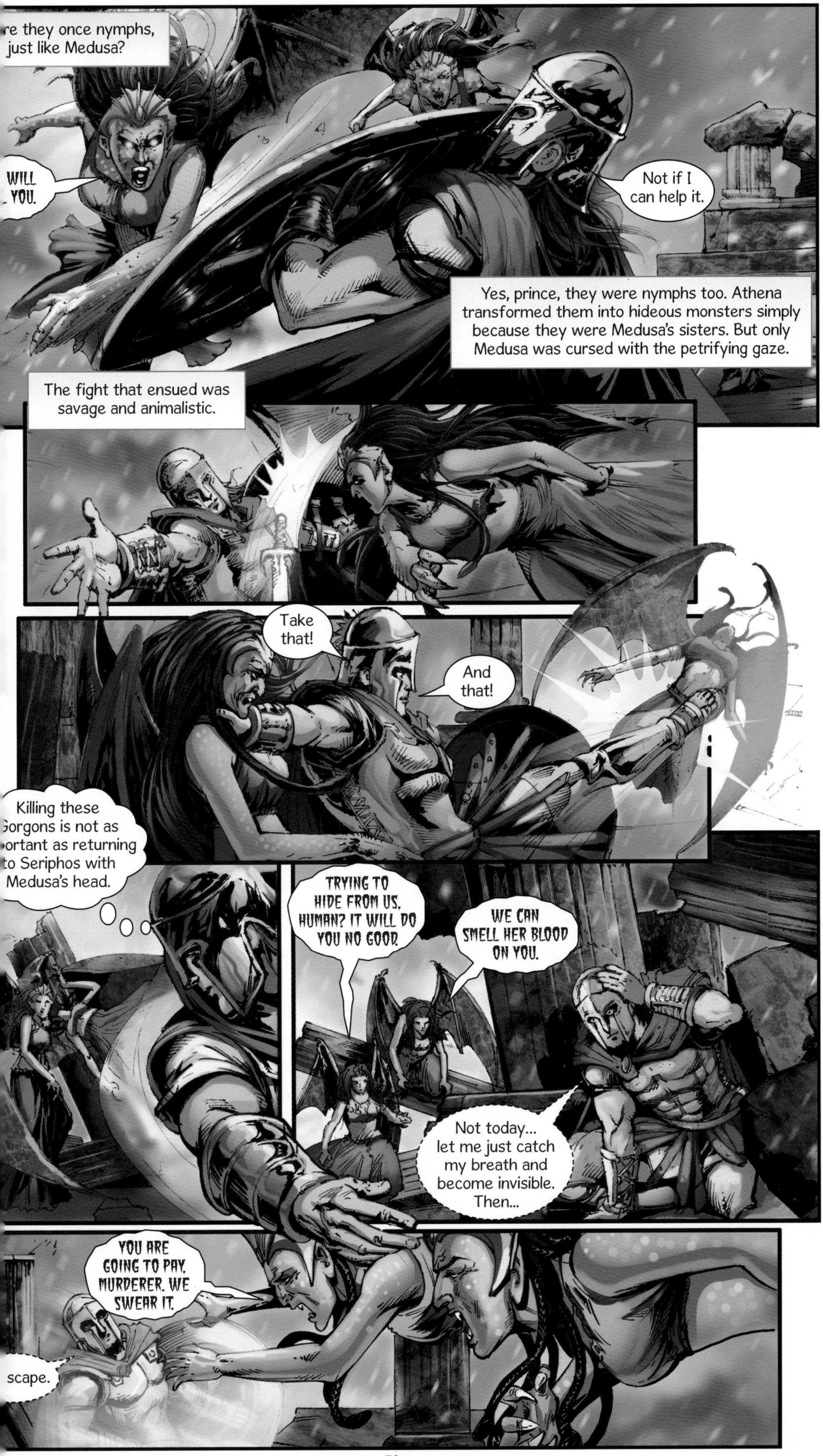
re they once nymphs, just like Medusa?
WILL YOU.
Not if I can help it.
Yes, prince, they were nymphs too. Athena transformed them into hideous monsters simply because they were Medusa's sisters. But only Medusa was cursed with the petrifying gaze.
The fight that ensued was savage and animalistic.
Take that!
And that!
Killing these Gorgons is not as ortant as returning to Seriphos with Medusa's head.
TRYING TO HIDE FROM US, HUMAN? IT WILL DO YOU NO GOOD.
WE CAN SMELL HER BLOOD ON YOU.
Not today... let me just catch my breath and become invisible. Then...
YOU ARE GOING TO PAY, MURDERER. WE SWEAR IT.
scape.

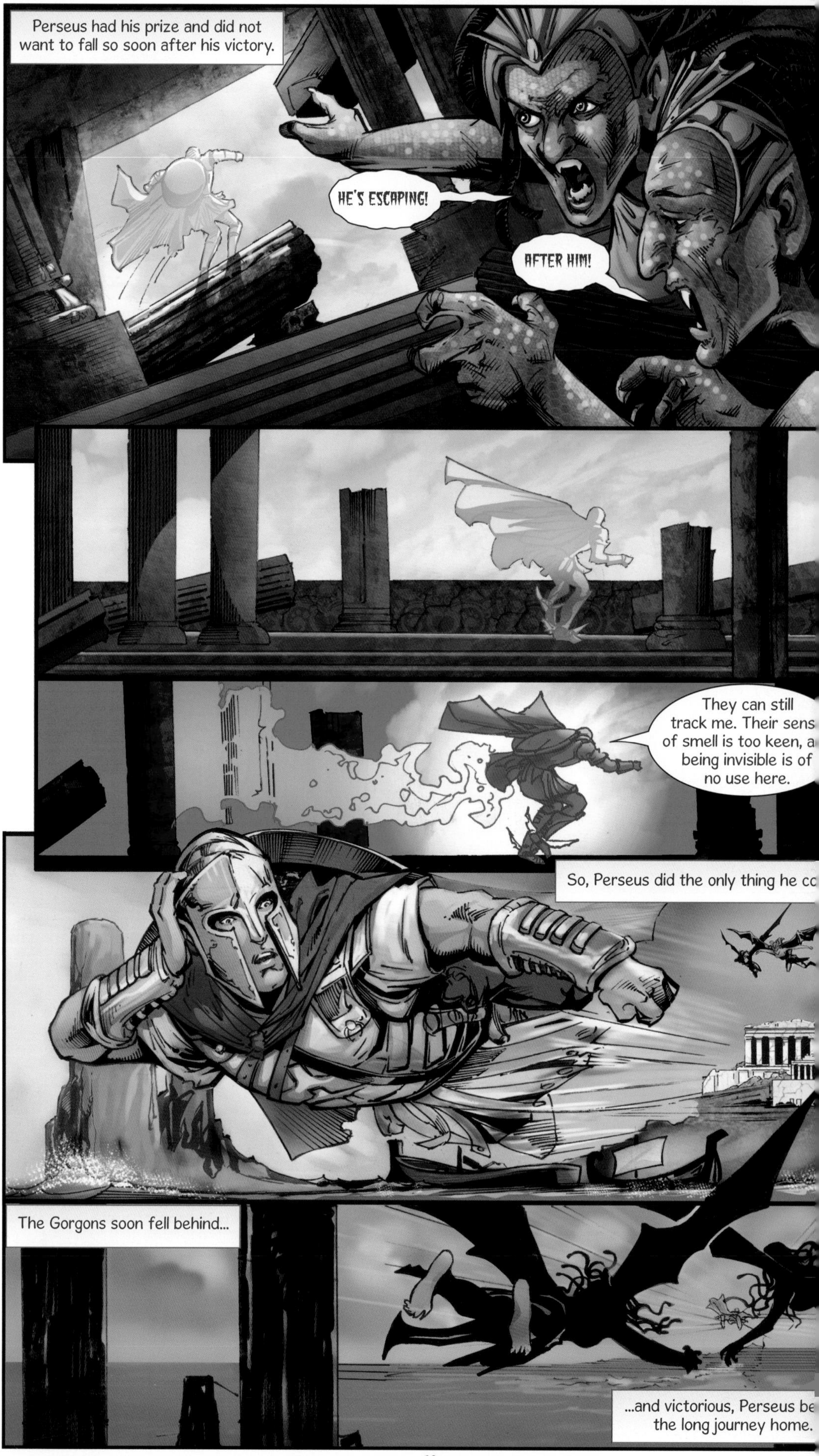
Perseus had his prize and did not want to fall so soon after his victory.
HE'S ESCAPING!
AFTER HIM!
They can still track me. Their sens of smell is too keen, a being invisible is of no use here.
So, Perseus did the only thing he co
The Gorgons soon fell behind...
...and victorious, Perseus be the long journey home.

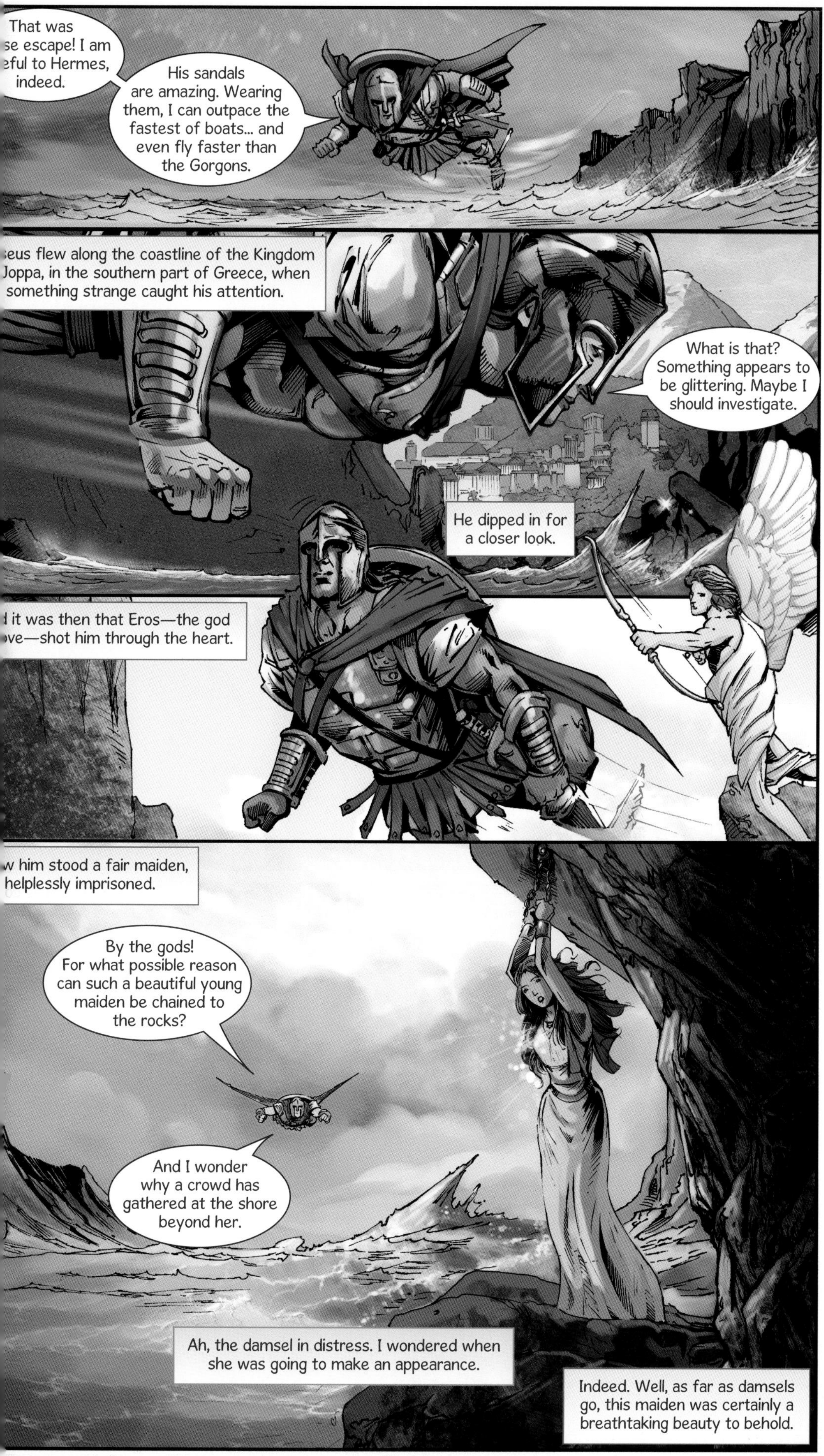

That was se escape! I am eful to Hermes, indeed.
His sandals are amazing. Wearing them, I can outpace the fastest of boats... and even fly faster than the Gorgons.
eus flew along the coastline of the Kingdom Joppa, in the southern part of Greece, when something strange caught his attention.
What is that? Something appears to be glittering. Maybe I should investigate.
He dipped in for a closer look.
it was then that Eros—the god ve—shot him through the heart.
w him stood a fair maiden, helplessly imprisoned.
By the gods! For what possible reason can such a beautiful young maiden be chained to the rocks?
And I wonder why a crowd has gathered at the shore beyond her.
Ah, the damsel in distress. I wondered when she was going to make an appearance.
Indeed. Well, as far as damsels go, this maiden was certainly a breathtaking beauty to behold.

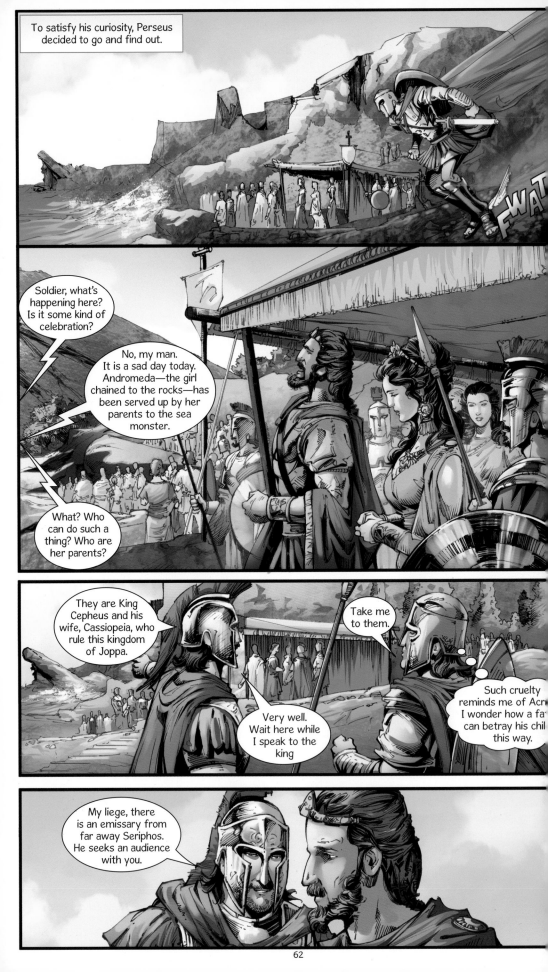

To satisfy his curiosity, Perseus decided to go and find out.

FWAT

Soldier, what's happening here? Is it some kind of celebration?

No, my man. It is a sad day today. Andromeda—the girl chained to the rocks—has been served up by her parents to the sea monster.

What? Who can do such a thing? Who are her parents?

They are King Cepheus and his wife, Cassiopeia, who rule this kingdom of Joppa.

Take me to them.

Very well. Wait here while I speak to the king

Such cruelty reminds me of Acri I wonder how a fa I can betray his chil this way.

My liege, there is an emissary from far away Seriphos. He seeks an audience with you.

62

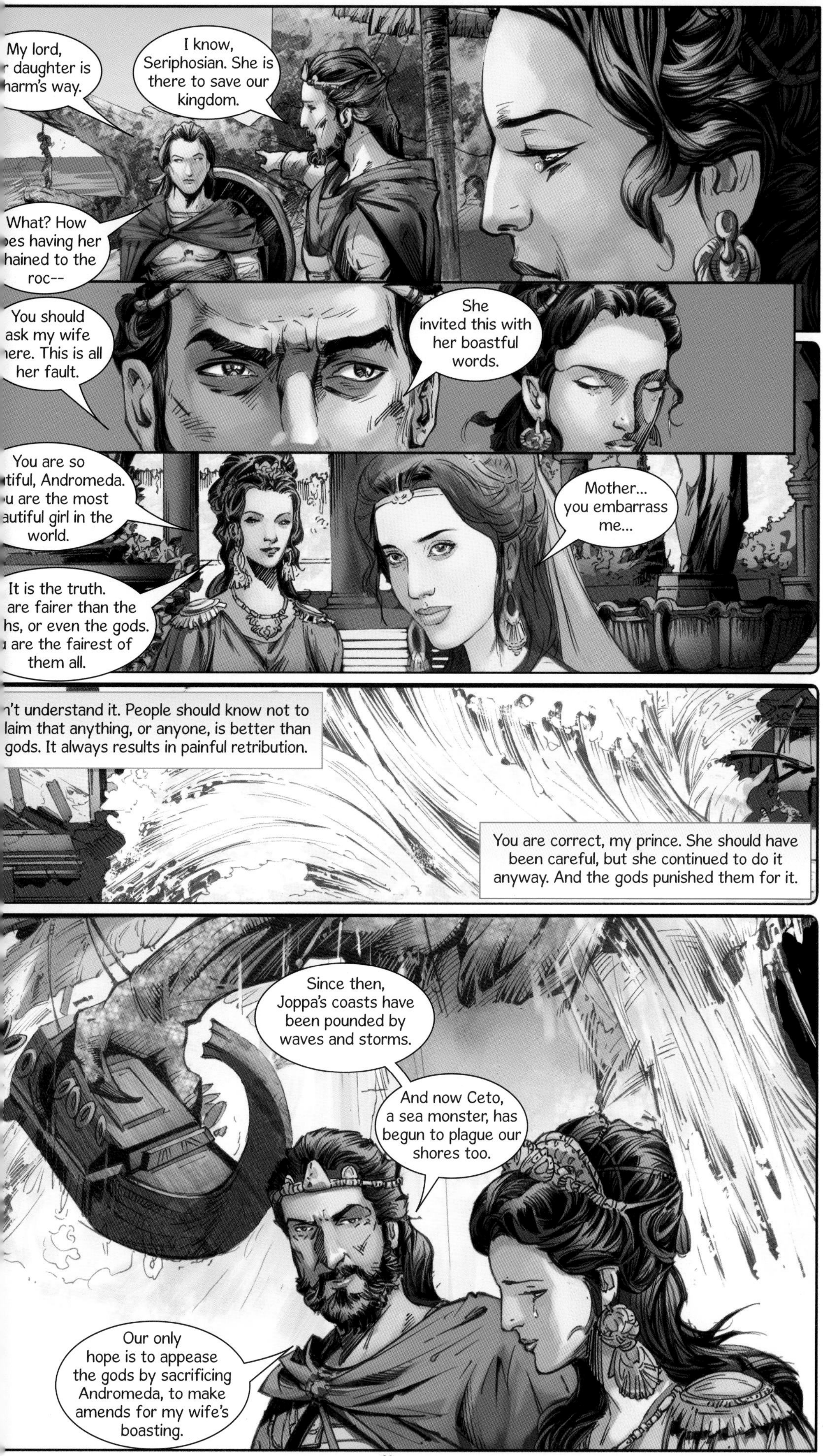

My lord, daughter is harm's way.
I know, Seriphosian. She is there to save our kingdom.
What? How es having her hained to the roc--
You should ask my wife ere. This is all her fault.
She invited this with her boastful words.
You are so tiful, Andromeda. u are the most autiful girl in the world.
Mother... you embarrass me...
It is the truth. are fairer than the hs, or even the gods. are the fairest of them all.
't understand it. People should know not to laim that anything, or anyone, is better than gods. It always results in painful retribution.
You are correct, my prince. She should have been careful, but she continued to do it anyway. And the gods punished them for it.
Since then, Joppa's coasts have been pounded by waves and storms.
And now Ceto, a sea monster, has begun to plague our shores too.
Our only hope is to appease the gods by sacrificing Andromeda, to make amends for my wife's boasting.

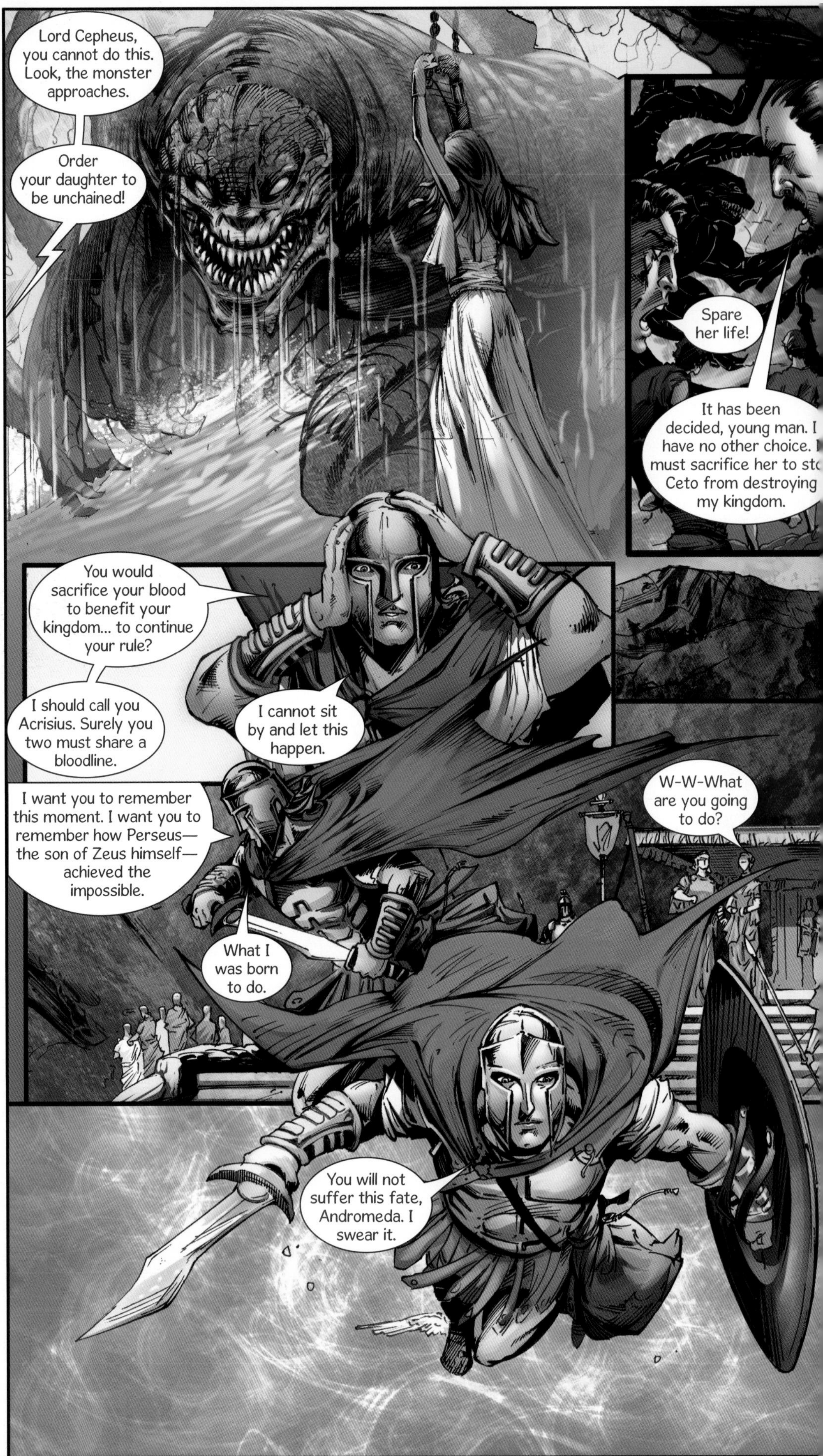

Lord Cepheus, you cannot do this. Look, the monster approaches.
Order your daughter to be unchained!
Spare her life!
It has been decided, young man. I have no other choice. I must sacrifice her to sto Ceto from destroying my kingdom.
You would sacrifice your blood to benefit your kingdom... to continue your rule?
I should call you Acrisius. Surely you two must share a bloodline.
I cannot sit by and let this happen.
I want you to remember this moment. I want you to remember how Perseus— the son of Zeus himself— achieved the impossible.
What I was born to do.
W-W-What are you going to do?
You will not suffer this fate, Andromeda. I swear it.

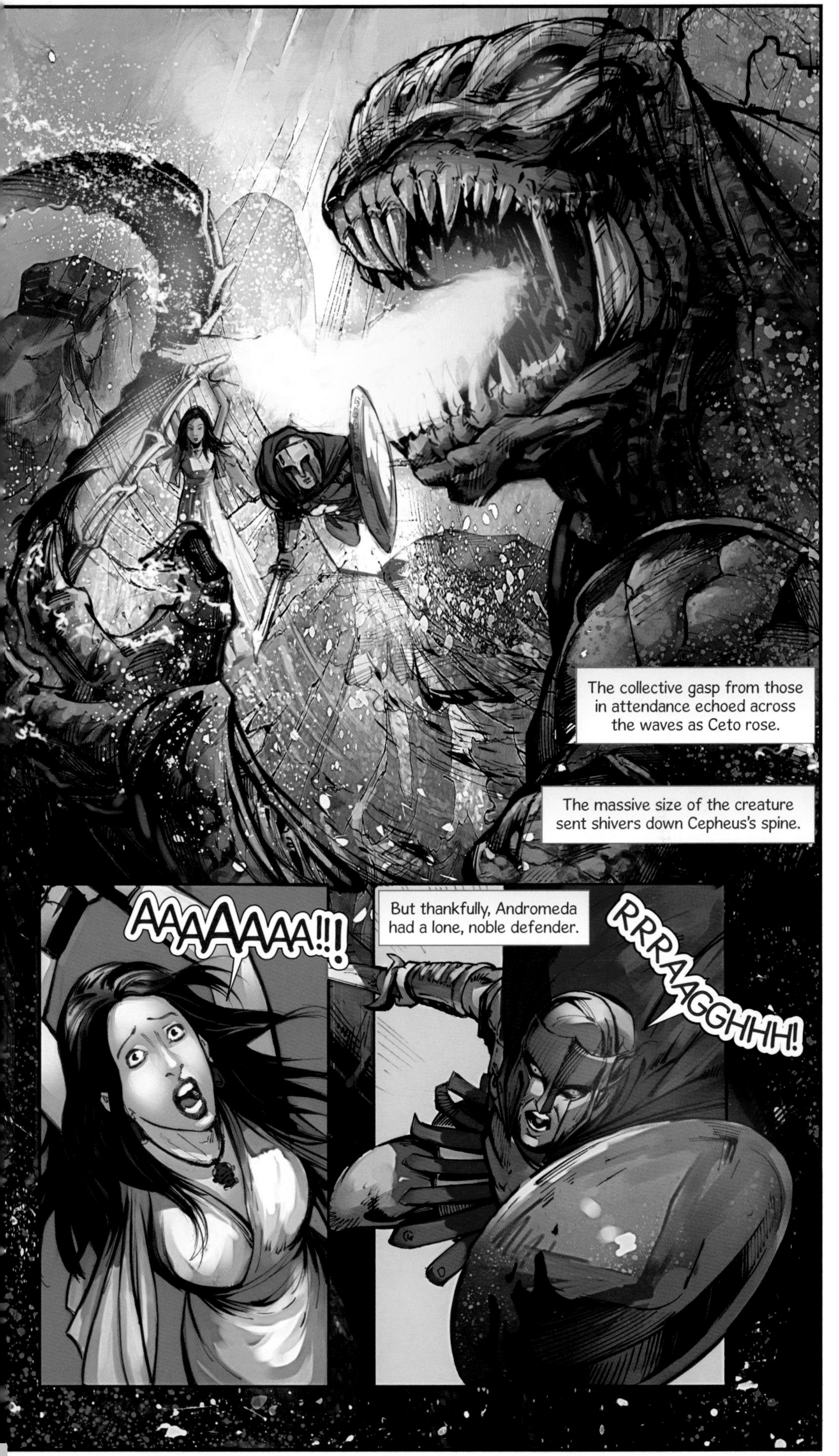
The collective gasp from those in attendance echoed across the waves as Ceto rose.
The massive size of the creature sent shivers down Cepheus's spine.
AAAAAAA!!!
But thankfully, Andromeda had a lone, noble defender.
RRRAAGGHHH!

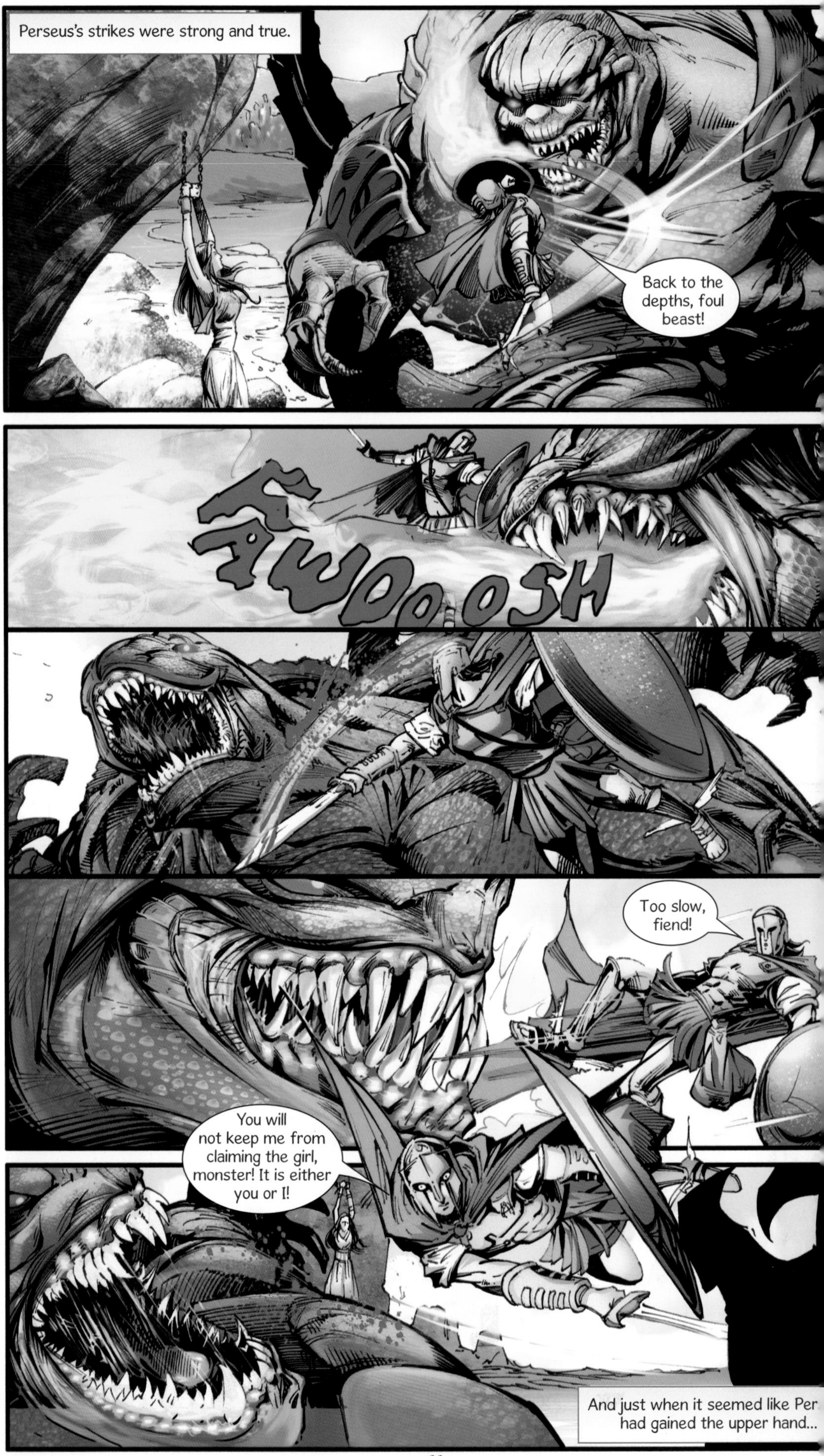

Perseus's strikes were strong and true.
Back to the depths, foul beast!
FAWOOOSH
Too slow, fiend!
You will not keep me from claiming the girl, monster! It is either you or I!
And just when it seemed like Per
had gained the upper hand...

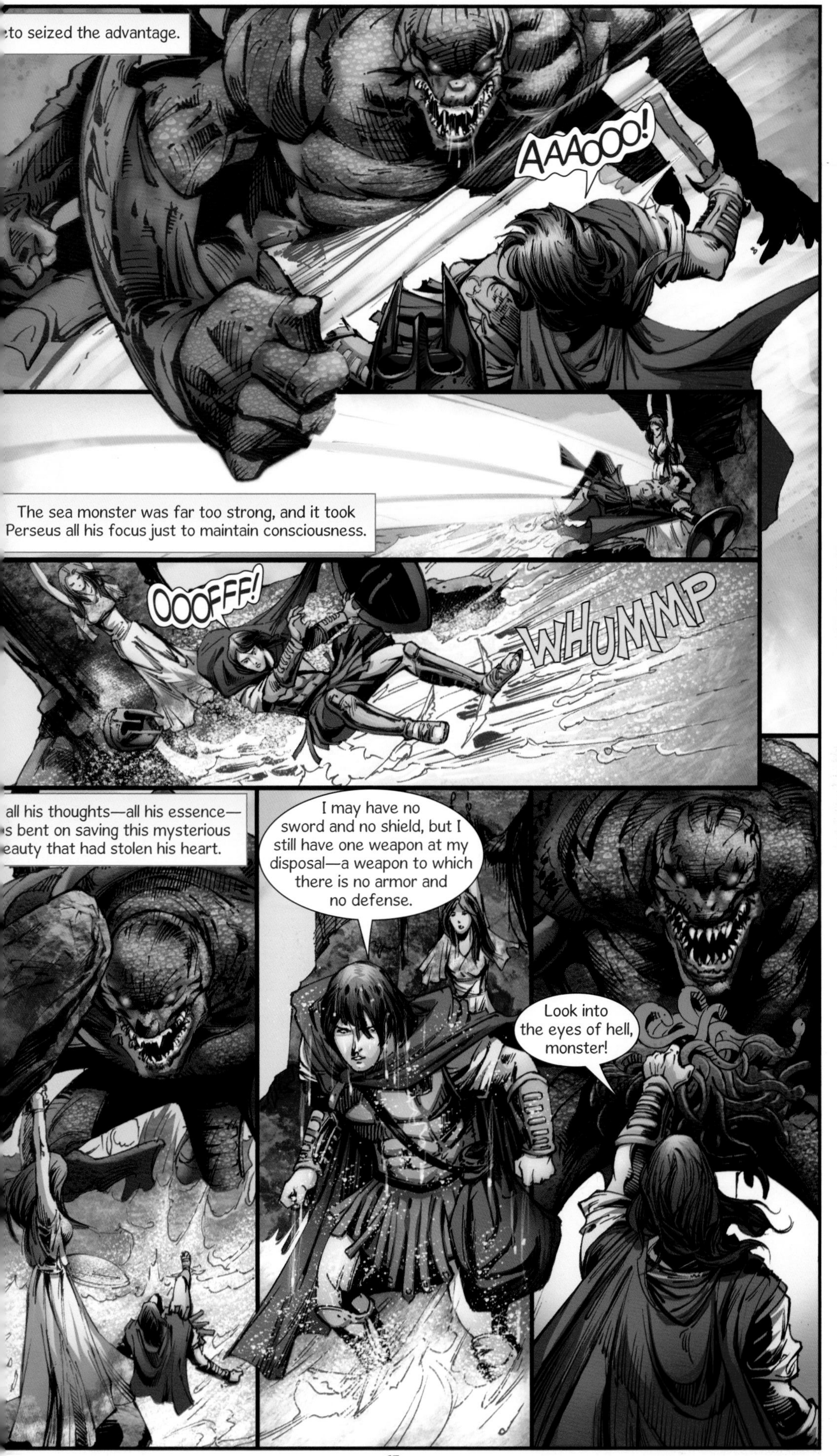

to seized the advantage.
AAAOOO!
The sea monster was far too strong, and it took Perseus all his focus just to maintain consciousness.
OOOFFF!
WHUMMP
all his thoughts—all his essence—
s bent on saving this mysterious
eauty that had stolen his heart.
I may have no sword and no shield, but I still have one weapon at my disposal—a weapon to which there is no armor and no defense.
Look into the eyes of hell, monster!

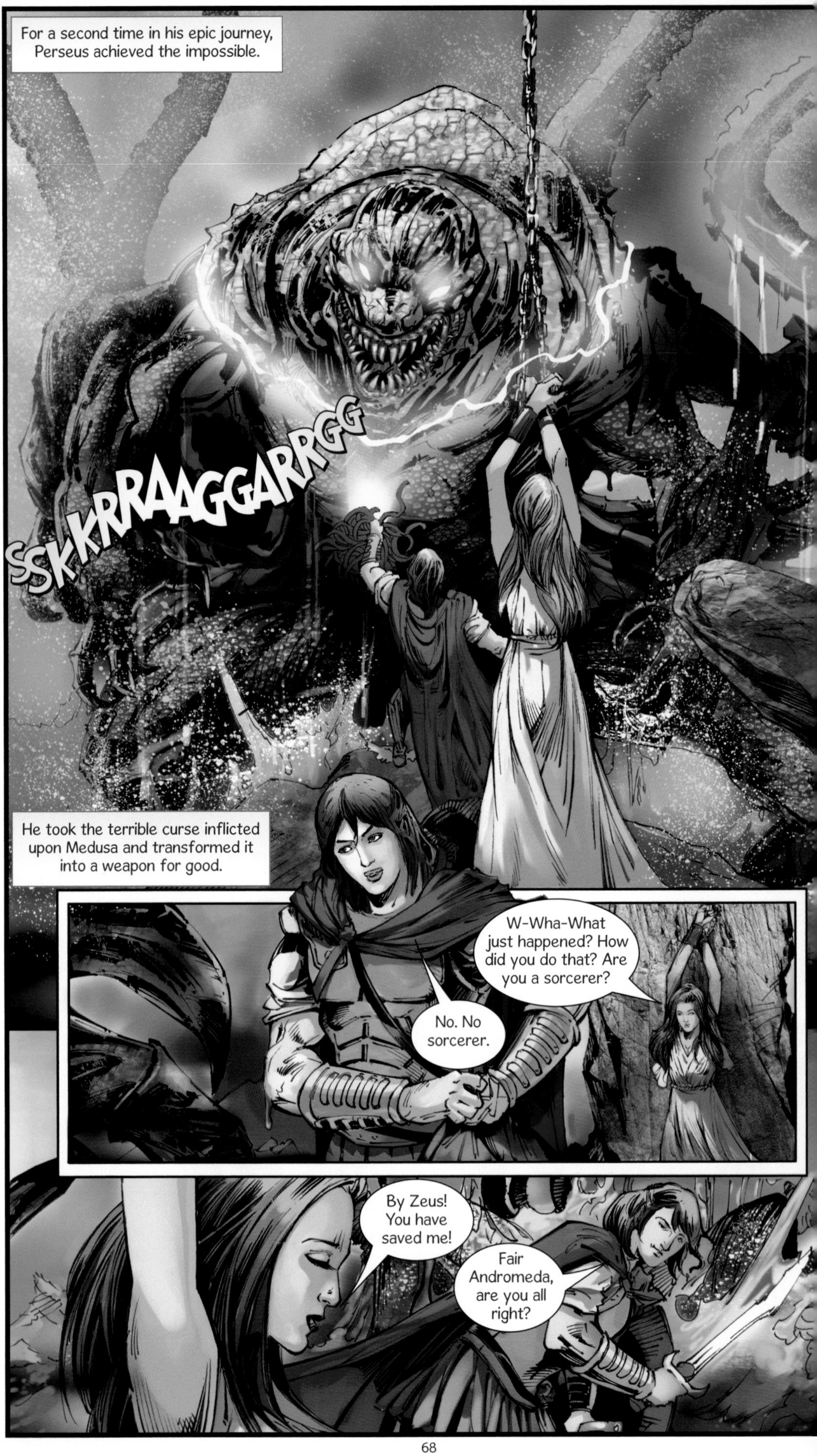
For a second time in his epic journey, Perseus achieved the impossible.
SSKKRRAAGGARRGG
He took the terrible curse inflicted upon Medusa and transformed it into a weapon for good.
W-Wha-What just happened? How did you do that? Are you a sorcerer?
No. No sorcerer.
By Zeus! You have saved me!
Fair Andromeda, are you all right?

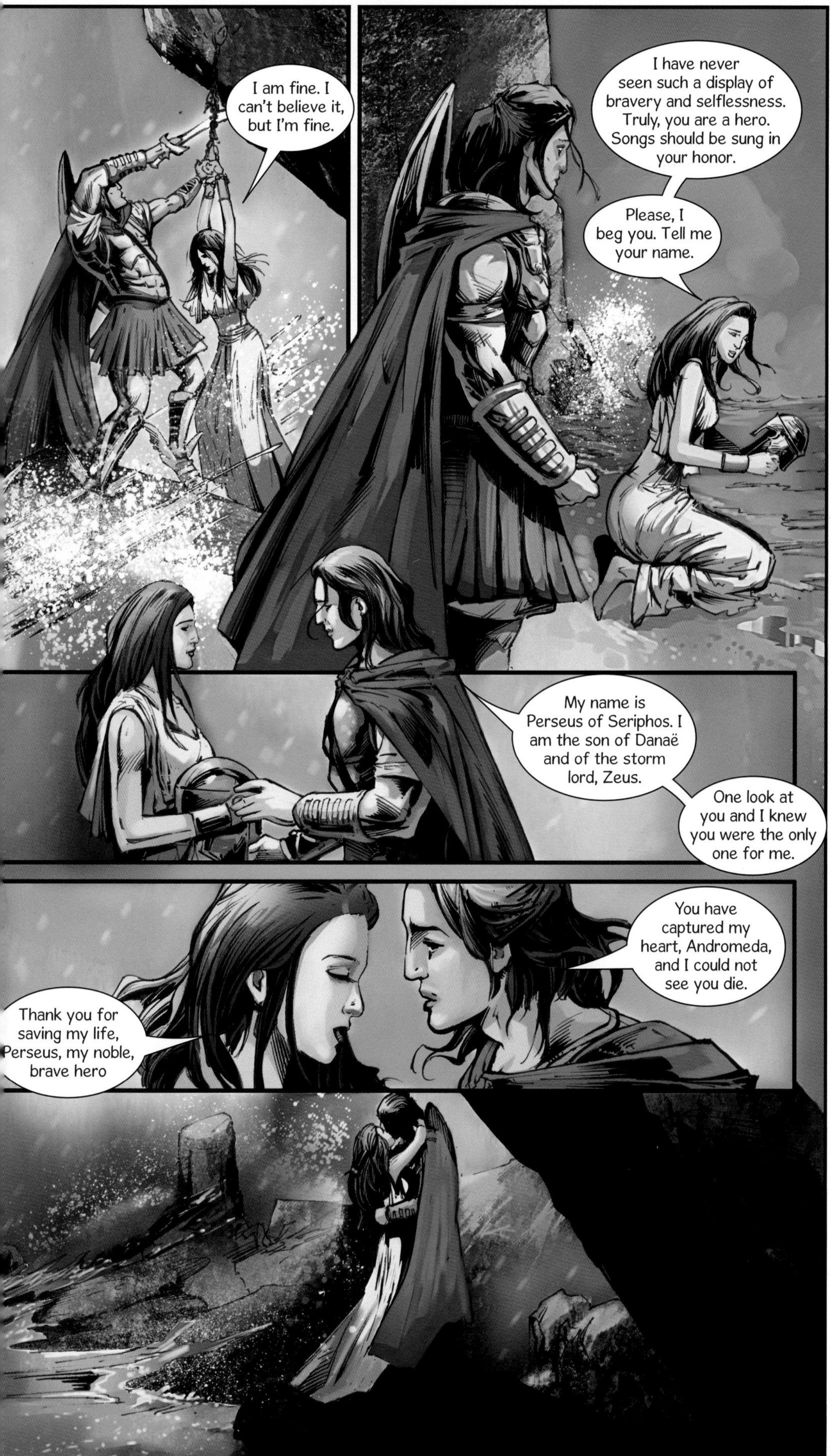
I am fine. I can't believe it, but I'm fine.
I have never seen such a display of bravery and selflessness. Truly, you are a hero. Songs should be sung in your honor.
Please, I beg you. Tell me your name.
My name is Perseus of Seriphos. I am the son of Danaë and of the storm lord, Zeus.
One look at you and I knew you were the only one for me.
You have captured my heart, Andromeda, and I could not see you die.
Thank you for saving my life, Perseus, my noble, brave hero

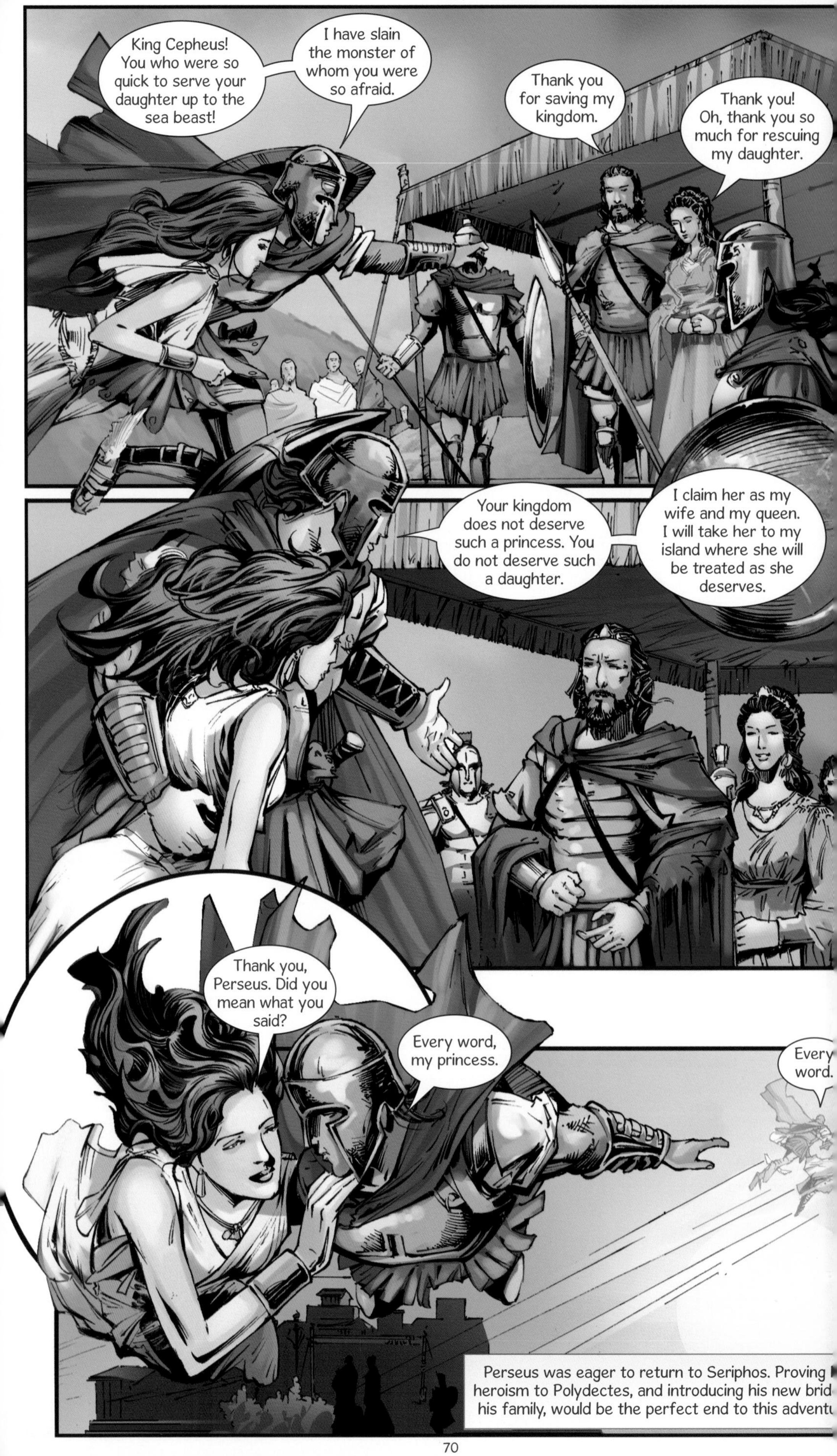
King Cepheus! You who were so quick to serve your daughter up to the sea beast!
I have slain the monster of whom you were so afraid.
Thank you for saving my kingdom.
Thank you! Oh, thank you so much for rescuing my daughter.
Your kingdom does not deserve such a princess. You do not deserve such a daughter.
I claim her as my wife and my queen. I will take her to my island where she will be treated as she deserves.
Thank you, Perseus. Did you mean what you said?
Every word, my princess.
Every word.
Perseus was eager to return to Seriphos. Proving heroism to Polydectes, and introducing his new brid his family, would be the perfect end to this adventu

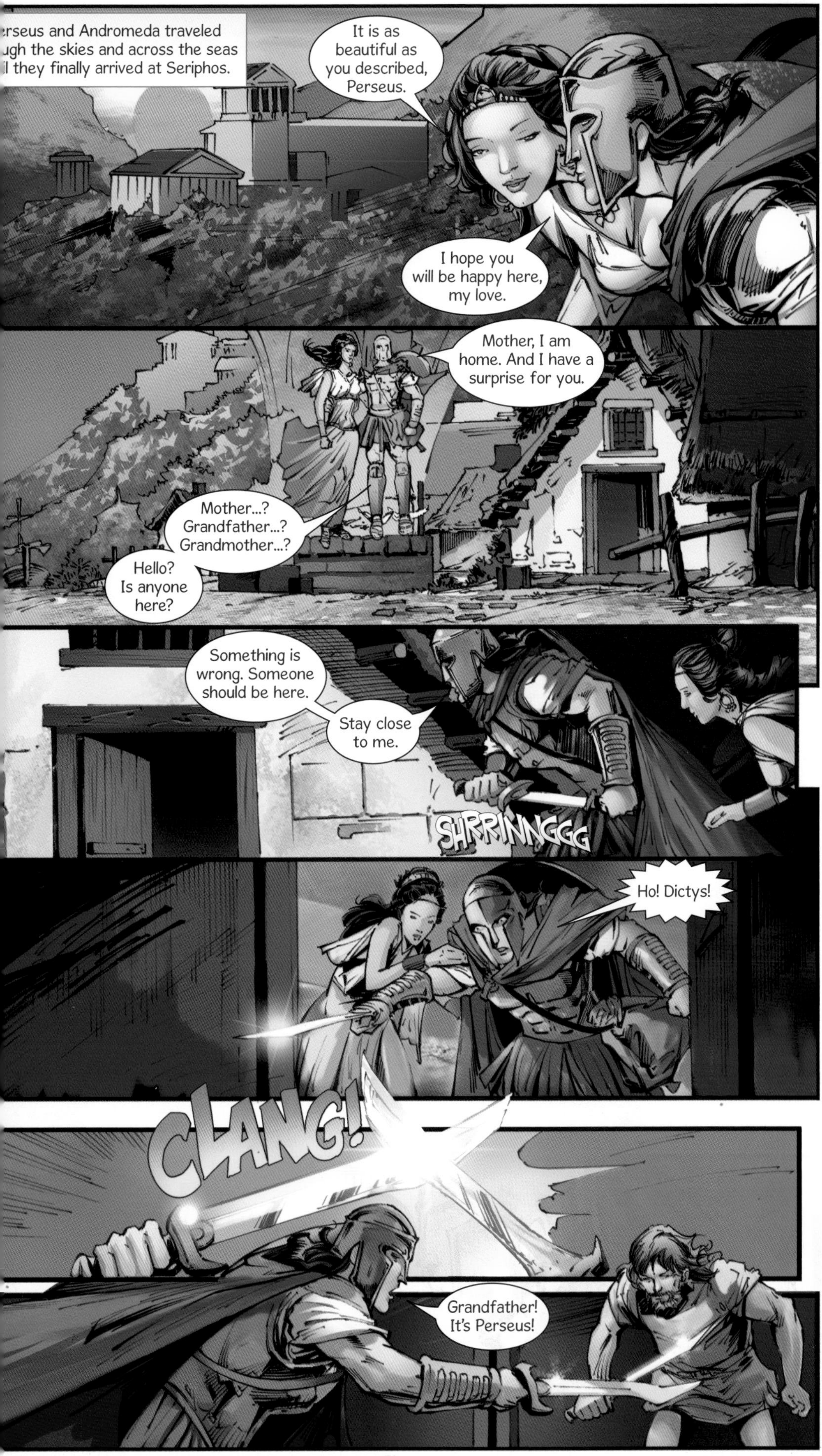

rseus and Andromeda traveled
ugh the skies and across the seas
l they finally arrived at Seriphos.
It is as beautiful as you described, Perseus.
I hope you will be happy here, my love.
Mother, I am home. And I have a surprise for you.
Mother...? Grandfather...? Grandmother...?
Hello? Is anyone here?
Something is wrong. Someone should be here.
Stay close to me.
SHRRINNGGG
Ho! Dictys!
CLANG!
Grandfather! It's Perseus!

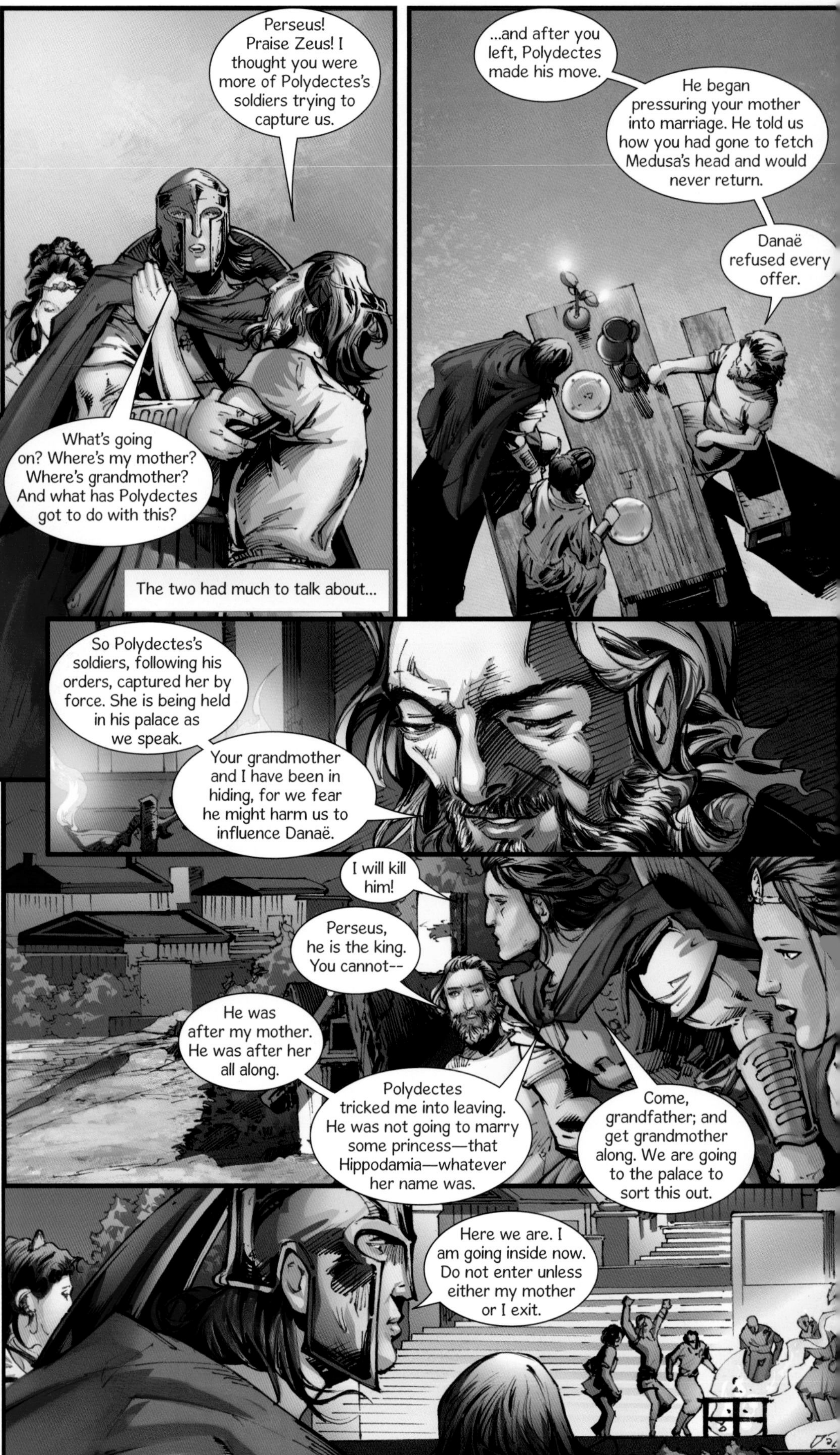
Perseus! Praise Zeus! I thought you were more of Polydectes's soldiers trying to capture us.
What's going on? Where's my mother? Where's grandmother? And what has Polydectes got to do with this?
The two had much to talk about...
...and after you left, Polydectes made his move.
He began pressuring your mother into marriage. He told us how you had gone to fetch Medusa's head and would never return.
Danaë refused every offer.
So Polydectes's soldiers, following his orders, captured her by force. She is being held in his palace as we speak.
Your grandmother and I have been in hiding, for we fear he might harm us to influence Danaë.
I will kill him!
Perseus, he is the king. You cannot--
He was after my mother. He was after her all along.
Polydectes tricked me into leaving. He was not going to marry some princess—that Hippodamia—whatever her name was.
Come, grandfather; and get grandmother along. We are going to the palace to sort this out.
Here we are. I am going inside now. Do not enter unless either my mother or I exit.

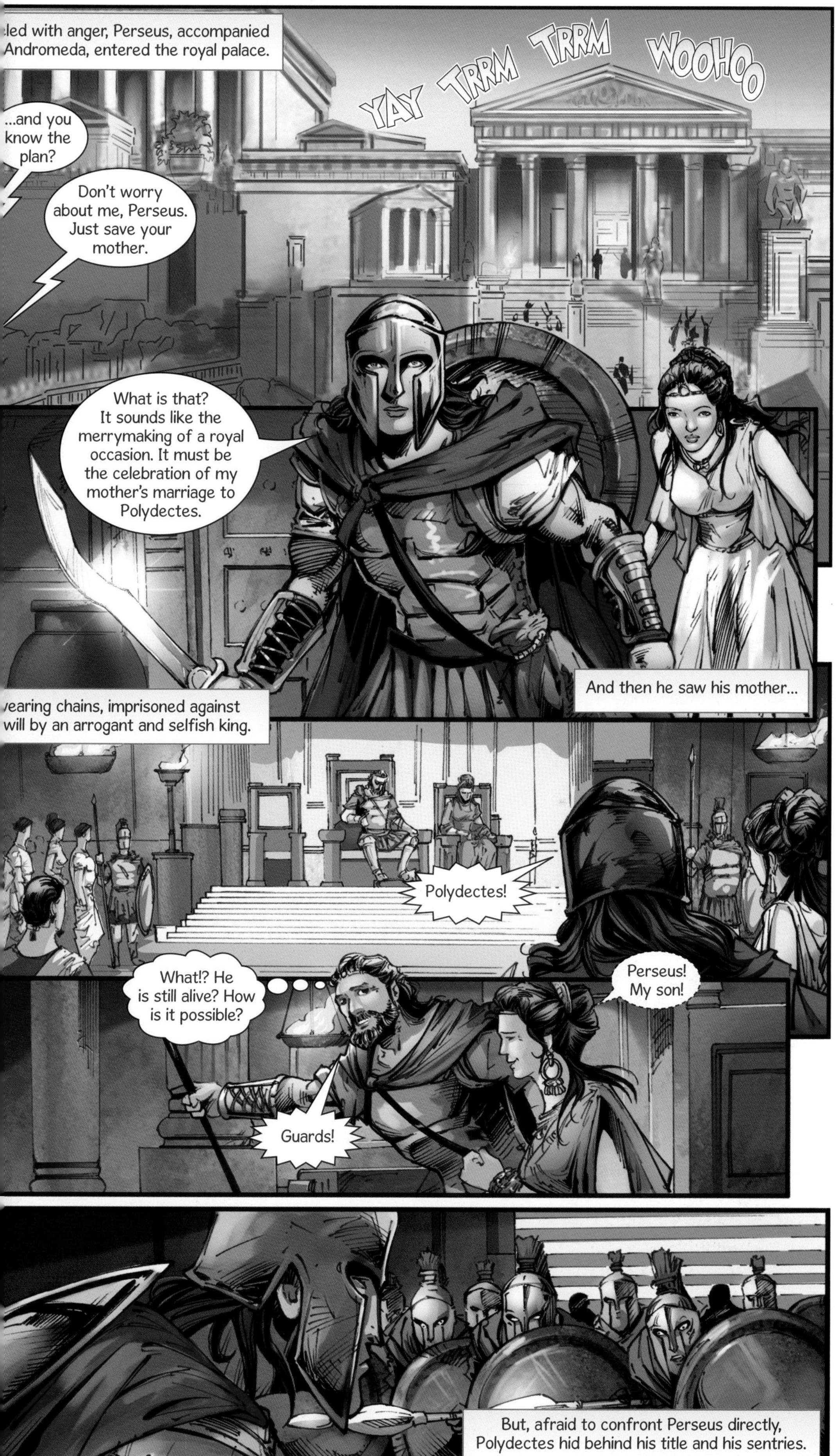

led with anger, Perseus, accompanied Andromeda, entered the royal palace.
YAY TRRM TRRM WOOHOO
...and you know the plan?
Don't worry about me, Perseus. Just save your mother.
What is that? It sounds like the merrymaking of a royal occasion. It must be the celebration of my mother's marriage to Polydectes.
And then he saw his mother...
vearing chains, imprisoned against will by an arrogant and selfish king.
Polydectes!
What!? He is still alive? How is it possible?
Perseus! My son!
Guards!
But, afraid to confront Perseus directly, Polydectes hid behind his title and his sentries.

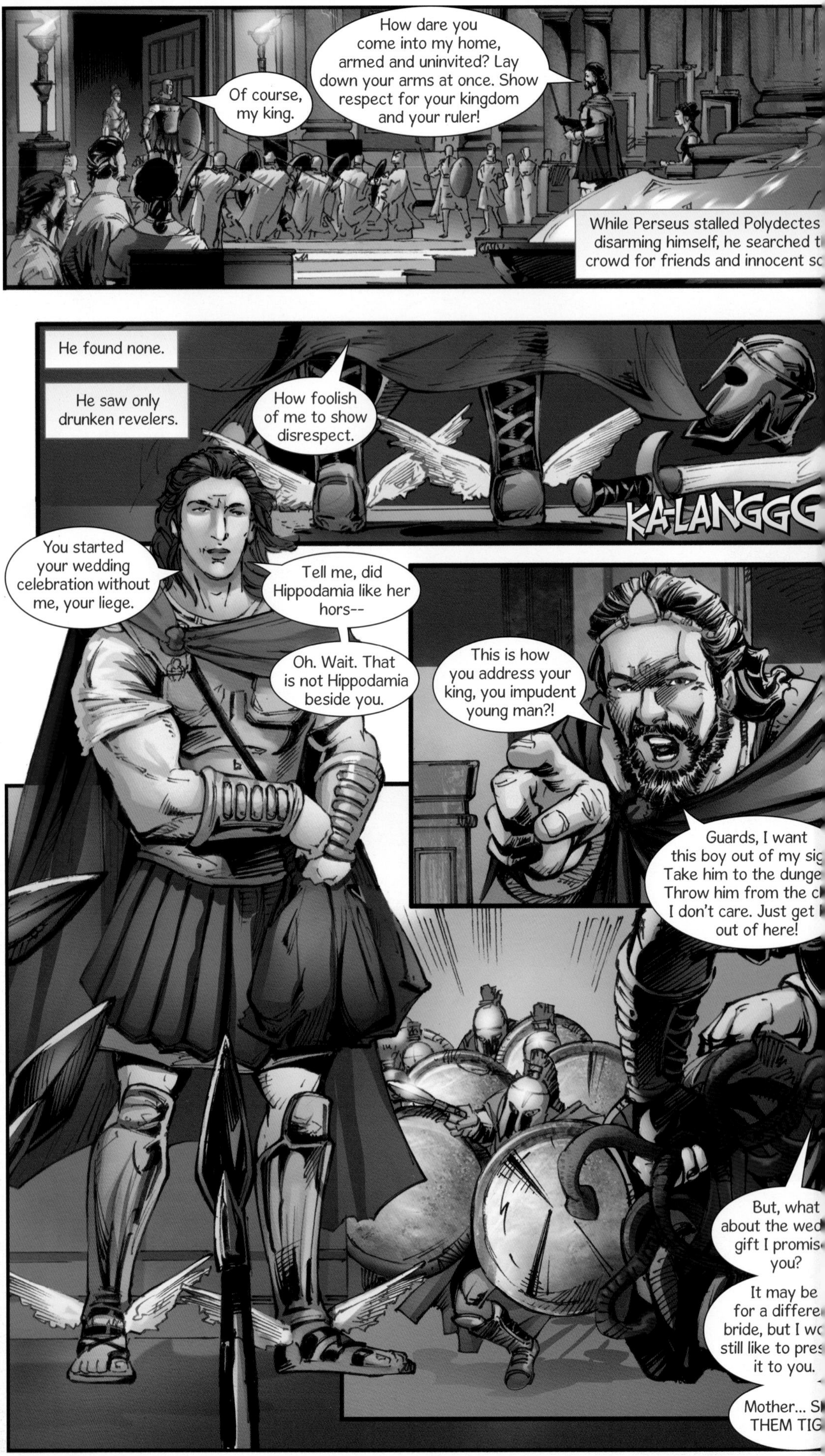

How dare you come into my home, armed and uninvited? Lay down your arms at once. Show respect for your kingdom and your ruler!
Of course, my king.
While Perseus stalled Polydectes disarming himself, he searched t crowd for friends and innocent sc
He found none.
He saw only drunken revelers.
How foolish of me to show disrespect.
KA-LANGGG
You started your wedding celebration without me, your liege.
Tell me, did Hippodamia like her hors--
Oh. Wait. That is not Hippodamia beside you.
This is how you address your king, you impudent young man?!
Guards, I want this boy out of my sig Take him to the dunge Throw him from the c I don't care. Just get out of here!
But, what about the wed gift I promis you?
It may be for a differe bride, but I w still like to pres it to you.
Mother... S THEM TIG

From the moment he was born, Perseus and Danaë had shared a phrase. She would whisper it to him after nightmares or during terrible storms.

They were words of comfort for the small boy. The instructions were simple.

Shut them tight.

On hearing these words, Perseus would close his eyes and banish his fears. It was their secret code which no one else knew.

a--

Now, those same words saved Danaë's life.

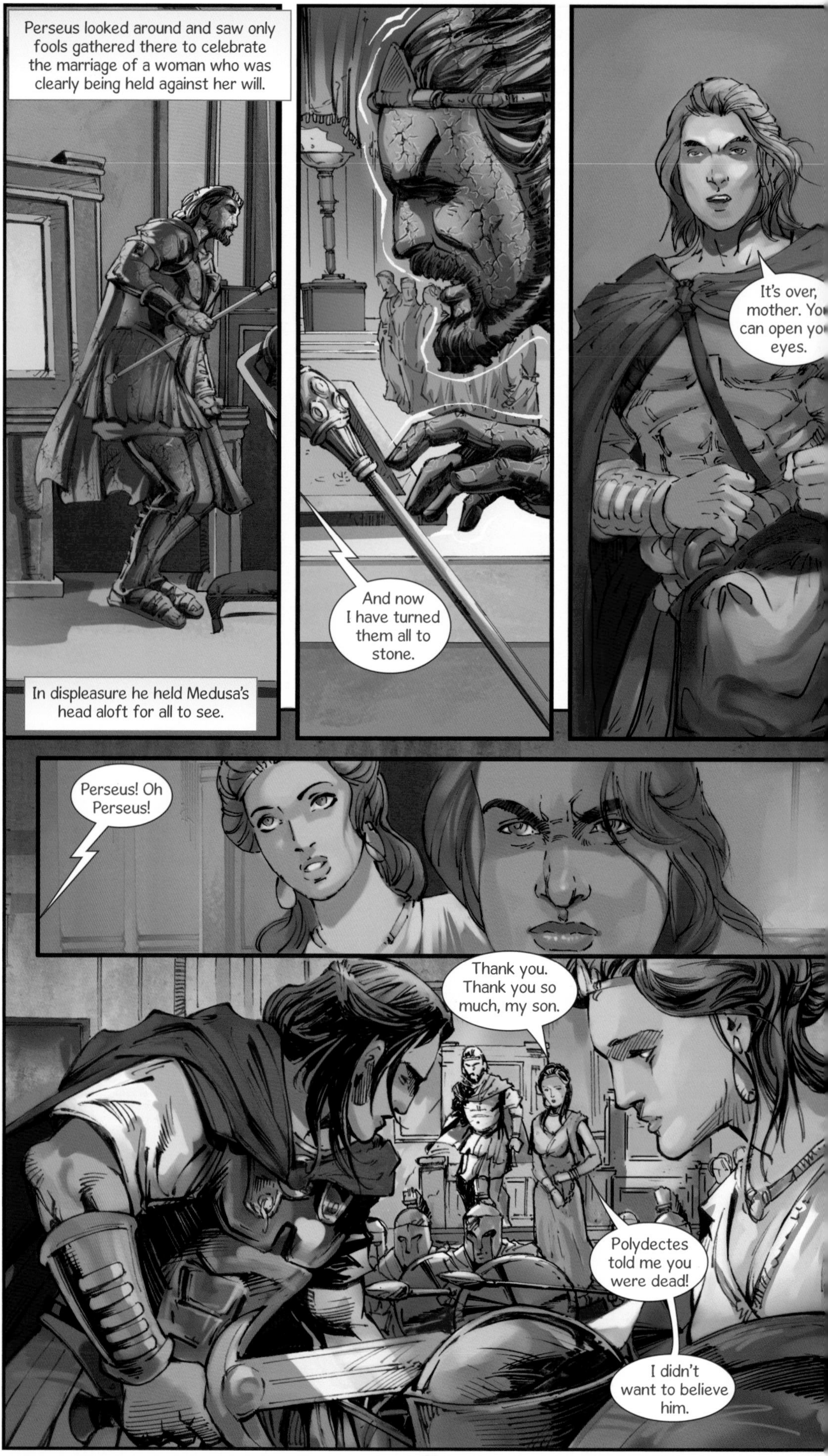
Perseus looked around and saw only fools gathered there to celebrate the marriage of a woman who was clearly being held against her will.
In displeasure he held Medusa's head aloft for all to see.
And now I have turned them all to stone.
It's over, mother. Yo
can open yo
eyes.
Perseus! Oh Perseus!
Thank you. Thank you so much, my son.
Polydectes told me you were dead!
I didn't want to believe him.

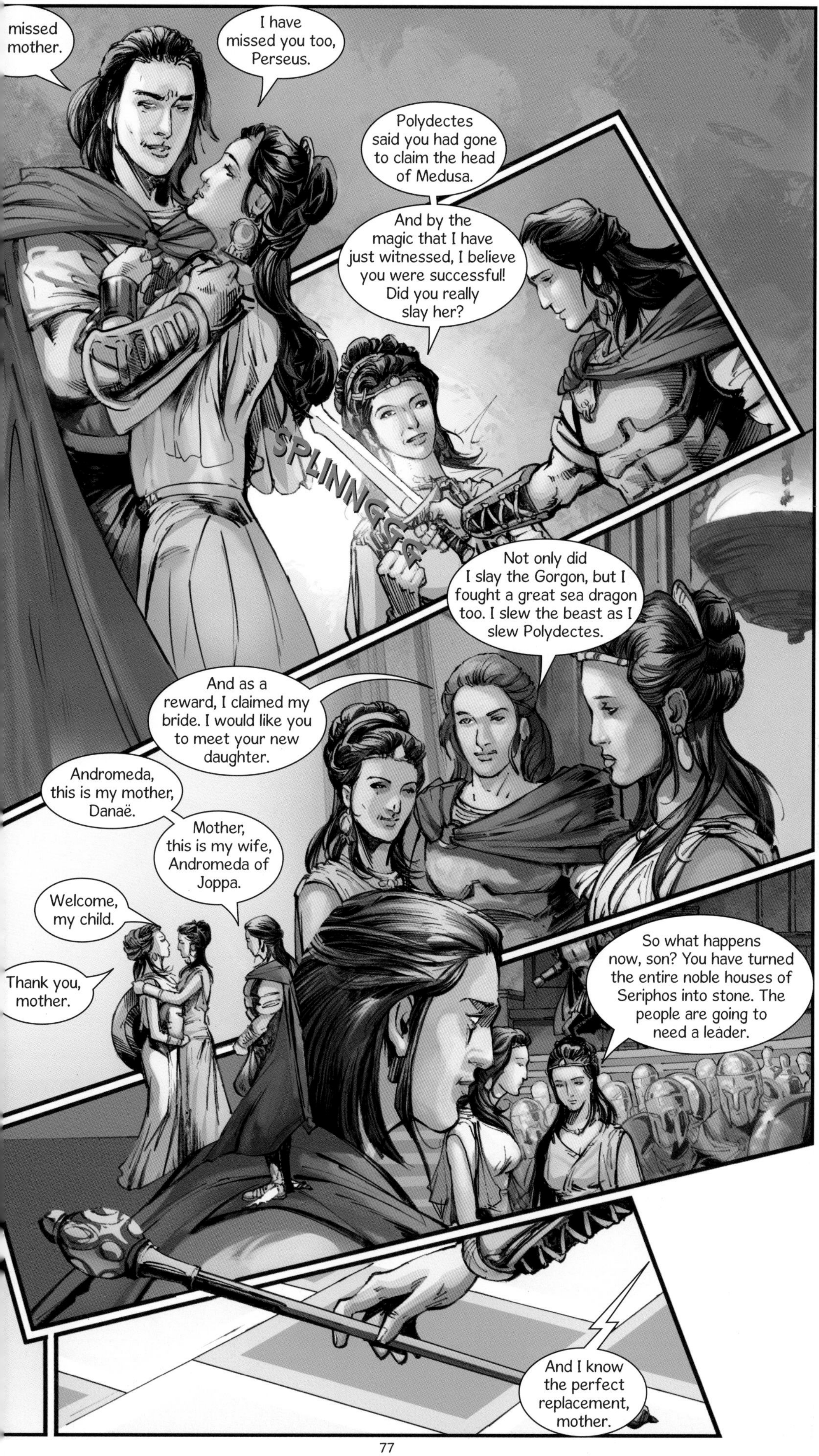

missed mother.
I have missed you too, Perseus.
Polydectes said you had gone to claim the head of Medusa.
And by the magic that I have just witnessed, I believe you were successful! Did you really slay her?
SPLINNGGG
Not only did I slay the Gorgon, but I fought a great sea dragon too. I slew the beast as I slew Polydectes.
And as a reward, I claimed my bride. I would like you to meet your new daughter.
Andromeda, this is my mother, Danaë.
Mother, this is my wife, Andromeda of Joppa.
Welcome, my child.
Thank you, mother.
So what happens now, son? You have turned the entire noble houses of Seriphos into stone. The people are going to need a leader.
And I know the perfect replacement, mother.

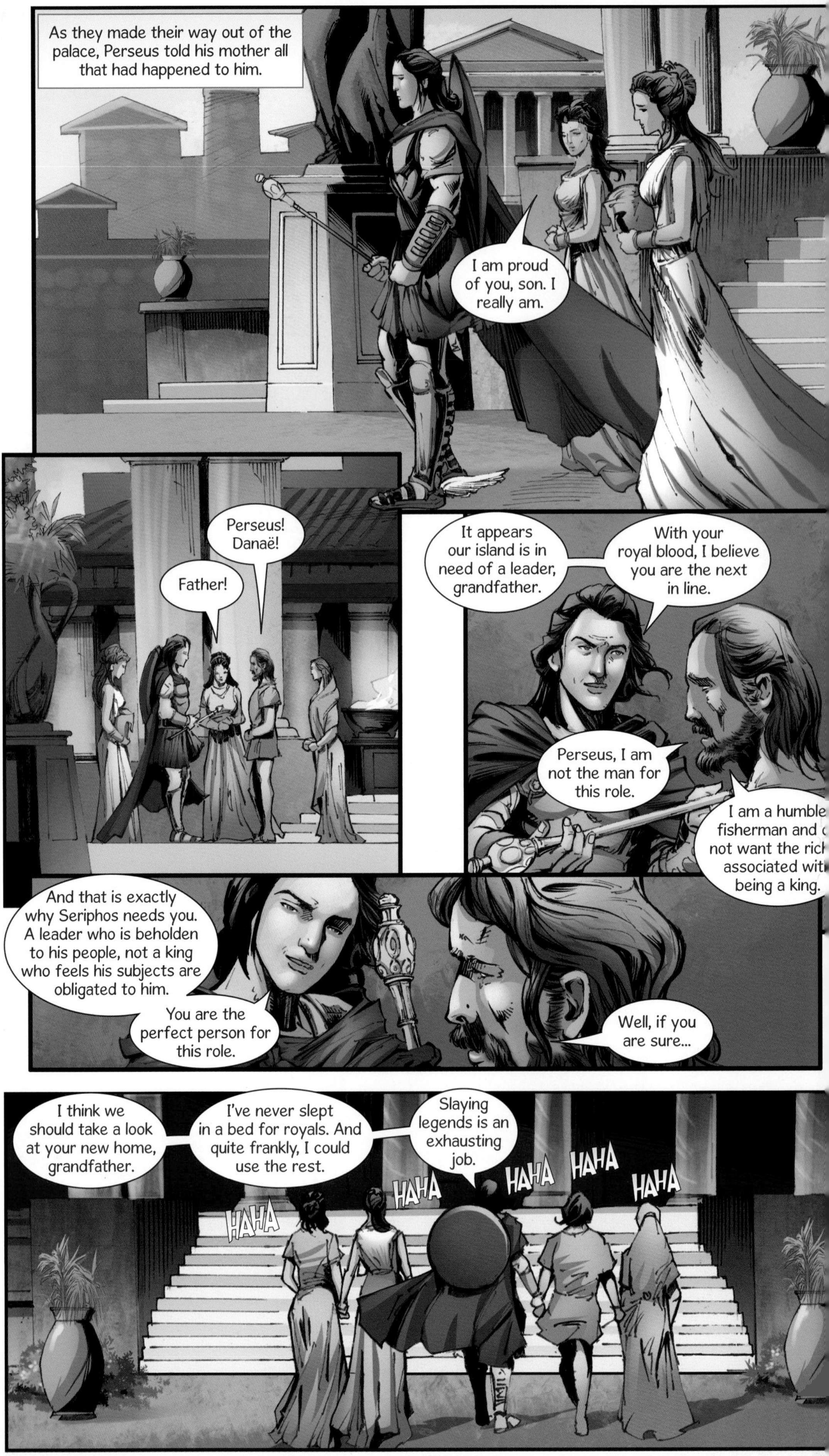

As they made their way out of the palace, Perseus told his mother all that had happened to him.
I am proud of you, son. I really am.
Perseus! Danaë!
Father!
It appears our island is in need of a leader, grandfather.
With your royal blood, I believe you are the next in line.
Perseus, I am not the man for this role.
I am a humble fisherman and not want the ric associated wit being a king.
And that is exactly why Seriphos needs you. A leader who is beholden to his people, not a king who feels his subjects are obligated to him.
You are the perfect person for this role.
Well, if you are sure...
I think we should take a look at your new home, grandfather.
I've never slept in a bed for royals. And quite frankly, I could use the rest.
Slaying legends is an exhausting job.
HAHA
HAHA
HAHA
HAHA
HAHA

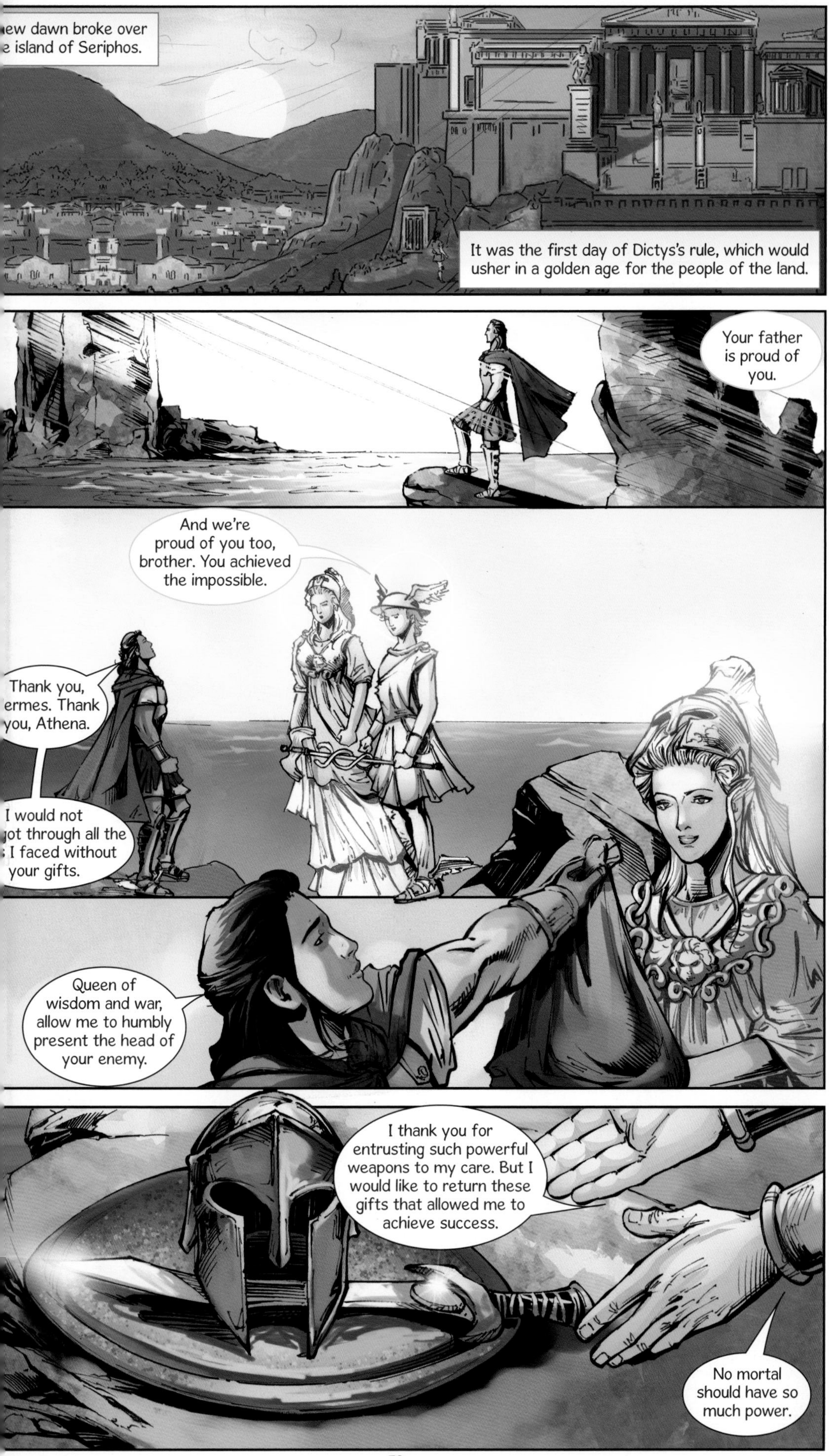
ew dawn broke over
e island of Seriphos.
It was the first day of Dictys's rule, which would usher in a golden age for the people of the land.
Your father is proud of you.
And we're proud of you too, brother. You achieved the impossible.
Thank you, ermes. Thank you, Athena.
I would not jot through all the I faced without your gifts.
Queen of wisdom and war, allow me to humbly present the head of your enemy.
I thank you for entrusting such powerful weapons to my care. But I would like to return these gifts that allowed me to achieve success.
No mortal should have so much power.

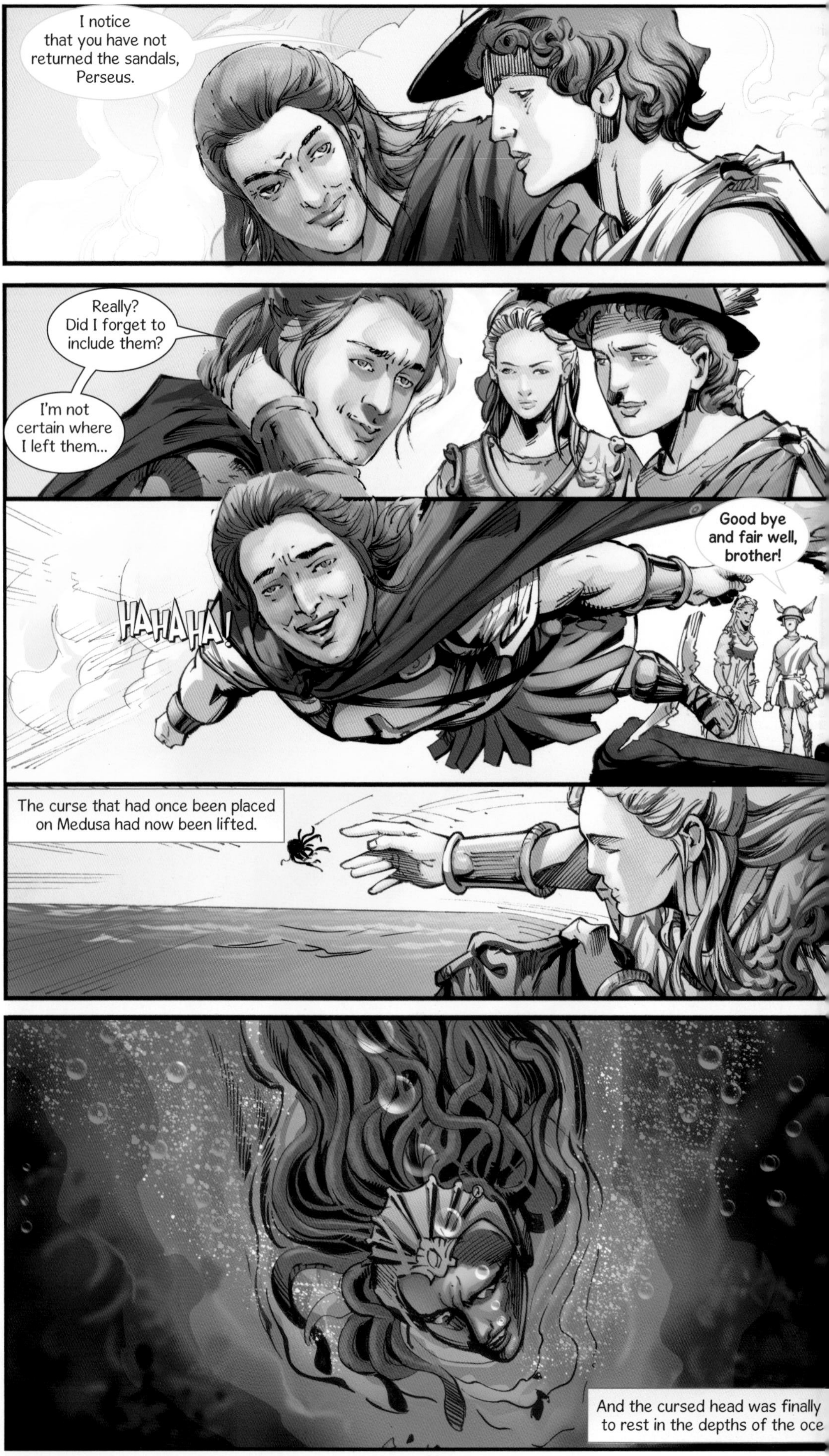
I notice that you have not returned the sandals, Perseus.
Really? Did I forget to include them?
I'm not certain where I left them...
HAHAHA!
Good bye and fair well, brother!
The curse that had once been placed on Medusa had now been lifted.
And the cursed head was finally
to rest in the depths of the oce

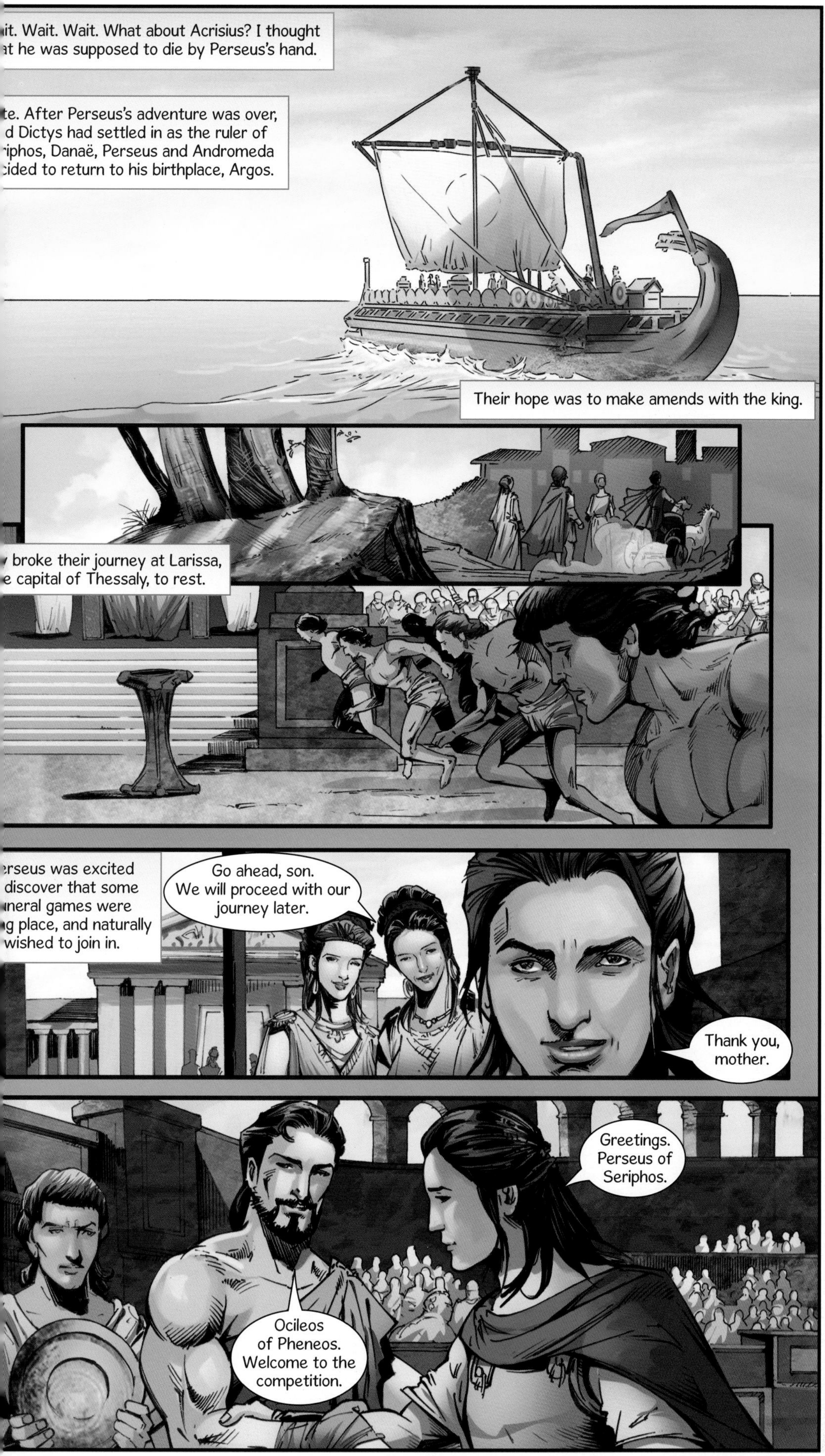
it. Wait. Wait. What about Acrisius? I thought
at he was supposed to die by Perseus's hand.
te. After Perseus's adventure was over,
d Dictys had settled in as the ruler of
iphos, Danaë, Perseus and Andromeda
cided to return to his birthplace, Argos.
Their hope was to make amends with the king.
broke their journey at Larissa,
e capital of Thessaly, to rest.
rseus was excited
discover that some
neral games were
g place, and naturally
wished to join in.
Go ahead, son. We will proceed with our journey later.
Thank you, mother.
Greetings. Perseus of Seriphos.
Ocileos of Pheneos. Welcome to the competition.

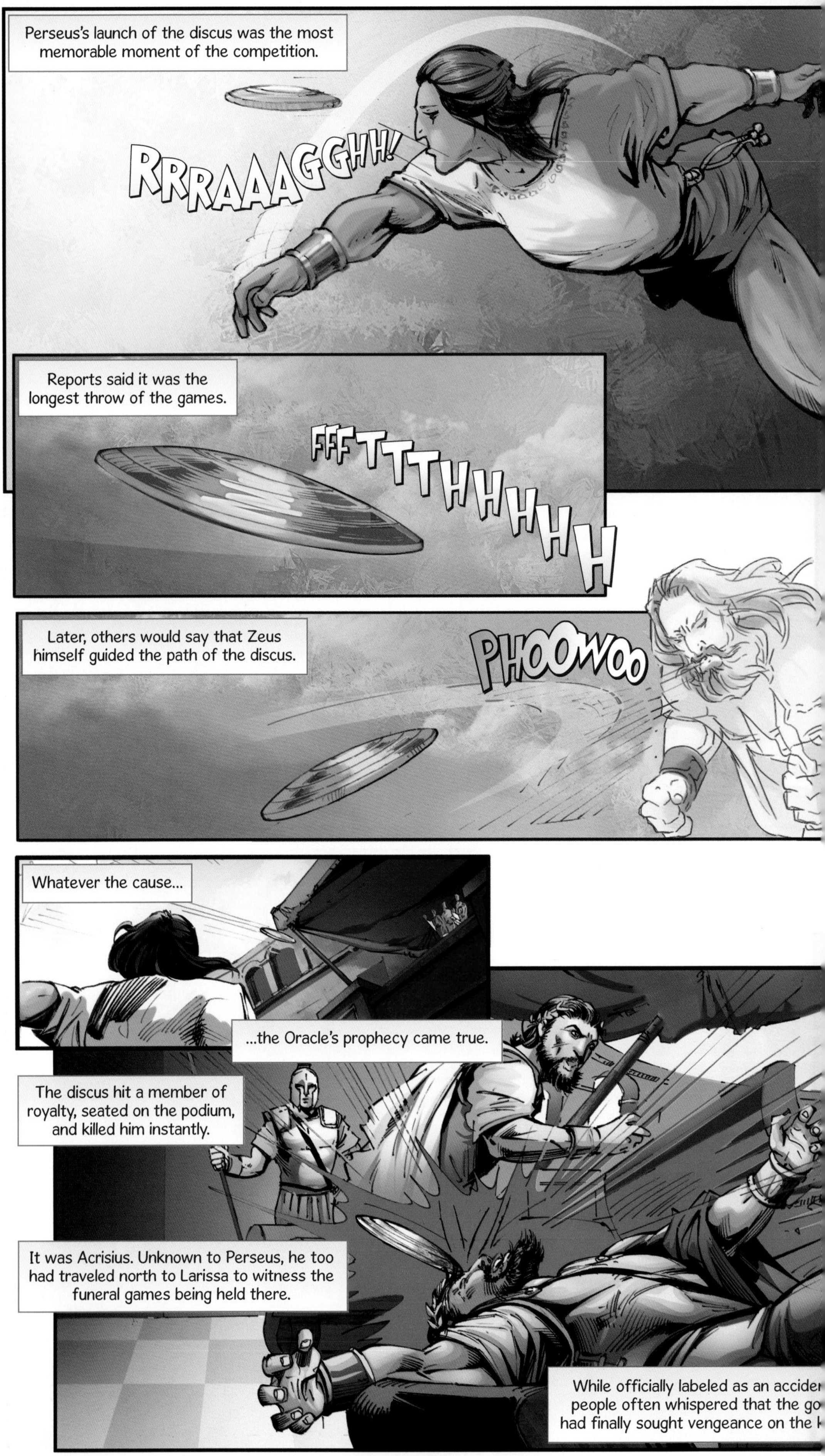
Perseus's launch of the discus was the most memorable moment of the competition.
RRRAAAGGHH!
Reports said it was the longest throw of the games.
FFFTTTHHHHHH
Later, others would say that Zeus himself guided the path of the discus.
PHOOWOO
Whatever the cause...
...the Oracle's prophecy came true.
The discus hit a member of royalty, seated on the podium, and killed him instantly.
It was Acrisius. Unknown to Perseus, he too had traveled north to Larissa to witness the funeral games being held there.
While officially labeled as an accide
people often whispered that the go
had finally sought vengeance on the k

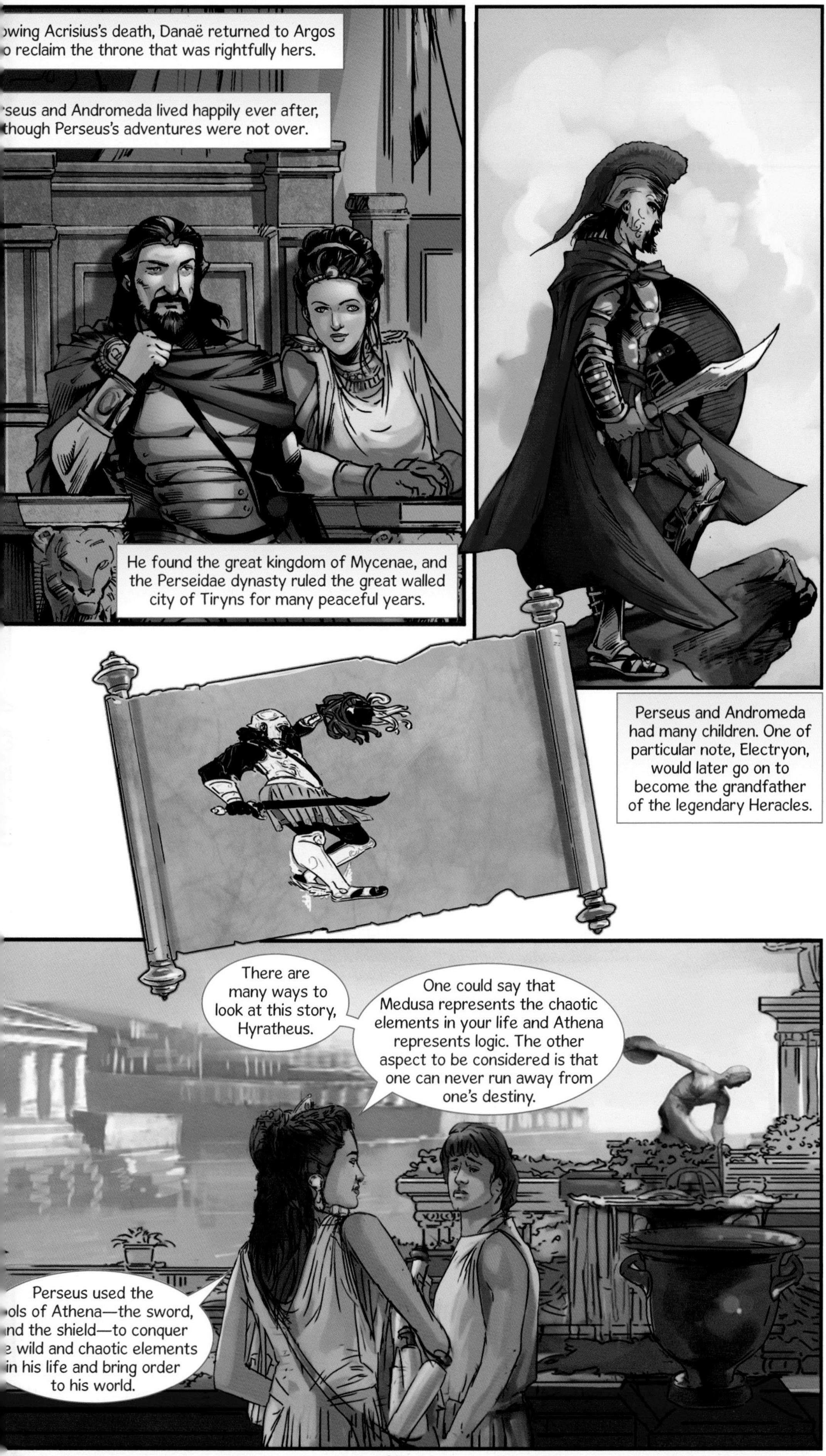

›wing Acrisius's death, Danaë returned to Argos
›o reclaim the throne that was rightfully hers.
›seus and Andromeda lived happily ever after,
›though Perseus's adventures were not over.
He found the great kingdom of Mycenae, and the Perseidae dynasty ruled the great walled city of Tiryns for many peaceful years.
Perseus and Andromeda had many children. One of particular note, Electryon, would later go on to become the grandfather of the legendary Heracles.
There are many ways to look at this story, Hyratheus.
One could say that Medusa represents the chaotic elements in your life and Athena represents logic. The other aspect to be considered is that one can never run away from one's destiny.
Perseus used the ›ols of Athena—the sword, ›nd the shield—to conquer › wild and chaotic elements in his life and bring order to his world.

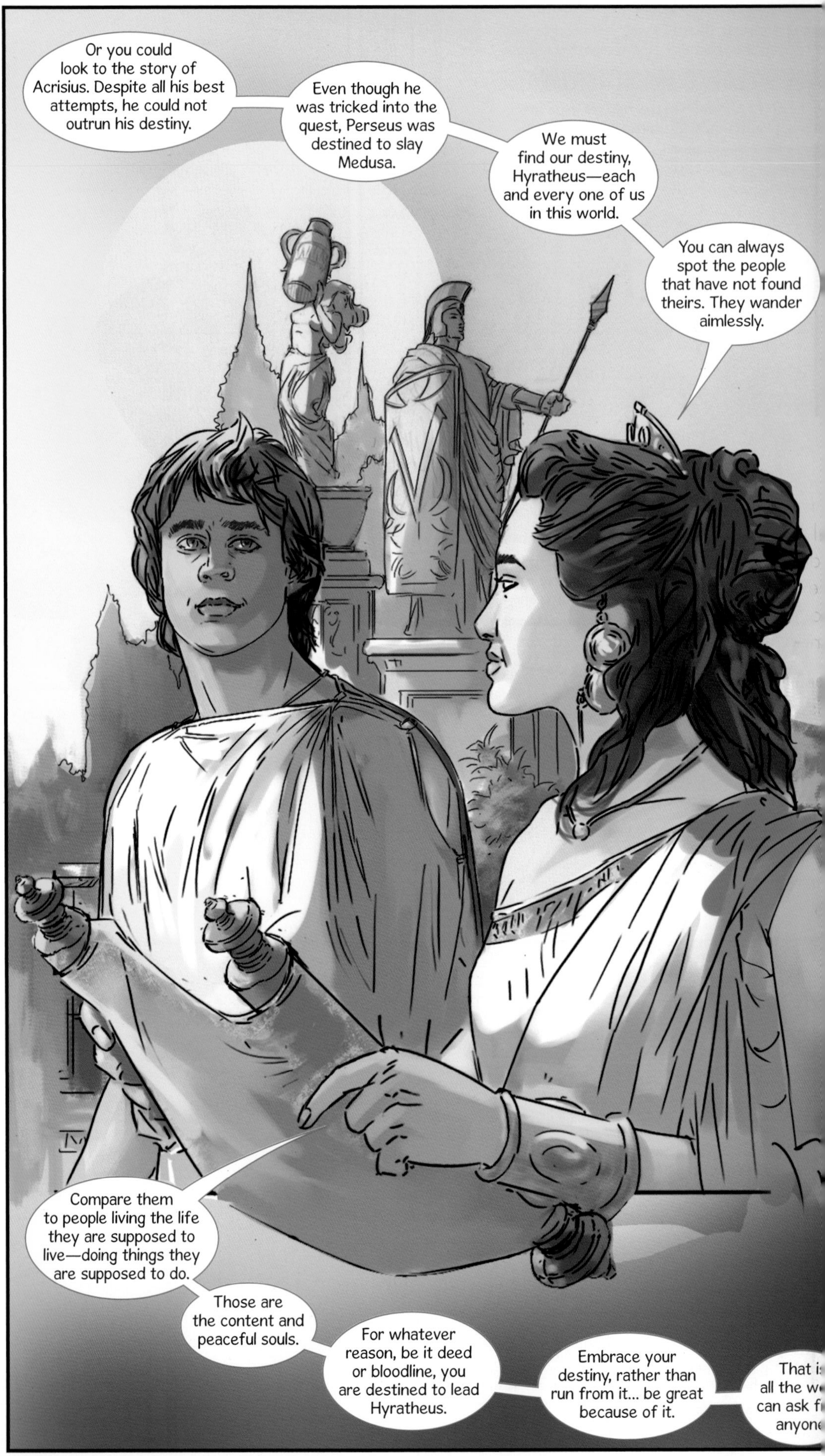

Or you could look to the story of Acrisius. Despite all his best attempts, he could not outrun his destiny.
Even though he was tricked into the quest, Perseus was destined to slay Medusa.
We must find our destiny, Hyratheus—each and every one of us in this world.
You can always spot the people that have not found theirs. They wander aimlessly.
Compare them to people living the life they are supposed to live—doing things they are supposed to do.
Those are the content and peaceful souls.
For whatever reason, be it deed or bloodline, you are destined to lead Hyratheus.
Embrace your destiny, rather than run from it... be great because of it.
That i
all the w
can ask f
anyone

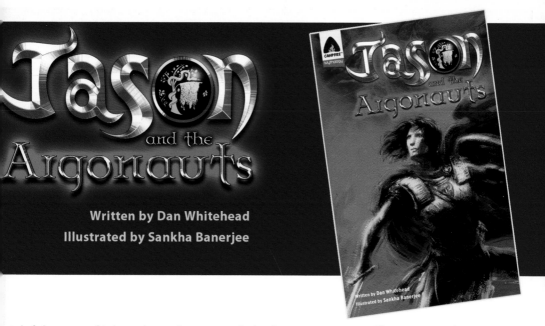

Jason and the Argonauts

Written by Dan Whitehead
Illustrated by Sankha Banerjee

CAMPFIRE
Mythology
Jason and the Argonauts
Written by Dan Whitehead
Illustrated by Sankha Banerjee

rightful prince of Iolcus, brought up in exile by the great centaur Chiron, Jason has just one l in mind—to save his people from the tyrannical rule of his uncle, Pelias. Warned about downfall by Apollo's Oracle at Delphi, Pelias challenges Jason to do the impossible— eve the Golden Fleece from the kingdom of Colchis—in return for the throne. Thus flags one the greatest voyages in Greek mythology—the voyage of Jason and his group of riors, the Argonauts.

ercoming tremendous odds, Jason moves relentlessly toward his goal. But he is not unaided is mission. Insanely in love with him, the sorceress Medea ensures Jason's success at every , while being unaware of the larger divine intervention at work. So then what is Jason's ievement, what is his victory in a preordained world? Does Jason remain ignorant of the 1 of his triumph, or does he come to terms with his flaws to gain a deeper realization of destiny?

old in the graphic medium with amazing visual effects, this enduring tale of adventure, nradeship, temptation, and betrayal makes one reflect on the true meaning and value of oic success.

CAMPFIRE™

www.campfire.co.in

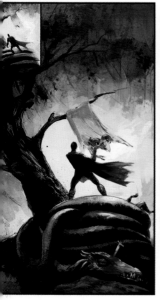

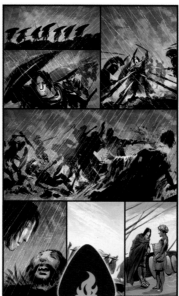

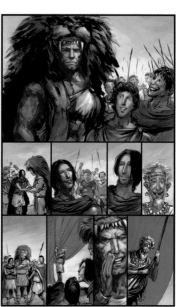

Myth, magic and more

All kinds of magical objects are used by the heroes and villains in Greek mythology, to make themselves stronger, to fly, to battle evil, to wreak havoc... and much more.

TALARIA

Talaria are magical, winged sandals, which Hermes owned a pair of. The ones which belonged to him were made by Hephaestus, the god of blacksmiths, and were designed to help Hermes in his role as messenger of the gods, by allowing him to deliver any messages at super fast speed. In the story of Perseus we see how Hermes lends his talaria to our hero and how they help him greatly in succeeding in his mission.

INTERESTING, ISN'T IT?

Although Hermes was the Greek name for the messenger of the gods, the Romans called him Mercury. And he, the swiftest of gods, gave his name to the planet in our solar system which takes just 88 days to orbit the sun—Mercury.

AEGIS

The aegis, an all-powerful, magical device, belong to Zeus and made him invincible. Designed for h by Hephaestus, it could take the form of a protecti shield with Medusa's head in the center, or become cloak covered with scales and fringed with serpen

INTERESTING, ISN'T IT?

As with many old Greek words, 'aegis' is now used in the English language, and is particularl popular in a phrase you may have heard. To be 'under the aegis' of someone or something means to be under the protection of someone or something powerful.

Did you know?

Adolf Hitler was fascinated by all mythical and magical objects. He was convinced they would grant him absolute power and immortality. So strong was his belief that he is said to have ardently searched for both the *Holy Grail* and the *Ark of the Covenant* during World War II. The *Ark* was a sacred chest where the ancient Hebrews kept the stone tablets containing the Ten Commandments, while the *Grail* was a cup used by Jesus at the Last Supper and is said to possess miraculous powers.

POSEIDON'S TRIDENT

he trident of Poseidon was a gift to him from the yclopes (one-eyed giants). With this powerful eapon he created new land masses in the water d calmed the stormy seas. And when he became ngry, he would violently strike the earth with it to use earthquakes, tsunamis and storms.

NTERESTING, ISN'T IT?

he trident is the traditional weapon of the Hindu god, Shiva. It even finds a place of honor in e US Navy Special Warfare insignia. This insignia is worn by the US Navy Seals, and represents e three areas in which they operate—sea, air and land.

APHRODITE'S GIRDLE

The golden girdle was a magical belt that belonged to Aphrodite, and was a gift to her from none other than her husband Hephaestus. The belt was so potent that whomsoever she desired would fall in love with her. Hera, the goddess of marriage, would often borrow it to reunite quarreling spouses and encourage suitors.

INTERESTING, ISN'T IT?

Even today, witches often wear girdles dedicated to Aphrodite, to attract men and make them fall in love.

MAGIC IN THE SKY

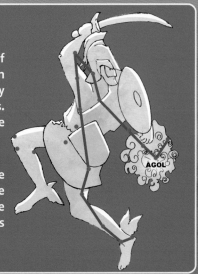

Although the story of Perseus dates back thousands of years, his legend lives on as a constellation and can be seen in the winter sky, in the Northern Hemisphere. It is easy to spot his form, with a triangular body, legs and hands. In one hand he seems to be holding a weapon, and in the other, Medusa's head.

Agol is the primary star of this constellation. It means the 'demon star' and is very easy to identify as it forms the eye of Medusa. Ancient sky-gazers considered it to be cursed as the star's brightness is not constant and flickers continuously.

LEGEND
THE LABORS OF HERACLES

Heracles has it all: a beautiful home, a loving family, and a reputation as a great soldier who would stop at nothing to defend his homeland. As a result of a vicious plot, he is hypnotized into committing the worst crime of all. He finally finds solace in the fact that he can atone for his sins by completing ten impossible tasks. Where other men would give up and accept defeat, Heracles is undeterred in his mission. Will he succeed? Or has destiny other plans for him?

STOLEN HEARTS
THE LOVE OF EROS AND PSYCHE

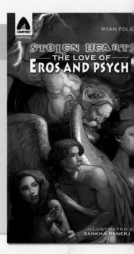

Aphrodite, the Greek goddess of beauty grows jealous of the praise being heaped upon a young mortal girl named Psyche. Under her instructions, her son, Eros, the god of love, performs a nasty trick that backfires when he falls in love with Psyche. But then Psyche is tempted to see Eros in the light, something he had forbidden her to do, and is spurned by him. Nevertheless, she sets out against impossible odds to regain the trust of her one true love. A wonderful story of love, penance, and redemption.

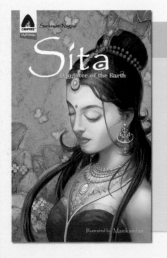

SITA
DAUGHTER OF THE EARTH

Sita is the kind-hearted and intelligent princess of Videha. Married to Rama, Prince of Ayodhya, her journey in life takes her from exhilaration to anguish. Ensnared in the evil plans of the wicked demon-king Ravana, Sita is abducted and hidden away. Will Rama muster up a strong army to rescue Sita from the demon's clutches? Will Sita return to Ayodhya to become queen of the land? Adapted from the ancient Indian epic, the *Ramayana*, this is a touching tale of love, honor, and sacrifice in an unforgiving world.